ROPERS CAN'T TIE THE KNOTS

Contents

One
Gabe

There's a certain freedom that comes with age and a successful career.

You can choose holidays when you want, the boss leaves you to your own devices most of the time, and you can eat dessert for breakfast.

In my case, it also means you can decide to walk away from a position that no longer serves you and move on to a fresh life challenge. With no mortgage or family anchoring me to this job or city anymore, it's time for a change.

When the law firm I work for passed me over again and still didn't offer me a partnership after ten years, I knew the time I'd been waiting for had truly arrived.

It was scary as hell to acknowledge I was ready.

Watching my best friend fall in love and enjoy his life made me wonder if perhaps I had it all backwards from the beginning. Happiness wouldn't find me when I holed myself up in my office sixteen hours a day, six days a week. Accumulating wealth and job experience before seeking a relationship seemed like a great idea in the beginning.

Over time, the only things that found me were loneliness, overeating, and self-induced heartburn. After several deep discussions with my best friend Riley and meetings with my financial planner...I resigned.

I won't lie and say I wasn't terrified to walk away to parts unknown, because I was. Working as an attorney for a prestigious civil law firm filled every moment of my life, and I enjoyed it. But the call to find the missing piece has intensified.

At forty-one, I have a lot of life to live yet, and with the increased time I spend with Riley and his friends, it's painfully obvious I've let too much of the past ten years slip through my fingers.

But a man still needs to work. While I don't mind an extended leave of absence, I'd need to work again, eventually.

Which is how I've found myself moved to the small town of Kissing Ridge, where my best friend lives. Fate must have been thinking of me when I came across the ad for a law practice for sale in the small town.

I liked the business the previous lawyer had built, and I was bursting to make the change, not just in my career, but in my life. I wanted to attend rodeos with Riley and walk to the farmer's market for fresh food twice a week. Most importantly, I wanted to be a part of the friend group Riley invited me into.

They're a close-knit group of rodeo cowboys and welcomed me without question. Well, the one guy was a little prickly, but I could manage him.

Parking my car in the lot of my new favourite coffee house, I exit the vehicle with a smile and enter The Thirsty Cow. City life has most things I adore, but it doesn't have this quaint and cozy coffee house with the bubbly barista named Diamond.

Diamond looks up from the espresso machine and flashes a smile my way.

"Well, hello, Mr. Handsome. What can I get you today?"

His tone is flirty, and while he's an attractive man, he's not the type to set the butterflies off in my gut. He's like a warm hug from an old friend.

"I'd love a mocha, please." Scanning the seating, I wave to Riley. "I'll be over there. No rush, darling."

Diamond nods with a wink, drawing a small laugh from my lips before I walk across the room to meet Riley.

I wasn't expecting him to be here alone. "Is it just the two of us today?"

After hugging each other, he returns to his place, and I sit beside him, angling so we can speak face to face.

"I'm afraid so. The boys have some kind of pressing rodeo thing, and it didn't sound like any fun to me." He smiles and reaches over to squeeze my knee. "Some days I still can't believe you're here." His voice clogs with emotion. "Everything going okay?"

We've spent too much time apart. Sometimes it doesn't seem real that I'm here permanently, either.

"It's great, Rye. In fact, we signed the final papers today. I have officially bought the practice."

His hand covers his mouth and mutes his squeal of joy. "Oh my god, this is so amazing! You'll love it here, Gabe. Honestly."

Diamond delivers my coffee with another wink, and I allow myself to appreciate the man a little longer. The legs he has go on for days, and while he's not my usual type, he'd probably be a fun fling.

"I'm not on the market, handsome. Eyes up here." He tsks, and Riley laughs.

"Busted." I join Riley's laughter. "They're a lucky person then, Diamond."

"Yes, they are." He quips before blowing me a kiss and returning to the counter.

"I don't think I've ever seen you shot down so smoothly before. Are you losing your touch?"

Reaching for my mocha, I can only keep laughing. "I don't think so. He said he was taken anyway, so that doesn't count. I'd hate to be a home-wrecker." Riley watches as I sip from my mug, and I turn away from his gaze.

One-night stands aren't my thing anymore. Riley probably knows that even though I've not voiced it out loud yet. He's always been able to read me well, and part of the reason we just clicked.

Riley clears his throat. "So, when will you plan to be here permanently?"

"I still need to find a place to stay. The unit I had hoped to rent while I house hunted had a sewer backup and is no longer rentable."

"Well, that's shitty." We both chuckle at his joke. "Aunt Agnes said she'd love to have you if she still had a spare room." Riley offers.

"Tell her I appreciate that, and I'll still be by for visits." Even if she still had a room, I'm not sure I'd like to live with an eighty-year-old. While I don't plan on stringing together wild nights with strangers, if I met someone, how could I bring them back to my place with her on the other side of the wall? Just...no.

"I'll figure it out. Now, tell me about you and Jackson's hydroponic thing. Catch me up."

Riley speaks with such joy. His eyes glow and the smile on his face is one I envy as he tells me about their dogs, the growing hydroponics business and Riley's romance planning. He's currently arranging several student promposals and I have to say, I didn't know that was a thing.

"Let me get this straight. He wants to ask a girl out using a cow?"

Riley snort-laughs and slaps my arm. "You're in the country now, Gabe. We do things a lot differently here."

I think that's an understatement. His phone pings, and he reads it with a smile before rapidly typing a response. "Are you free tomorrow? There's a big party to kick off the rodeo season." He wiggles his eyebrows. "Lots of wrangler butts, Gabe."

I *do* like a cowboy. Not something I thought I'd ever say, but after last year and my first rodeo, I admit I see the appeal. I never got close enough to touch, though, last time. But I observed one closely.

"Yeah. I'll be there."

Riley's answering smile is one that confirms I did the right thing moving here. "I've really missed us hanging out, Gabe. I'm so happy you're here. Can I invite you for dinner every week, or is that too much?"

Laughing, I sip my mocha and eye the rest of the cheesecake on his plate.

"Are you going to finish that?"

He pushes the plate towards me with a smirk.

"Your sweet tooth hasn't changed."

No, it hasn't. Lots of things have, but not my love for homemade desserts.

"Are you having fun?"

Jamieson, the bull rider friend of Riley's, shouts across the table, and I raise my glass with a nod. "I am, thank you."

He nods his head and smiles like there's nothing better than being in a crowded hall filled with cowboys, belt buckles, and tight asses. To be fair, I can agree with that to a point.

If you have any kind of western kink, this is the place to be. It's a denim-clad ass buffet and in case you're not an ass man, there are loads of shiny belt buckles. And more than a few cowboy hats. Although Riley mentioned earlier that the guys at the bar still wearing hats are just using them to get laid.

Whatever works, I say.

Turning my back to survey the dance floor, my gaze falls on the man who caught my attention last year. It wasn't his belt buckle that drew me in, although I can appreciate a man proud of his achievements. The dark and handsome cowboy with a smouldering gaze and a chip on his shoulder was all I needed to be intrigued.

Hunter Burke.

Jackson's former rodeo partner, and a man with one hell of a cactus exterior. I had hoped last year he'd be up for a little fun, but he had one hell of an attitude, and I thought it best if I left him alone. Dealing with someone's thorns wasn't on my list.

This time, though, I think I want to chance it and see if he draws blood.

Hunter stands against a wall while he speaks with a young woman. She touches his arm, and he slides it away with a smile and a shake of his head.

She pats his arm again and walks away just as I step into his line of sight and his smile fades.

"Ouch. I'm not sure what I've done to get that look already. I'm just coming to say hello."

Hunter sips his beer with a cocked eyebrow.

"What look? This is literally my face...Gabe."

Smiling, I take a sip from my glass. The way he says my name sends a beacon of hope that maybe he noticed me last time, too. "You remembered my name. I must've been memorable for you."

Hunter draws another swallow from his beer and looks out at the dance floor. "Riley talks about you all the time. It's hard to forget."

What a dirty liar he is. It's more than that, and I know it. We're playing the same game here, and we should both be winners.

"Still...you remembered." Moving closer, I test his limits and brush a finger along his hand. He stills, but I don't miss the bob of his throat. "And I definitely remembered you."

"Is that so?"

Hunter's brown eyes meet mine as he turns his head back to me and I sip my drink, pleased when his gaze drops to my lips.

"Do you want to taste it?"

"What?"

Swirling the ice cubes, I raise my cup. "My drink. You can taste it, Hunter. I don't mind."

His nostrils flare, and the flash in his eyes sends a spark to my groin. This man is absolutely gorgeous in an untamed way. Just like the last time I saw him, he has this whole wild stallion vibe going on. He's unpredictable and I'm fucking here for it.

Hunter leans in close, his lips ghosting against my ear. "You can't handle me...counsellor." He lingers, and I swear he blows a soft caress across my skin. "As attractive as the offer is, I'll have to decline."

My hand wraps around his wrist before he steps away. His skin is hot against my palm, and I smooth my thumb across the inside of his wrist, feeling the steady pulse under my touch. "I've handled a lot more than you. I don't need to know why you're turning me down now, but if you change your mind...I'll be around."

Dropping his wrist, I turn around and walk away.

He might say no this time, but I'm nothing if persistent. I live here now. There *will* be a next time.

I'm sure of it.

Draining my glass, I drop it on a table as I walk by on my way to say goodnight to Riley.

"Enjoy the rest of the night, Rye." Leaning in, I kiss his cheek. "I think I'll get an early sleep. I'll talk to you this week."

"Thanks for coming, Gabe." Riley isn't a big drinker, but the flush on his cheeks is a giveaway that he's had more than a few. "No luck tonight?"

"I'm not feeling it. It's okay. Say goodbye to Jackson for me."

Weaving through the crowd, I exit the bar towards the parking lot. A few small groups cluster, sharing a cigarette, and I nod as I walk by. The late spring air still carries a chill in the evening, and I quicken my steps to get to the warmth of my car.

The lights flash when the doors unlock, and I turn my head to look back towards the bar.

An unmistakable figure stands at the edge of the shadows from the streetlight.

"Well, well...you couldn't just let me walk away after all, could you?" Opening the car, I slide behind the wheel with a victorious grin. But when I look towards the figure, it's no longer there.

But my smile remains.

Seems Hunter Burke doesn't always make things easy.

Game on, cowboy.

Two
Hunter

"You can go right in, Mr. Burke."

The secretary in the lobby of the swanky law firm buzzes me through, and I navigate the halls to my lawyer's office. I would've preferred keeping this matter with a lawyer in town, but most had dealt with my grandfather at some point, and I wanted an unbiased opinion.

Which proved harder than I initially thought.

With a light knock on the door before opening, I step inside to meet with the man who has hopefully untangled some of the mess my grandfather left behind.

"Hunter. Nice to see you."

Jonathon Conway thrusts his hand forward with a nervous smile. He always carries this air of uncertainty when we meet, and I really hope it's just me being overly sensitive and not that he lacks confidence in his profession. I have a lot hanging on him being competent and not another asshole in a custom fit suit.

"Likewise, Jonathon." That's a lie. I'd rather not see him, but I still know how to operate with a bit of social decorum. Most days anyway.

After taking our seats, he opens a file on his desk and passes me a large manila envelope.

"I have good news and bad news." He starts, and my heart sinks.

"Can we please start with the good news?" Fuck me. If this is another shitty day that comes at me when I'm not prepared, I might actually weep. "I could use some." So could my lines of credit and bank account. Probably my fucking blood pressure, too.

"Yes, of course." He taps his fingers on his desk and clears his throat. A nervous sound that has me on edge more than I was when I sat down. "I secured you access to the first trust for physical property. The account to maintain the costs of the ranch should have had you listed at the financial institution. I believe it was an intentional oversight as it clearly states in clause 5.3 that the current inhabitant should draw funds as needed for property and business maintenance."

My chest loosens with his words. I can believe it was intentional. Not a stretch in the least, and yet another example of how money can influence people to do the wrong thing.

"So I can submit all the receipts I've kept for the animal and equipment care, property taxes and the like?"

"Oh yes. The trust specifically states for care of the animals and property under the ranch name."

If you could name what relief feels like, it's the decision to hire a lawyer and help with this bullshit. The last eighteen months have been hell. I thought I'd lose everything. While it wasn't directly willed to me, I wasn't kicked out and trusted to care for the property.

But I couldn't pay for it all on my own. The taxes on the land alone were staggering. The only thing that kept me afloat was my name on the business of breeding rodeo livestock. My name was only on it because I registered the paperwork. Since it was my efforts running it, and essentially my company, I put my name on it all. Jeremiah Burke was furious, but he also never changed it.

Maybe he never changed it because he knew he'd bend me over in the will and I'd have to see all my hard work dismantled piece by piece.

I had to sell it all off, though. It broke my heart, and if it wasn't for Jackson pushing me to get a second opinion on this, I might be living out of my horse trailer now.

"It's all summarized in the envelope for you. I've already sent all the legal documents to the trustee with instructions and you should be able to get your money back in the next week, if not sooner."

"Thank you so much, Jonathon. Now, what's the bad news?"

He fidgets with the papers in front of him, and I brace myself. I'm used to bad news these days, but it doesn't get any easier each time it's delivered.

"The second trust about the estate residue…I couldn't get to it. Your retainer only covered my time for the first trust."

Oh. That's not as bad as I thought.

"I understand. You don't work for free."

I also can't afford to pay him another three grand right now to help with the other trust.

"I do require payment up front for these cases, and I'd be happy to help again when you're able to handle the fee."

"You've been extremely helpful so far, and this helps. I'll be in touch then when I'm ready to continue, if that's okay?"

"Of course. You have my card. Just schedule an appointment and we can tackle what's next."

After leaving the law office, I take a walk to the small park nearby and grin when I find a hot dog cart. It's still early, and she's just setting up for the day, but I want to celebrate with a hot dog. Is it odd? Probably, but I'm hungry and hot dogs make me happy.

"Good morning! When will you be ready to open?"

The young woman smiles as she continues to load drinks into a cooler.

"If you come back in five, you can grab the first dog of the day. I just put them on the grill."

"That's perfect."

Finding a bench nearby, I sit and dial Jackson's number to relay the good news.

"Oh man, Hunter, this is the best news ever. I'm so happy for you! Does this mean you won't lose the ranch then? Your money problems are solved?"

"Yes, and no. I still need to submit all my receipts and get the money back. It will clear up all the debt I incurred to keep things going, but the reality is there isn't anything left to keep going."

"Because you sold all the stock, you have nothing to provide an income and with no rodeo..."

Jackson trails off while I nod, even though he can't see me.

"Right. I dismantled the entire stock breeding operation, Jack. I have a few old bulls and that one bronc nobody wanted, but they aren't good enough to rebuild from. Thankfully, their care won't drain my resources now, but...what the fuck am I supposed to do for money now?"

Not that I expect Jackson to have a solution. It's my fault I stayed working for my grandfather when I knew damn well it wouldn't end with a good outcome for me. If you look up petty bastard in the dictionary, it's his picture. I knew that and still stayed.

But I refused to let go of this place even when he treated me like a stranger and voiced his hatred of same-sex relationships frequently. Through some twisted dream in my head, I hoped he'd do the right thing and remember how our lives used to be back when my grandmother was alive.

"What about the other will stuff? The guy was loaded. There's nothing for you there? You kept that place running and did more work than you should have. You deserve something."

The growl in my best friend's voice brings a small smile to my face. Jackson is as loyal as they come and I'm forever grateful he stuck with me all these years.

"There's another trust I don't understand for the residue, and my lawyer said he needs another fee payment to continue. I can use my credit again, I suppose, once I get all the back payments, but I just need a bit of time to get things caught up first."

And to breathe and celebrate that I didn't cry in the lawyer's office.

"You know, Gabe would probably help and let you work out a payment plan or something. Or maybe instead of rent, you could swap for his services? That might work, you know, and get this closed out faster for you."

My skin heats at the name of the sexy lawyer. The one who's also set to move into my home temporarily. Which if I had my way wouldn't be happening, but when your friends all agree in front of the man that it's a great idea to rent him one of your empty rooms, you have to say yes or look like the biggest dick in town.

Which is now even more awkward since he hit on me and made my dick hard with a single touch. He's trouble for me, and it feels like I've set myself up for an awkward roommate situation before it even starts.

"Maybe. I'll have to see how we get along first. No sense letting him know my business if I don't like the guy, you know?"

I'm just grasping for reasons not to have to speak to him for extended periods. I know that, but Jackson sure doesn't. Gabe throws strong, *'I want a white picket fence and 2.5 kids vibes.'* I might be wrong about that, but with the way Riley has talked about him and how often Gabe dotes on his best friend, I don't think I'm too far off base.

I'm not a family guy, and I certainly don't want kids. Having me as a father wouldn't be fair to the child. It's the only reason I went back into the bar after watching him get into his perfectly safe, family-friendly, full of safety features Lexus. I don't need that kind of commitment, and perhaps it's self-centered for me to think he wants more than just sex, but if I hang on tight to that thought, nobody gets hurt.

Besides, it can't be casual if we share a roof for any amount of time.

"I suppose so," Jackson muses. If we were face to face, he'd have that knit in his eyebrows when he thinks too hard. I can hear it in his voice. "Feel him out, at least. It could be an answer to your problems."

My periphery catches the hot dog cart lady waving, and I wave back as I stand.

"Listen, Jack, I'm going to let you go. I have a celebratory hot dog lined up, then I'm driving home. Just wanted to share that the worst of this nightmare is over."

"Thanks, buddy. I'm so happy you have this off your mind, and the ranch stays. Let me know when you make it home."

Shoving the phone in my pocket after a goodbye, I switch the phone for my wallet and hand the woman a ten-dollar bill.

"What are the chances you have fried onions?"

"Very good, my friend." She removes a dome from her grill with a flourish to reveal a pile of onions in all their fried, delicious glory.

"You are a gift! Load me up, please, and don't skimp on the onions."

She passes me a heavily loaded jumbo hot dog, and I step off the path to enjoy it. It's hot-dog-and-onion goodness, and it's also a mess that leaks into my hand. I can't be mad about that one bit because it's fucking delicious.

Once I'm finished, I grab a few extra napkins and clean my hands. I'm three steps back towards the truck before I turn around and reach into my pocket for the change she handed me.

"Ginger ale, please."

There's always a price to pay for eating those things, and I'll never learn. With a gulp of the calming ale, I smile as the sun shines on me.

Good lawyer news and a hot dog.

Heartburn or not, life is good today.

Gabe sent me a text last night that he was planning to arrive late Sunday afternoon. After confirming the address and directions, I set to work organizing all the receipts for the ranch and animal upkeep since my grandfather died.

The piles are large, and I organized them by date, then by property or animal expense. By the time I was finished, my head was pounding, and I cursed my past self for not keeping better track of things.

Last night I went to bed early, intending to have it all cleaned up before Gabe arrived. But it's now late Sunday afternoon, and I'm just a tired cowboy, staring at paper piles and wishing they'd take care of themselves.

The muffled slam of a vehicle door outside sounds, signalling the arrival of my temporary roommate. I'll have to get to this after Gabe is settled. If he has an issue with a messy dining room table, I hope he keeps his mouth shut.

When several minutes pass and there's no knock at the door, I pull on my boots and go out to ask if he needs any help to find the entrance. He's a city boy, so you just can't tell sometimes. With all his fancy clothes and car, maybe he's waiting for the bellhop or something equally absurd.

Gabe's fancy ass car sits parked next to my truck, but the man himself is nowhere to be seen.

A high-pitched shriek sounds from close to the barn, and sure enough, there's my new lawyer roommate standing on the rung of the fence and clutching at it like the ground is lava.

"Lord, they didn't warn me wild animals were this close to the house."

Gabe's voice remains shaky, and a bark of laughter escapes my lips, though it's not like I tried to keep it in. I can't *not* laugh at the grown-ass man in khakis and dress shoes clutching at my fence like it will save him from whatever made his voice rise like he took a dodgeball to the nuts.

He turns his head towards me before dropping his head with a groan. "Ugh. This is completely embarrassing." He says without letting go of the fence pole.

"What exactly is embarrassing, Gabe?"

Settling against the fence next to him, I look into the pasture to find Jackson's horse grazing alongside mine. An older mare I couldn't sell is also out there, but I don't see what might make Gabe screech like he was being murdered.

"The, ah, the giant fuzzy thing that ran that way."

Squinting, I look in the direction he's pointing and can only come up with one possibility.

"You mean Lewis?"

"Would Lewis be a fuzzy thing with giant teeth that whistles like it's possessed by a demon?"

Laughing again, I shake my head. Gabe is just as out of place here as I am at the lawyer's offices in the city.

"Lewis is a groundhog. He whistles if he's scared or trying to get your attention. You probably scared him because you're new."

When Gabe still doesn't step off the fence, I tap his shoulder. "He's harmless, Gabe. You can get off the fence."

He does, and I shake my head at his shoes. Fancy loafer sort of things. Not even a sensible running shoe for moving, but a...loafer. Does he ever dress down?

Gabe steps to the ground and dusts his hands off while casting a wary glance toward Lewis's burrow.

"It won't bite?"

"If you try to feed him, he might. He's a wild animal."

"Oh." Gabe releases a shaky breath, and while I normally have zero patience for teaching city slickers about harmless wildlife, something about his fear makes me bite my tongue. "Are there, ah, more wild animals around I should know about?"

"Tell you what. Why don't we get your stuff inside, and you can ask all your questions then?"

He clears his throat with a nod. "Sure. That would be great, thanks."

He has brought little with him. A few suitcases, mostly, and I'm surprised he doesn't have boxes of books.

"I thought you'd have loads of reference books or something."

Now it's Gabe's turn to poke fun as we carry the last few bags in from the car.

"The few books I have are at the office, but it's all online. I don't own shelves of encyclopedias with case law. I'm not a lawyer from an '80s TV show."

He smirks, and I just can't let him have the last word. "That makes sense. You just like to wear loafers to a ranch like an '80s sitcom character, then?"

He snorts and laughs. "Okay. We've established we both know the '80s."

Gabe kicks off his loafers that make me question how the fuck this living situation will work out. If he fills the bathroom with fancy lotions and shit, I might have to change my mind and tell him to leave.

We each carry two of his bags, and he follows me up the stairs. The first door at the top is his, and I enter, dropping the bags in the middle of the room.

"This is your room. It's nothing fancy."

Gabe looks around the room with a smile. It really isn't fancy. It could use a paint job and a new light fixture, but I don't get many guests here. Fixing it up isn't high on my priority list.

"This is great, Hunter. It really is." He opens the closet and mumbles under his breath. "I appreciate you doing this."

"Not like I had much choice," I respond with a pointed look. "If Jamieson hadn't put me on the spot, I wouldn't have offered."

Gabe's smile falters. "Are you always this prickly?"

"No. I'm usually worse."

We stand there staring at each other. I can't read his expression, and I give nothing away either. I'll let him draw his own conclusions about why this arrangement might not end well.

Gabe just shrugs off my admission and smiles, carrying on like we both didn't just make each other uncomfortable.

"Yeah, well, sorry about that, but your friends wouldn't let the idea go once it came out. Thanks anyway, though. The housing market in Kissing Ridge is more competitive than I thought."

I don't know if that's true or not, but he has no reason to lie about it.

"It's fine. Listen..." I might regret this, but if he's living here, maybe I should at least try not to be a complete asshole. I owe that to Jackson and Riley, at least. Gabe is important to them, and if the roles were reversed, I'd want them to treat my friend better than how I've just welcomed Gabe.

Not to mention, my grandmother would likely cuff the back of my head for being rude.

"It's getting late, and I know the grocery store closes early on Sundays...you're welcome to join me for dinner later. It's nothing fancy, but I don't mind sharing until you get settled."

Jesus Christ, why did that hurt so much to say? Has it really been so long since I've been a gracious host and polite human that it physically pains me to be nice?

Gabe nods quickly and smiles. His eyes crinkle at the edge, and he pushes his wire-rimmed glasses up. His adorable glasses.

"That would be super helpful, Hunter. Thank you so much."

"Okay. Good. I'll, ah, be downstairs then. Happy unpacking, I guess."

Happy unpacking?

What the fuck is wrong with me?

Three
Gabe

I only meant to lie down for a quick nap, but when I wake up, night has fallen.

I clearly needed the rest, but when my stomach growls, I remember Hunter's dinner invitation and hope he saved me some. I wasn't expecting him to be so...puzzling. But after laughing and trading barbs before his admission that he didn't want me here, he softened right in front of me.

Like he knew he was rude simply because he could be, and maybe reconsidered his actions. I certainly don't mind giving people second chances, and I can't fault him for being honest. But if we're to live under the same roof together, even for a few months, we might snap at each other more often than I'd like.

After changing into a T-shirt and lounge pants, I creep down the stairs towards the kitchen. There's still a light on in the dining room, and Hunter sits at the table—shirtless. A glass of amber liquid close by, he punches numbers into an old adding machine, missing the paper roll, before taking a sip from his glass. Something about the scene makes me pause and wonder how many layers there are to this man, because I wasn't expecting to find him using an adding machine and sipping what I hope is whiskey.

He notices me then and after swallowing, he says, "You were asleep when dinner was ready. There's a plate in the fridge for you if you're hungry."

Hunter shuffles through a pile of papers and clips them together after scribbling a note on top.

"I only meant to take a nap. Thank you. I'm starving."

He nods and gets back to his task, jabbing at numbers with a chewed-up pencil, and I make my way to the kitchen. When I open the fridge, I find a dinner plate covered in tinfoil, and it reminds me of my sister. A sharp pang of loss hits me, and I shake it off as I peel off the foil to find a grilled chicken breast, broccoli, and mashed potatoes.

Nothing fancy by any means, but it's food cooked in a home and not takeout. After sliding the plate in the microwave, I find a glass in the cupboard and pour a glass of water, before guessing the cutlery drawer right on the first try.

While the microwave works its magic, I look around the well-loved kitchen. It's spotless without a single thing out of place. A small table sits snug in one corner with a single chair, and I find it odd that there's only one.

The microwave sounds and I carefully remove the plate. With the plate in my hand, I turn to the single chair first, but change course after a few steps instead. His earlier invite was to join him for dinner, so that's what I'm doing. I'm just late.

He raises an eyebrow when I sit but says nothing, and I wonder if he always eats at the table in the kitchen by himself.

"Is it okay for me to eat here? I just thought you might want company, and I've been eating alone for years, so another person would be great."

Hunter puffs a breath, but he doesn't tell me to leave. I cut into the chicken, and I'm pleasantly surprised to find it stuffed with cheese and more broccoli.

"It's stuffed! This is so good." I say around a mouthful, and this time a ghost of a smile plays on his lips.

"It's just chicken, but thank you."

Hunter sips his drink as I eat, and he says nothing else. He just watches me, and it doesn't even feel creepy. Part of me wants to make a show of it and discover a way to make eating cheese-stuffed chicken erotic just to see if he'd still turn me down, but there's a vibe here, and it's not a flirty one.

Something has changed since I arrived.

"Can I ask what you're working on? Looks like you're behind on your taxes or something."

Hunter takes a sip again, his deep brown eyes giving nothing away. My gaze slides to his naked chest. He's toned, the evidence of manual labour etched into his upper body distinctly differently than muscles born in a gym. His complexion is either on the darker side naturally, or he spends a lot of time out in the sun with his shirt off.

Which is a thought I shouldn't entertain right now while I cough around a mouthful of food.

"Do you need help?" His concern is unexpected as he rises to come closer. I sputter and take a drink while motioning I'm fine, and Hunter returns to his seat. After a moment, his attention returns to the papers in front of him. Scribbling a note on one pile, clipping them and moving to the next.

"What kind of lawyer are you, anyway?"

"A good one."

Hunter raises his gaze to mine, and I grin. "It's true."

"Okay, Gabe." Hunter leans back in his chair, tapping his chewed-up pencil on the table. "What kind of law are you good at? Is that better?"

Placing my cutlery on my plate, I lean back in the chair to study the man. My gaze then slides to the piles of papers and the adding machine before going back to Hunter. Ah, there it is. Whatever these papers are about is something legal. Maybe he's in financial trouble.

"If you need to ask me something as a lawyer, it remains confidential if that helps."

He exhales slowly and places the pencil on the table. A single finger plays with the rim of his glass.

"I'm not very good at asking for help." He says quietly. "But Jackson told me I could trust you and that maybe...maybe we could make a deal."

I don't know Hunter well, but I know Jackson since he's my best friend's boyfriend. Jackson is a man of his word and a wonderful soul. If he's urged Hunter to ask me for help, it's only logical for me to assume I can trust Hunter that way, too.

"I'd be willing to do that if you tell me what you need help with."

Far too much time passes as he sits in silence. His gaze remains on the mess of paper in front of him. For one flash of a moment, my legs coil to burst out of my chair and hug him. Thankfully, I don't act on it, but the need to want to comfort him remains, even though I don't know why.

Finally, he nods and reaches for a manila envelope sitting nearby.

"I'm not very smart about legal stuff. My grandfather's will is complicated. He left two trusts. One deals with the property here and the livestock. I just got that one sorted." He gestures to the piles of paper on the table. "This is fallout from that. But the second trust for the residual estate...I don't understand it, and the lawyer here wouldn't help."

"Why wouldn't a lawyer help you?"

With another heavy sigh, he leans back. "He doesn't like gays."

Hunter delivers that bit like he's used to saying it, and while it's still common to encounter, it enrages me all the same.

"Sounds like this town needs a lawyer like me who doesn't have any prejudice, then."

Hunter finally passes me the envelope. "If you could help me figure out how or if I can even access the residual, you don't need to pay me any rent."

"That's a generous offer, Hunter, but figuring out a will doesn't cost two months' rent."

"I won't allow you to do it for free, Gabe."

His stern tone makes that clear, and I appreciate that, but I can't in good conscience take his deal for a task that will probably only take a few hours.

"How about this? Let me look it over to get a feel for how much work is involved. If I feel two months' rent is fair, I'll accept or...I'll counter with something else."

I'm not ashamed to admit I let the words hang as my gaze raked over him there in his own dining room. He already knows I'm interested, and I'm curious if he'd sell himself out or not. Is it a bit sleazy? Of course, but I kind of want to know how he'll answer.

"You don't give up, do you?"

"Not usually. I'm trying to respect your space and not make you feel uncomfortable in your own home, but you cooked me dinner, and you're sitting here without a shirt. A guy has to shoot his shot, and make it known I'm open to other forms of payment."

Hunter stands and walks to my end of the table with his now-empty glass. I smell it now, peach-flavoured whiskey, and that seems like a perfect fit for him. "I won't enter into a deal for sex, Gabe." He leans in, lips close to my ear. "When I have sex with you, it won't be out of obligation, but because I want to."

"Noted." Also noted, he said *when*…not *if*. That's a victory for me. Not that I would ever make a deal for sex, but Hunter at least admitted he's attracted to me.

He takes my plate and nods towards the envelope. "I'll clean up and let you have a look. Take as much time as you need. I never gave you the house tour earlier because I thought you'd be down before supper, but the living room is comfortable."

Without another word, he leaves for the kitchen, and I head towards the sunken living room off the dining room. An overstuffed chair sits under an old Tiffany light with a view out the large picture window. I imagine Hunter here with his whiskey after a long day, and I hope he doesn't mind me taking what must be his favourite seat.

The document he handed me has some heft, and immediately from the first page, I conclude two things. First, the lawyer who did the will is an asshole out to make money before protecting a man's legacy and two…Hunter's grandfather was loaded.

He's right, though. There are loads of unnecessary stipulations here, and I'm just skimming the first trust.

"Hunter? Do you have a notepad and a pen I could borrow?"

He enters the living room and lifts the lid on the ottoman next to me. "You should find what you need in there."

"Do you want a second opinion on the first trust, or skip that?"

"If you need to read it to understand the second one, I'm not sure."

He rubs a hand to his neck and clears his throat. "There's a summary page in there if it helps from the guy who helped me."

"Okay. I'll do what I can."

Ignoring the summary, I fish around to find a notepad and pen and start reading. After returning to the start and reviewing the first trust, I agree with the lawyer's summary. Including the suspicion that it was an intentional oversight to keep Hunter from accessing it.

It's a legal fucking document and stated clearly he had access to funds for property upkeep. My bet is that's what he's got spread all over the dining room table. At least he kept records.

Yawning, I check the time and notice it's almost ten 10 PM. I'd like to know what this will take to sort before I head to bed. I get back to the second trust with a renewed focus. It's just as complicated as the first, with far too many clauses that don't need to be there or make much sense. A lawyer who gets paid by the hour and loves to make it look like he knows a lot by being extra wordy without cause is clear.

I hate guys like that. Don't be purposely vague. Get to the point.

But slogging through, I weed out all the conditions that make sense for Hunter to access this and sit back with a hand in my hair. This is...odd.

"Hunter? Are you free?"

A chair scrapes back in the dining room, and he walks over.

"Did you already sort it out?" He's hopeful, and a small smile graces his face. I'm not sure how long it will stay there, though.

Motioning to the couch for him to sit, I nod. "I think so."

He huffs a surprised laugh. "Seriously? I paid the last guy three grand to work out the first one, and it took him months to get back to me."

"Well, he probably had other cases and didn't make yours a priority, but to be fair, the first one was more complicated, and I agree with what he said. So no worries there."

Hunter closes his eyes and sighs. "Thank god. You don't know how stressful that was."

A nervous laugh escapes my lips, and his eyes snap open.

"Okay, so...um, this residual trust isn't all that complicated. In fact, I had to read it twice to make sure I got it right because..."

It's like a Band-Aid, right? I should just blurt it out and not try to sugarcoat it. Hunter is a man of action and not games. He's blunt and honest.

"Gabe, just tell me. Did he leave it to his favourite horse, and I already sold it or something?"

"You're his only surviving family member, correct?"

"Yes."

"The residual of his estate, all his wealth that isn't used to manage this property, is left to..." I flip to the page and read directly from the document. "'*The residual of my estate shall be bequeathed to my sole heir in its entirety. As my partner in the rodeo stock breeding, he shall inherit the sum of my wealth.*'"

"So he left it all to me? Holy shit."

"There's a catch." Inhaling a breath, I continue to read. "'*My wealth shall be distributed to my sole heir in increments when milestones of the nuptials are reached.*'"

Hunter blinks. "What?"

"It lists dates that sums will be released to you, Hunter. He doesn't name you by name, which is odd, but he at least named you as his business partner for the rodeo stock. There wasn't a third name, was there?"

Hunter shakes his head. "No. Just the two of us. But...nuptials?"

Flipping the page, I find the passage and read it. "'*Failure for my heir to sustain a marriage for the full duration will result in forfeiting any remaining sum to Broken Rainbow charity.*'"

Hunter remains completely still. He doesn't even blink, and I wonder if this is what it's like in the eye of a tornado. Pure calm before chaos.

"He wants me to get married and if I don't, he'll leave the money to a fucking anti-queer charity!?" He launches off the coach and strides to the end of the room. "Are you absolutely sure, Gabe?"

Hunter's voice is barely a whisper with his back to me, but I hear him. To the depth of my soul, I feel what that question doesn't ask.

"Yes. If you want me to ask a friend for another opinion, I can, but most of the wording in this will is all garbage. I suspect it was drafted that way on purpose to hope you didn't figure it out. Maybe even give up on it."

He grabs the edge of a serving cabinet and, still shirtless, I notice all the muscles in his back tense as he hangs his head.

"Thank you, Gabe. If you don't mind, I'd like to be alone for a while."

"Of course. I'll just grab a glass of water and head to my room."

He's still like that when I head upstairs, and while I wish I could comfort him, I feel like it's the wrong thing to do right now. Maybe another day he'd be open for it, but right now, Hunter Burke has a lot to process.

And I wish I could help.

Instead, I close my bedroom door softly and hope tomorrow is a better day for both of us.

Four
Hunter

No way in fuck do I want to be married.

It's not that I don't believe Gabe. He wouldn't just make shit up like that, but why would my grandfather do this?

After Gabe closed his door behind him, I broke down for the first time since my grandmother died. I'm so fucking tired of holding it all in and pretending I don't care. Tears of anger and loss for something I never had flowed freely. My heart, already ripped and jagged at the hands of my grandfather, finally fell apart. I care too much, and I can't just turn it off.

Grabbing tissues from a box in the living room, I wiped my face and sagged onto the sofa.

It's not even about the money. Yes, it would help, and while it's his wealth and he can leave it to whoever he wants, I poured almost thirty years of my life into this ranch. I worked harder than any hired help, and my pay was laughable, but I stayed first out of obligation. Like I owed it to my father to be better for the man who shunned him.

But I also stayed because there was a time I worshipped Jeremiah Burke. He loved me once when I was a child, and I so desperately wanted that man back. The warm hugs and the walks in the barn, talking about horses and ranch life. I wanted to be like him then.

Family was something everyone I knew had, and I craved it. I wanted to be the one he could count on, and I just wanted him to see me. Really see that I was capable. To be proud of his grandson again and flash his smile my way. For just one short, *'good job, Hunter.'*

It never happened.

I was foolish to live in a world where I hoped he'd change, but I suppose I'm just as thick as the lawyers who made the will thought I was.

When the tears finally stop flowing, I head up to my bedroom.

Sleep won't make the problem go away, but it will help me forget about it for a while.

"Here you go, handsome." Diamond sets my cheesecake down on the table with my coffee. "I gave you extra chocolate sauce. It looks like you could use some happiness."

"Thanks, Diamond."

I force a smile, and he pats my shoulder with a friendly squeeze before he returns to the front counter. His long legs eat up the distance as he crosses the room, and I admire not just his legs, but how he's turned his place into a unique business that all the cowboys flock to.

With the uniform of cut-off shorts and cowboy boots—but only if his staff are comfortable wearing them—The Thirsty Cow's brand of playful sex appeal, alongside coffee and amazing hand-crafted desserts, draws people in like nothing else. Diamond isn't just another pretty face. He's smart as hell.

"Hey...sorry I'm late." Jackson plops into the chair across from me and pats his messy hair. "I thought I had a ball cap in the truck, and now I'm...yeah. I'm late."

Jackson is usually calm and mostly put together, but it takes me less than three seconds to bark a laugh when I figure out why he's late.

"You, ah, missed a few buttons there, Jack. Next time, just wear a T-shirt if you're getting lucky with a deadline." I touch the side of my neck. "Also...he left a mark."

Jackson groans and runs a hand down his face. "It's just...he was...and then —"

"Do *not* explain it. It's fine. You made me laugh, at least."

Diamond stops next to us and sets a coffee in front of Jackson with a smirk. "If I was a betting man, I'd say you haven't had breakfast yet either. I have scones coming out of the oven in ten. I'll drop a few over right away. They go great with cheesecake."

He winks and leaves us be while Jackson shakes his head as he sips his coffee. "My life isn't boring. I'll say that. But we aren't here to talk about me."

I called him first thing this morning because the best thing to ease some sorrow is a talk with a good friend and a slab of homemade cheesecake. It doesn't matter that it's only 10 AM. Desperate times and all that.

"Right. I need to tell you something and I trust you'll be honest with me."

"You know I will."

I launch into telling Jackson how Gabe arrived, and I was still going through all my receipts when Gabe asked if he could help me.

"Ah! So you asked him to look at the will, then?"

"I did, and I'm pretty sure I can trust him. Riley wouldn't be friends with a guy who isn't honourable, would he?"

Jackson shakes his head hard. "No, and you know they're close. Remember when Riley's Aunt Agnes fell just as we got serious? He called Gabe, and I found them sleeping together."

"What? Like...sleeping or fucking?"

Jackson laughs at my question and shakes his head.

"Sleeping, Hunter. Riley was upset and needed comfort, which Gabe gave him. They used to do that a lot, from what Riley says."

"Can I go back and ask what you did when you found them like that? Honestly, I probably would have punched first and asked questions after."

Diamond shows up with fresh scones for each of us and little pots of homemade jam. Blueberry is one of the flavours. I should tell Jamieson since he loves this stuff. "I'm sorry I can't offer clotted cream right now. The delivery guy is late. I'm so sorry."

Diamond is truly apologetic for the oversight. "I'll survive Diamond. Thank you. Just tell any of the English folk before they order, so you aren't mobbed."

We both laugh as Diamond hurries away to the long line of customers that have just arrived.

"I almost punched him." Jackson says as he slathers a scone with strawberry jam. "But I knew Riley enough to keep calm. He wouldn't have been with me then fucked someone else forty-eight hours later. Plus, Gabe immediately identified himself, which helped."

We eat quietly for a few minutes. Exclaiming about how great it all tastes, fresh cream be damned, while inside I'm a nervous mess. But I'm not leaving here without having a plan of action.

"So...Jesus...I don't even know how to say this, Jack." Running a hand over my face, I puff out a breath before summoning the courage to just say it. "According to the residual trust, it's mine if I meet the conditions."

"That's amazing!" I hold up my hand and shake my head. "Oh. How is it not amazing, then?"

"I need to be married." Jackson sputters his coffee and I pass him a napkin. "My bad. I should've let you swallow that first."

"Married!?" Jackson's eyebrows raise as he processes my info drop. "Like, say '*I do*,' and have a proper husband married?"

"If there's another kind of marriage, please share," I say dryly.

Jackson blinks a few times before puffing out a breath. "So, what are you going to do?"

"I was hoping you had an answer."

Jackson's eyebrows return to earth and this time draw into a scrunch on his forehead. He does that when he's thinking, and it's something I've seen plenty of times when we were rodeo partners. "Okay, tell me what else it said. Let's workshop this." Jackson cracks his knuckles and sits forward. "We'll solve this together."

And that's why I called Jackson. He's always in my corner, even when I'm an asshole. Sometimes I think I don't deserve a friend like him, but fuck, I'm glad I have him right now.

"There aren't a lot of details. Gabe said the only heir inherits the rest at certain intervals if they're married and stay married. I think he said three months, six months, and a year."

"What exactly happens at those times?"

"A portion of the money is released from the trust to me to do with as I wish." I bring my mug to my lips. "As long as I'm married." I wash the words away quickly with warm coffee.

Jackson nods and rubs his chin. "I feel like there's a catch. Unless you being married is the catch." Jackson presses his lips together. "Actually, do you think he'd do that?"

"Do I think he'd force me to get married, which I never wanted, because he thinks it will make me miserable just to receive the money? Abso-fucking-lutely."

"If you don't get married, what happens to the trust?"

"Oh, get this...it goes to the Broken Rainbow."

Jackson's mouth drops open.

"Are you fucking kidding me? Jesus, he was a real piece of work. Make you miserable being married or make all our lives miserable because he funds a bullshit straight-rights group." Jackson's hand curls into a fist. "That group isn't a charity. They spread hate everywhere and are actively lobbying the government to repeal everything we fought for. Hunter, please tell me you won't let that happen."

Jackson didn't have to point out everything my grandfather did. It kept me awake most of the night already. I thought of my friends here in Kissing Ridge, especially Riley and Jackson. Riley plans same sex weddings, and that enriches his life in ways I can't understand because romance was never my thing.

Weddings are enormous expenses just to say two words in front of hundreds of people you barely send Christmas greetings to, and it's never appealed to me. But that sort of thing makes many people happy.

Including the two men or women who might be there, not just because they love each other, but because it was something we had to fight for. It's a statement, and I could never live with myself if I was part of the reason the basic right was taken away.

"No, Jack. I don't want that to happen. But I don't know how to not have it happen. That's why I called you."

We sip our coffee in silence for a moment, and I don't really know how the hell I can just marry someone and parade them around to have funds released.

"I have an idea," Jackson says.

"Tell me."

Jackson chews at his lip and leans forward, dropping his voice like we're planning a bank robbery and not finding me a fake husband.

"Gabe. You should marry Gabe." Jackson rushes on. "He already lives at your place. He's a lawyer, and he'll make sure you don't break the rules of the will, and he'll definitely support the reason for not forfeiting funds to Broken Rainbow."

As far as ideas go, it's not the worst one.

"You think he'd go for it?"

Jackson grins. "Only way to find out is to get a ring and ask."

He chuckles a little, and I do, too, because me proposing is just ridiculous…but it makes sense. It also gives me hives, but it makes sense.

"I'll talk to him tonight."

After I left Jackson, I stopped at the jewellery store downtown.

Ring prices were…something. After trying to be polite by asking vague questions, I finally just asked the girl for the cheapest ring they had. A $149 thin gold band now sits in a box in my pocket in what possibly is the biggest twilight zone moment of my life.

If Jackson is right, Gabe will agree this is a great idea and we'll arrange a date to get our marriage licence and walk over to the courthouse as soon as it's in hand. We'll submit the proof to the trustee for the clock to start and meet up again in three months.

I feel hopeful for the first time since the old bastard died. This battle with lawyers and wills might finally have an end in sight. Which, if I'm honest, has been more stress than I could handle. I was close to breaking a few times, and now, with some resolution, it's like I can breathe again.

By the time I came home and fed the animals, it was late, but they didn't give me too much shit for it. Even Lewis. He accepted the carrot I threw his way, and I lingered along the fence, watching him eat it with his little paws and chubby cheeks. Such a funny little animal.

The nerves don't hit me until after I've showered and started dinner. I don't even know Gabe's schedule. We didn't have time to talk about any of that, but he's a lawyer in Kissing Ridge. He can't work that late... can he?

The ring in my pocket feels like a bomb, and I just want this over and done with. I'm almost positive proposals shouldn't make people feel like the world is about to end, but maybe if you're in love, it's completely different.

The front door opens while I'm chopping carrots for the steamer, and I hold my breath for Gabe to announce he's home.

"It smells amazing in here. I should pay extra for you to be my chef," he jokes as he loosens the tie at his neck.

My palms sweat, and I wipe them on my jeans and attempt a smile.

"Are you okay?" Gabe asks with a tilt to his head.

"I'm fine?"

"Are you asking me? That sounded like you're not sure." His eyes narrow, and I hold my breath as he scrutinizes me like a bug under a microscope.

"I'm sure. I usually cook for two, so I have something for lunch the next day, but you're welcome to join me again."

"Really?" His eyes light up like it's Christmas, and he heads to the stairs. "Give me a minute to change, and I'll help you."

Gabe disappears, and I return to my task.

"Just ask him, for god's sake," I mutter to myself and slam the knife through the carrot harder than I should.

If he says no, it'll be even more awkward than it is now. If he says yes, well, maybe we can go for ice cream or something. What do people do to celebrate this kind of thing?

I'm so out of my comfort zone here. I'd be more comfortable running naked down Main Street.

Which I'd likely choose over what I'm about to do.

Five
Gabe

Today was a day that could have gone better.

Arriving home to find Hunter cooking and another invitation for dinner definitely turned things around. This morning began with two major pending land transactions pulling me as their counsel of choice because I wasn't '*country*' enough. Whatever that was supposed to mean, but it quickly deflated my good mood.

After changing out of my suit into a pair of khakis and a short-sleeved button-down, I return to the kitchen and find Hunter clutching the counter while inhaling deeply.

I'm positive he's not just inhaling the aroma of garlic.

"Hunter?"

He bolts and stands ramrod straight. "Was just, ah, doing one of those breathing exercise things." He nods and puffs a breath. "Yeah, just getting in the zone."

He needs to be in a zone to cook?

"Um, okay. What can I do to help?"

"Do you like to drink? I could use one." He runs a hand through his hair and brushes past me towards the living room. When he doesn't return for several minutes, I turn the elements off on the stove and go search for him.

He's standing in front of the liquor cabinet, this time with a hand clutching a glass of whiskey, and I'm not sure I should interrupt. His lips move silently, like he's having a conversation or singing a song. I'm not sure which, but he's focused, so I wait.

Hunter downs the rest of his drink and blows out a breath. When he turns to see me watching him, his eyes widen.

"If there was anyone else, I'd ask them, but will you marry me?" He pauses, like he forgot something, and digs in his pocket. "I got a ring." Hunter steps towards me and thrusts the small box at me like it's a relief for someone else to hold it. "Okay, that wasn't so bad," he breathes.

I suppose that depends on what end is judging if it was bad or not.

"I'm sorry, but...did you just ask me to marry you?"

He gestures to the box in my hand like that's the magic answer, and when I flip it open, a thin gold band sits inside. It's plain and not at all fancy, sort of like the man who apparently just proposed to me.

"Please don't make me say the words again. I thought I was going to pass out."

I'm not overly romantic like my friend Riley, but when I imagined a proposal, it certainly wasn't like this.

"Let's back up. Is this because of the will thing?"

Hunter nods. "Yeah, I...oh shit. Dinner!" He rushes by me, so I follow him back to the kitchen.

"I turned it all off since it looked like you were having a...crisis of sorts." Looking at the box in my hand, I huff a laugh. "Guess I wasn't far off."

Hunter busies himself at the stove while I consider getting a drink myself. "It's okay. We can still eat it. I'll just finish up the chicken and reheat the veg. It's good."

While he does that, I shove the ring box in my pocket and pull out the plates and cutlery, working alongside him in the large country kitchen like I've been here for more than a day.

We settle at the dining room table again, but this time with Hunter at the end and me next to him. After a few bites of dinner in silence, and it's clear he's not about to start the conversation, I do.

"Hunter, you need to explain what this is about."

With a sigh, he leans back and sets his fork down. "I talked to Jackson this morning. I told him what you said about the trust, and he suggested I ask you to marry me."

"And what were his reasons for why it was a good idea?"

Hunter motions around him, and I make a note that we should never play charades because I'm clueless. When I remain silent, he continues.

"Gabe...you already live here. We can sell it as an actual relationship. I want the money, I'll admit that, but I also don't want the money to go to an organization that funds hate against people like us." Hunter pauses and swallows, his tough bravado mask slipping for a moment. "He didn't approve of me being gay and I refuse to be ashamed of that or let him attack us even after he's died. That's too far, Gabe."

Pain drips from his words before he resumes eating, and my mind spins with so many questions. I don't know how much money we're talking about, but to leave it in the trust with checkpoints to distribute it must be significant. But aside from that, if it's only a dollar, I don't want it going to that organization either.

"I don't want money sent to them either, Hunter. But, and I hate sounding like a dick about this...what's in this for me? Marriage for a year is a big deal. My life is on hold."

He drums his fingers on the table.

"What would you like? I can't pay you, obviously, until I get the money." His nose wrinkles. "That sounds...awful. But if you want compensation, it could be done."

"Actually, there is something you could help me with. I had a problem with some farmers today."

Hunter furrows his brow. "What kind of problem? They're usually decent people around here."

"Oh, they were very polite when they took their real estate business elsewhere because, and I quote, *a city man like you won't understand.* I won't lie to you. I'm concerned if it's happening now, it will keep happening, and I can't keep losing business."

"So, how can I help with that?"

Shrugging, I push my plate to the side and steeple my fingers in front of me. "Teach me about this area and what makes a land deal with farmers or ranchers so different that a city guy can't handle it. Make me a country boy, I guess."

Hunter's laughter booms in the small room, and I can't help but smile. He's a striking man when he smiles and laughs. Beautiful, even. He probably doesn't even know it.

"Make you a country boy? If I do that, will you promise to listen to my suggestions?"

"Of course."

"You won't like most of them."

Hunter's eyes twinkle with a playfulness that makes me wonder what the fuck I'm doing in this town. Moving to a small town from the city. Buying a sleepy law practice and leaving the high-paced prosecution office behind. Living with a man who just asked me to marry him, and I'm actually considering it.

I wanted to slow down and make a change, but all of this sounds like the product of a fever dream

"Like what?"

He leans forward. "Lose the suit and tie. You're in farm country. They want to know that you're not a stuffy suit and you're not afraid to get dirty. They work with their hands and bodies, Gabe. Suits don't make them comfortable."

"Are you serious?"

"Completely."

"Okay, so, if I marry you, you'll get the money, and I'll get to use you as I see fit to help the business. I can ask you to attend events or explain things when I need?"

"Sure. That's pretty easy."

"What about when the year is up?"

Hunter shrugs again. "We get a divorce and go on our way again."

He says it so matter-of-factly. Like it means nothing to just do this and end it in a year, but I suppose this kind of thing happens more often than either of us knows.

"You should protect yourself, though. I'll ask a friend to draw up a prenup before we do it."

"So, is that a yes?"

"Yeah. We both get what we need. Why not?"

Hunter's smile is blinding.

"Nice. Thank you."

Hunter rises and takes his plate to the kitchen. We just negotiated a marriage over baked chicken and carrots. Removing the ring box from my pocket, I pull it out and slide the ring on.

Riley is going to have a fit when he learns how this went down.

"OMG...Gabe! Tell me everything!"

After hugging Riley, we settle at our table in Avocadabra, a trendy bistro he loves, for a quick lunch.

"It's not real, Rye," I whisper. "You know that, so there's no big romantic moment to tell you about. I put the ring on myself and everything."

He frowns and reaches for my left hand, running his thumb over the gold band.

"You're married before me. I never thought I'd see the day. I'm not sure what I should say. Congrats doesn't feel right."

I know Hunter had already been over to talk to Jackson, so Riley has the details behind the why I'm getting married to someone I don't even know. His conflict about it is understandable.

"Yeah, I know. I never thought I'd get married, but if I did, it wasn't over a plate of chicken and putting the ring on myself, you know? I hate to say it, but...some romance would be nice."

"Oh, Gabe." Riley squeezes my hand. "When you find the real one, I'll make sure it's done right." He sits back and reaches for his tablet. "So we won't go too overboard with this wedding. Have you picked a date? Thought about what to wear? Anything?"

"Uh...we're getting the licence tomorrow and just planning to cross over to the courthouse after."

Riley's tablet almost hits the floor. "What?" He hisses. "You can't just get married at a courthouse without any personal details. I know it's not real, but like...don't you want to have a nice corsage or something?"

"Well, if Hunter was doing it for reasons other than money, sure. But it's just to make it legal. My friend Erik sent me a draft of a prenup already. Hunter wants to get this started, and I can't blame him. His life is in limbo. So we'll just do this for now."

The server stops at our table, and after taking our orders, Riley leans in again. "Can I at least come?"

Riley's eyes shine with unshed tears, and I feel like an idiot. "Fuck, Rye. I'm sorry. Yes, you can come. We need witnesses, too, and I'd love for you to be there. I imagine Hunter will ask Jackson, too."

"Sorry for being emotional, but you're my best friend, Gabe. This might mean nothing to you, but it's still a huge moment. You're getting married, and there's a chance it could last forever. I don't want to miss it."

Riley was always the more sensitive of the two of us. He has a giant heart, and the more I think of it, the more I think he's right. I don't think it will last forever, but what if it's the only time in my life I get married? I should make some sort of effort.

"You know what? You're right. It's a life-altering moment. Reasons aside, let's pretend it's a real wedding. What can you pull off for tomorrow afternoon?"

His grin is real as he checks his schedule. "With Jackson's help, lots. Let's do this."

Somehow, over a plate of vegetarian pasta, Riley and I pull a few details together for my real wedding to a fake husband. It's ridiculous, but Riley's statement that it could last forever still echoes with me.

Stranger things have happened.

Just in case, I tell Riley to find a photographer.

Six
Hunter

"**I** don't know how Gabe wears a suit every day. This would drive me nuts."

Thankfully, it's a cool day, the full summer heat isn't on us yet, but I'm already feeling the chafe on my balls with this suit.

"It's only for a few hours. You'll survive." Jackson quips as he smooths his tie before helping me with mine. "If you showed up in jeans and T-shirts, Riley wouldn't be happy with you."

"He's your problem, not mine."

Jackson just laughs as he adjusts my tie and smooths it down with a pat to my chest. "I know this isn't real, but I'm still honoured you asked me, Hunter. It's a big deal no matter what. Thank you for letting me do this."

Jackson's sincerity has me pause. "You're always my go-to, Jack. Real or fake. You're the only one I trust with anything important. I hope you know that."

"Hunter...dammit. That means a lot, and you made my eyes water."

He pulls me into a hug and slaps my back before letting me go with a laugh. "Save the mushy stuff for the husband to be." He checks his watch and motions to the door. "We need to get to the license office asap. Riley runs a tight ship, so let's get moving."

We take my truck since it's not covered in dog fur like his and drive into town. The entire time, Jackson makes small talk, and I feel like I'm surrounded by a cloud of an alternate reality. I've not given too much thought to this wedding because it's not real. I've successfully compartmentalized it as just a deed to achieve a means...until now.

"Do you think we need to share bedrooms? How in-depth will these people look to confirm we're married? They wouldn't do that, would they?"

I'm not ready for that kind of commitment. My bed is mine. Lots of couples keep separate bedrooms, though. At least they used to. Is that still a thing?

"I don't think anyone will ask to see your bedroom, Hunter, but have you talked to Gabe about how you'll handle hookups? I don't think it's wise for either of you to be seen out with other people."

Shit. No, I hadn't thought of that either.

"Do you ever wonder if someone could fuck up their life more than me? I was so focused on getting him to marry me to get this money, I didn't think about what the next year will look like." I like sex just as much as the next guy, but I'm not on the circuit as much as before. The easy bed partners aren't as frequent, but...a year without it will suck.

Jackson reaches over and squeezes my shoulder. "Nobody is perfect, Hunter, but definitely make sure Gabe is on the same page. You don't want to risk anything."

Spotting Gabe's car out front of the registry office already, I park next to it and once again shake my head at how different we are. His fancy luxury car and my full-size pickup. I certainly hope this arrangement works for both of us.

Jackson leaves me at the registry office to go to the courthouse, where Riley waits. Entering the registry office, I follow the signs to the right room for marriage licences. As I round the corner, Gabe comes into view, and I almost turn around and change my mind.

Gabe is...beautiful. I see him in a suit every day, but not like this. It's moulded to his body perfectly, and paired with his short, trimmed beard and perfectly styled black hair, he's a showstopper.

Gabe smiles and awkwardly wraps an arm around me in a half hug and kisses my cheek. "Dashing as always, Hunter."

His blue eyes smile behind his glasses, and I clear my throat. "Thank you. You look good. Great, actually."

We fidget in the hallway for a moment and Gabe holds up the numbered ticket. "We're third in line. She said it won't take long."

"Oh...good." Because I can't seem to find other words today. Thankfully, Gabe talks a lot for a living and takes it in stride.

"Have you ever had a pet?" Gabe asks.

"Does a horse count?"

"Of course. What about a house pet? Cat, dog, snake...anything."

Despite the nerves, I laugh. "No snake, for sure. I caught a garter snake once, and my grandma nearly fainted when I showed her."

Gabe laughs, light and easy. "I'd have loved to see that. I never had pets either. We couldn't afford the care for one."

Gabe offers me that information with no reservation, and it catches me off guard. "Why are we talking about pets?"

"To get to know each other. We're about to be married, and it would be nice to know something about you."

"Number three!" A woman's voice calls, and Gabe holds up the ticket. "That's us."

"Is that something that's important to you?" I ask as we approach the counter.

Gabe cocks his head. "Knowing you? Yes. No matter what happens between us, I'd like to know you."

"Gentlemen. How can I help you?"

"A marriage licence, please," Gabe says, and I take a moment to digest what he said as we both fish out our identification from our wallets.

The woman begins our form, and I figure if he's making an effort, I should, too.

"What's your favourite colour?"

"Teal," Gabe says. "What's yours?"

"Does black count?"

Gabe snorts. "I think so. Why black?"

"It hides dirt." I laugh. "My grandma always called me a dirt magnet. One time I had a new white T-shirt and within ten minutes I had a grass stain, and I didn't even go outside."

I laugh softly, remembering that day. Still a mystery where the grass came from.

"Your grandma, you talk about her a lot. You were close?"

The memory of my grandmother is one that's mixed. She was the only light most days in a dreary childhood filled with adult-sized work and not enough positive reinforcement. Without her, I don't know if I would be half the person I am today.

"We were. I'll tell you about her sometime."

Gabe picks up on my discomfort, thankfully, and before I can ask anything in return, he offers me something instead.

"I was raised by my two sisters. My dad literally disappeared. One of those *'oh honey, I'm going out for milk'* stories, you know?

I was ten. Then my mom got sick and was gone before I turned twelve."

He offers me a small smile, and with great clarity, I realize that maybe me and Gabe have more in common than I thought. His gaze locks on mine, and there's a glimmer of something there, like he might understand me.

Which is absurd, because nobody ever does and I'm certainly not going to entertain thoughts of finally finding a match or some other bullshit.

"Okay, gentlemen. Your licence is ready. I just need your signatures here."

Gabe charms the woman as he signs and replaces his ID in his wallet. She continues speaking while I do the same.

"You're the new lawyer in town, then?" she asks after Gabe mentions he just moved here recently and bought a business.

"I am. It wasn't just the business that brought me here, though. I couldn't stay away from this guy any longer. Long-distance relationships suck."

The woman sighs and nods my way. "You're looking a lot different in a suit, Mr. Burke, but congratulations. I hope you'll still be competing at the Kissing Ridge Rodeo as a married man this year."

"Of course I will." It's then that I finally place who she is. She's a member of the rodeo planning committee and also organizes a lot of the 4-H events for kids. "I didn't recognize you at your day job. I apologize for not saying hello, Christine."

She waves a hand and smiles. "I get that a lot. Don't worry about it."

"Is there a 4-H event happening soon? I'd like for Gabe to experience what it was like growing up country and bring him to a meeting if I could?"

The words are out of my mouth before I have more time to consider what it all means, but just like Gabe, I'm playing the part of a devoted husband.

Christine smiles and reaches for a slip of paper. "Yes, there is! Next week and my speaker just cancelled. If either of you could step in, I'd appreciate it." She passes me the paper with her number and meeting info. "Think about it if you'd like, and just call me. After the wedding, of course."

Showing Gabe the slip, I ask if he's free, and he enthusiastically nods. "I'd love to be there, Christine. Hunter or I will get back to you in a day or two."

We exit the registry office, a marriage licence tucked into my pocket and a slip of paper for a 4-H meeting in the other. Gabe is quiet until we step outside.

"Thank you for that, Hunter. I appreciate it, but I have one question before we go to that meeting."

"What's that?"

He pauses on the sidewalk with me, and I turn to face him.

"What the hell is 4-H?"

Throwing my head back, I laugh. "I'll fill you in. But first, let's get this wedding done so I can get out of this fucking suit."

The courthouse was busier than normal for a Wednesday afternoon, but Riley used his contacts, and we had a firm place in line.

In twenty minutes, I'd say I do to a man who I knew liked teal and was raised by his sisters, but never had a pet. Which is the sum of what I know about Gabe, aside from him being a lawyer.

"I know this is...you know, an arrangement," Gabe whispers next to me, "But I asked Riley to take care of a few details like it's a real wedding. I hope you don't mind."

"Uh...not like I can say no now, right?"

Gabe smiles sheepishly. "No. But that's your heads up. Here come Riley and Jackson."

Riley and Jackson each carry a small clear box and Riley, in all his romantic planning and romance-loving mode, audibly gasps when he reaches us before pulling me into a hug.

"You look simply amazing, Hunter. Thank you for letting us be here for this."

"Yeah, you're welcome."

He opens the box and pulls out a beautiful corsage before handing it to Gabe. It's a trio of white roses and baby's breath secured with teal ribbon and my lips betray me, smiling as Gabe steps forward to pin it to my suit jacket.

"Surprise," he murmurs as his fingers work to secure it to the material. "I didn't know your favourite colour, but I knew mine. Probably a good thing because weddings shouldn't have black flowers."

"Thank you. It's pretty. I've never worn flowers before."

Jackson passes one to me that's identical and after I take it, Gabe turns it over in my hand, showing me the giant-ass pin. "Riley can do it if you're not sure. It's okay."

"Is it? I feel like I'd stab you and that probably wouldn't be the right way to start this off."

Gabe motions for Riley, who steps forward and pins the flowers to Gabe like he does it in his sleep.

"There. Now that's two grooms who match."

"Davis and Burke? Please come inside."

"It's show time," Gabe says and grabs my hand before pulling me forward with Jackson and Riley behind us.

It's not fancy in the room. A man in an ill-fitting brown suit stands to the side of a desk. The clerk arranges us with Jackson beside me and Riley beside Gabe before sitting at the small desk with our marriage license.

The justice of the peace reads a non-denominational passage that Riley chose because it was a simple reading about the power of love and union or some other bullshit I couldn't give a flying fuck about. Gabe still holds my hand with a smile on his face as he listens, and my mind wanders.

While I can see the appeal if you believe in love, this *can* be a moving ceremony. Nothing is forever, though. People die and people leave. It's just the way things are in life. Even for our charade, this feels too much and—

"Hunter? Just repeat I do."

Shit. I wasn't even paying attention, and it's rather important to say those two words. Can I ask him to repeat the question just to be sure? It's like signing a contract before reading all the fine print.

"Sorry. Yeah. Uh...I do."

God, even I don't sound convincing, but Gabe keeps a smile on his face.

"Gabe, do you take this man and promise to be faithful? To love him and cherish him for all the days of your life?"

"I do."

Gabe smiles at me and if you've streamed a show online and it has that random buffering moment where you hang on the last word of the scene in anticipation of what comes next...that's how I feel. But with less anticipation and more anxiety.

"Do you plan to exchange rings?" The man breaks my thoughts and I nod. "I have one, yes."

Turning to Jackson, he hands me the same gold band I bought Gabe earlier this week.

"If you wish to say anything personal, you can do so now. If not, just repeat after me."

"Um, nothing personal for me, sir."

Gabe offers me his left hand as the justice speaks. "I give you this ring as a sign of our union."

"Gabe, I give you this ring as a sign of our...union."

The word union makes me stumble and remember what Jackson and I talked about earlier. Should I think about sex while we're exchanging vows? Thank god nobody can hear what I'm thinking.

"I have a ring as well," Gabe says and turns to Riley.

"What?" Realizing how that sounds, I correct myself. "I mean, you shouldn't have Gabe. I thought we were just keeping it at one?"

He winks at me, and I think he's enjoying this. "Sometimes I don't listen." He whispers.

"Repeat after me, Gabe." The man says and Gabe bites at his lip as the justice gives the same line he gave me.

Gabe grabs for my hand, which I haven't even lifted, and slides the same thin gold band I got for him on my finger.

"Hunter, I give you this ring as a sign of our union."

The ring fits perfectly, and while it looks foreign on my finger, it doesn't feel like I thought it would. There's no burning skin, so there's that.

"By the power invested in me by the town of Kissing Ridge and the province of Alberta, I now pronounce you husband and husband. You may now kiss."

Maybe it's the word kiss, or maybe it's because Gabe smells and looks amazing, or possibly because it's the societal expectations ingrained in me. No matter the reason, it's what I do.

With a hand on his hip and the other behind his head, I kiss Gabe. His lips are soft and part immediately with his tongue sliding next to mine like we've practiced for this moment.

My fingers flex on his hip as I tilt his head and get lost in everything Gabe. Kissing him is easy, and he presses against me while kissing me back with barely contained want. It's right there on his lips and I can taste it as sure as anything.

And this is why I've kept my distance from Gabe since we met. One kiss and it's like your first time with sugar. You want more.

It's not until someone clears their throat, I think it's Jackson, that I step away.

"Sorry about that. Kinda got carried away."

"S'okay," Gabe murmurs.

We sign the marriage certificate with Jackson and Riley, and in another few brief minutes, we're outside. My thoughts are a confused jumble, and my lungs burn for more oxygen.

The day is still the same outside as it was when we went in.

But I'm not.

Seven
Gabe

Most people dream of their wedding day. The first kiss, the first sight of your partner at the altar. Hell, even the food they serve their guests.

Marriage wasn't something I ever gave much thought to. I knew I wanted to share a life with someone forever, but marriage wasn't a deal breaker. It's just a piece of paper, after all. I may be a lawyer, but today I realized just how powerful a single sheet of paper can be.

After posing for photos in the park that I blamed on Riley, our marriage certificate firmly in my inner suit pocket, the enormity of this sat on my chest in a way I didn't expect. Riley drove my car home because Hunter insisted he wanted to drive.

The silence in the truck cab is heavy, and instead of happiness, a blanket of sadness sits. I should be elated that this man kissed the breath from me, finally. If someone hadn't cleared their throat, I might have let my hands wander to places not suitable for public eyes. Instead, my thoughts have turned to the family I miss who couldn't be here to watch me get married.

It may be fake, but it still would have been nice to include them somehow.

"Did you want to get an early dinner before we get home? Maybe takeout? People usually eat after getting married, don't they?"

Hunter interrupts my maudlin thoughts and I'm grateful for the distraction.

"I, uh...I arranged for that. It should be at the ranch already."

Hunter's gaze remains forward as he drives, and he clears his throat.

"Cool." His fingers flex on the steering wheel a few times and I catch the flash of the ring on his left hand. "So, now that we have a legal document to bring to the lawyer, I should be able to just drop it off, right? Or should we do it together?"

"We should go together. They will want our identification and all that to confirm I'm real. I can clear my afternoon on Friday if you can set up a meeting with them."

Hunter nods. "Great. I'll do that." A long pause sits between us, and things feel more awkward now than they did before. "Thank you."

Hunter pulls into the ranch yard, and I'm once again struck by the peacefulness this place radiates. I'm still not sure I can adapt like I need to in order to be successful here, but with Hunter's unexpected gift today to offer to introduce me, I'm cautiously hopeful.

After we step out of the truck, a single sharp whistle sounds, and I jump. Hunter's low chuckle aimed at me shouldn't stoke the fire to have him. I should be pissed he laughs at me for being scared of a wild animal with giant teeth, and yet...part of me wants him to always laugh at me like that.

"It's just Lewis, Gabe. He says hello when he hears the truck."

"Sorry. I'm not used to wild animals and their noises."

Hunter's eyes sparkle with a mischief that makes me take a step back, but he reaches for me, and his hand grips my wrist. "Come with me, counsellor." When I don't move, he softens his grip. "You can trust me, Gabe."

With a slight tug, he guides me to the barn and shows me where he has a bucket of carrots stashed for the horses and Lewis.

"I fill it up every few days. The smaller ones are for Lewis and the large ones for the horses. Sometimes they get apples, but carrots keep longer out here." He ducks his head as he fishes out two big carrots and one small one. "I only treat the horses with sugar cubes on Christmas."

Hunter doesn't make eye contact with that admission, but something in his voice tells me I might be the only one who knows that.

"Come on. You need to meet your new family."

"My what now?"

Hunter whistles and clucks his tongue before handing me a large carrot. "My horses." He grins, and it's easy for me to picture him as a young boy out there with horses and his grandmother making sure he doesn't wear white. "Dixie is the one I ride in rodeos. She's been my rock for almost fifteen years now and I need to think about training her replacement." He whistles again and three horses finally come into view. "My other horse is Mack. She's extra feisty and I need to spend more time with her. The third horse is Jackson's."

He breaks his carrot in two, and all three horses pause at the fence. They're huge this close and I step back, but this time Hunter grabs my elbow and pulls me closer to him. "They're gentle. Don't be afraid," he soothes, and despite my nerves, I let myself relax. He holds a half carrot to Dixie, who takes it with giant whiskered lips and crunches it down. Pieces fall to the ground, and she dips her head to pick up the pieces. Hunter takes my hand with the large carrot and covers my hand with his. "This one is for Jackson's horse." He gently pushes the head of Mack aside so Jackson's horse can take the carrot from me.

Hunter holds me steady, and the horse takes the carrot from my hand, chomping off half while I try not to scream like I did with the groundhog.

"See? Not so bad, right?"

Hunter feeds the third horse the other half carrot and pets their ears. Three giant heads stretch over the fence towards him, and Dixie nudges her nose against his suit jacket with a snort.

"I know, girl. You won't see me dressed like this again." He smooths a hand along her face and turns to me. "Would you like to pet her? She's curious about you." Dixie stretches towards me, and I lean back. "She's not a biter. Mack might nibble, but not Dixie."

I want to do this for him. He's so comfortable around these animals, and if I want to really know him or fit into this town, I need to be comfortable with the horses. He's a damn cowboy. What kind of fake husband would I be if I can't handle horses?

My hand shakes as I reach over to touch where Hunter's hand rests. Dixie's big brown eyes stare at me as she stretches closer. She huffs, and I jump while pulling my hand back.

"What's that mean? Does she like me?" My voice carries a hopefulness I hope Hunter doesn't pick up on.

"Yeah, Gabe." There's no laughter in his voice this time. His expression is nothing less than tender as he strokes Dixie's neck.

"She's just feeling you out, but she likes you. If she didn't, she'd pin her ears back and not get so close. She trusts me implicitly, so she feels safe to check you out." He turns his soulful brown eyes towards me. "Just like you should know that I'd not put you in danger."

No, I don't suppose he would. Hunter might present like someone who doesn't care, but watching him now? The man has a heart the size of the Rocky Mountains.

Dixie snuffles around Hunter a little longer until he playfully pushes her away with a promise of seeing her later. He's so relaxed here with his horse. He's not like the Hunter from the rodeo ring or bar with a ring of barbed wire around him. There's a definite change here in his demeanour.

Here, he's perhaps a little softer than most people see, and he just gave me that glimpse into what he's really like. The layers of this man must be plentiful, and I wonder if he'll show them all to me.

"If you throw that little carrot towards Lewis, he'll be your friend."

"He's not there."

Hunter shakes his head with a small laugh and points to the grass behind Lewis's hole where Lewis sits on his back legs, waiting.

"I thought they were called prairie dogs if they sit like that and not groundhogs."

"That's an entirely different animal and thankfully one I don't get here."

"Why?" I toss the carrot towards Lewis, and when it thunks on the ground, he waddles off his hill for it.

"Those are the ones I can't let stay here. They dig all over and make too many holes for the livestock to step in and get hurt."

"Oh. Lewis doesn't do that?"

"Nope. That's his only hole, and it's outside the pasture area."

I watch as the chubby animal eats the carrot, and he's rather cute.

"Hey, now that we're married, could we get a real pet? Like one that lives in the house and doesn't intimidate me?"

Hunter walks towards the house, still in his wedding-day suit, and I follow.

"You think talking about pets is the most important issue we have to cover right now?"

"It seems like a safe place to start. What do you want to cover first?"

Hunter pauses as we reach the front door and glances my way. "Sex."

The air leaves my lungs, and I suppose that's important enough. I mean...we all need it, right? God knows I've wanted it since I first saw him.

Hunter enters the house, and I follow. He leaves his boots at the door as he always does and heads down the hall to the living room.

"Gabe..." His voice trails off as I catch up to him and observe what Riley's help accomplished for my dinner surprise.

"Oh. This is...more than I requested." I laugh, a high-pitched squeaky noise, when Hunter stares at me. "I thought it would be nice to eat together out of the public eye while we figure out our next moves. Jackson said you like simple things, so it's—"

"You asked my friends what my favourite foods are?"

Hunter's gaze pins me in place, and thoughts of a sex talk evaporate. Have I offended him?

"Jackson said you love hot dogs even though they give you heartburn and that you'd appreciate all the toppings. So yeah, I asked and...I guess I delivered."

We have to cook the dogs, but a table sits in the living room with every single hot dog topping possible in small containers or chilling on ice. A row of foot-long hot dogs sits on a silver platter waiting to be grilled, and it would all feel like a kid's birthday party if it weren't for the bouquets of roses all over the room and the banner saying '*Husband and Husband.*'

Hunter remains silent, and I think it might be too much, but he throws his head back in laughter.

"Hot dogs and roses." He snort-laughs again, and I think that has to be a good thing. "I need to get out of this suit. Then we'll talk."

Hunter disappears up the stairs, and I watch him go, before finally taking the stairs to my room after I hear his door close.

I know I married Hunter Burke, but if today is any indication, he's not the man he appears to be.

Turns out the hot dog bar was a great idea. Not only did it make Hunter smile and laugh, but he opened up a little more, and we enjoyed conversation as friends.

I learned a little more about the mysterious man, but it's time to get to some real talk.

After pouring myself a glass of amaretto on ice and Hunter kicks back with a beer, our easy, friendly conversation screeches to a halt when I turn the talk to business.

"I don't know how long it will take for you to arrange an appointment with the lawyer, but just tell me when and I'll shuffle anything I have going on. Really. This needs to get recorded so you can access the funds as soon as possible."

Hunter swallows his beer and nods. "I appreciate you being so flexible about that. The sooner it's taken care of, the sooner we can get back to our lives." He sets his beer on the table and leans forward. "Speaking of our lives, we need to talk about how to conduct ourselves for the next year."

My heart rate kicks up, and I turn away from him. Another titter-like laugh escapes past my lips. "Is this the part where you ask me to pretend the strange men I find here are just friends?"

Hunter's dark gaze meets mine. "I don't bring people here. Ever." There's a flicker of something in his eyes that has me swallowing hard.

"Okay...I don't have to do that either. This is your home, and I'd never be that disrespectful." Hunter watches me closely and licks his lips after I sip from my glass. My cock aches as my imagination runs wild, dreaming of what his tongue might feel like on my body.

"I don't think we should risk being seen with other people." Hunter's voice is thick and raspy, and my mouth runs dry when I meet his gaze. We stare each other down and the room feels like it just had the air sucked out of it and I realize I haven't addressed his concern.

"That's probably wise. Hard to convince people you're married if you're out with someone else."

He leans back again and grabs his beer. His thick fingers wrap around the bottle and I wonder what those fingers would feel like wrapped around my dick. His throat bobs as he swallows the beverage down, and I think I know where he's going with this, but he has yet to come out and say it. When he remains quiet, I decide to take this where I want it.

Where I've wanted it since I first saw him on his horse over a year ago.

"I have a proposal." My voice sounds like I've just woken from the longest nap. Hunter's gaze shifts to me as I set my drink on the coffee table and move to sit next to him. Sitting this close to him, I catch his scent. A mix of horses and fabric softener that shouldn't be sexy, but somehow still is. "I can't go an entire year without sex, Hunter. Neither can you if I had to guess." He remains quiet, but shifts slightly on the sofa, and our thighs touch. "What if we keep it between us? It's convenient. We live together already." My hand slides onto his thigh, and the heat through his pants sears my palm. A soft breath passes from his lips, and the malty aroma left from his beer makes me want to taste it from his lips. "Casual sex while we're married."

He has to want this. There's no other way this could go.

"No feelings involved, and you sleep in your own bed at night," he rasps as he shifts towards me. My hand on his thigh drifts upwards and ghosts over the tented fabric in his pants.

"I can do that." Our chests rise and fall faster than a moment ago, and I lean in closer. "If we're exclusive, do we need protection?"

He reaches over and tugs at me to come closer. I stand and straddle his lap. God, he's beautiful, with flecks of gold in his brown eyes I never noticed before. I need him to wreck me...right now. My fingers curl into the soft fabric of his shirt, and his muscles jump under my touch.

"I'm on PrEP and my results are negative. If you're okay without, so am I." Hunter's hands slide to my ass, squeezing me in the rough, urgent way I crave.

My eyes close with a shaky sigh. "Same," I breathe.

When I open my eyes, Hunter's gaze is what I imagine a lion sees before it pounces on its prey; dark, dialled in, and hungry.

"You sure about this, counsellor?"

"I've never been more sure of anything in my life."

Hunter says nothing else. Instead, he pulls my head to his lips and steals my breath, just like he did in the courthouse. This time he doesn't restrain himself, and neither do I. We come together like a lightning strike.

His tongue still holds the flavour of his beer, and I suck on it, revelling in the growl that rumbles in his chest.

Hunter's hands are everywhere at once. My shirt comes off in record time and I'm scrambling to get him naked while still on his lap. His mouth on my neck bites down and I gasp.

"God, I want you," he growls against my skin, and if I weren't already sitting, I might melt in a puddle of goo.

"Take it all, Hunter. Whatever you want, I'm here for it." My teeth nip at his ear, and his body shivers. My arms wrap around his neck when he stands, lifting me with him. He turns us, gently lowering me onto the couch, before yanking my sweats down to my knees in one motion. My dick plumps under his gaze and his smirk is almost sinister.

"Fuck..." he whispers before bending to nip my thigh. "You hide all this under those fancy suits, counsellor. That's a shame." Hunter's mouth is hot and fucking perfect as he covers as much skin as he can before licking a line up my cock.

"Ahh..." My hips try to punch up, but he holds me down with a firm hand and an unspoken command to stay still. It's wild and hot, but I don't move. Even when he laps at my balls with a talented tongue and teases my hole with a tap of his thumb.

"I want to see you," I rasp. "For fuck's sake, take off your pants and let me see all of you, cowboy."

Hunter pauses and for one horrible minute, I think he'll change his mind and leave me here hard and horny, but he doesn't. Instead, he stands at my head and quirks an eyebrow as he looks down at me.

Scrambling up, my legs get twisted in my pants that are still at my ankles, and I work at kicking them off with my feet while yanking at Hunter's pants. He laughs, a quiet little huff. I wouldn't have heard it if he hadn't bent to pull my pants off the final ankle.

There's just something about that moment, that action specifically, that claws into me. I don't have more time to think about it because he's tapping his dick against my lips and I'm stretching open to swallow him with unbridled want.

He's heavy on my tongue, and I groan around him. I might be over-eager, but he doesn't seem to mind.

"Yeah, counsellor. That's it." He groans when I work him deeper into my throat. "I knew your lips would look pretty around my dick." His fingers curl into my hair, scratching my scalp, and I push forward to bury my nose against his skin.

"Fuck, Gabe…" Hunter drops his head back, losing himself to my mouth. I'm sloppy, gagging and drooling like it's my first time, but I'm so out of my mind with lust for this man that I don't care how I perform. I just want him to want this as much as I do.

"Flip around, counsellor," Hunter commands, and I instantly do as he asks, even though I didn't have nearly enough time with his dick in my mouth. Gripping the back of the couch, I spread my legs and drop my head when his hands smooth across my ass. "Everything about you is fucking refined, Gabe. This ass. Your mouth."

The moment his lips touch the small of my back and move south, my hands move to spread myself open for him. "I'm not refined. I'm horny and I'll beg if I have to."

There's that quiet laugh again as his breath puffs across my skin and I screw my eyes shut when he buries his face in my ass.

"Hunter…oh god…" I can't really find any words because there are none. Hunter rims me so fucking good that I can only push back into him as a silent plea for more.

When he pulls his mouth away, I don't have time to complain because his cock is there almost immediately and my fingers scratch along the fabric of the couch, searching for purchase as he pushes his way in. It's not soft, slow, or romantic. This isn't two people having tender, wedding-night sex in the throes of hearts and flowers.

It's all-consuming lust; hard, rough, and exactly what I want right now.

"I'm not made of glass, Hunter," I pant. "Don't hold back."

He curses under his breath and slams the rest of the way into me. The slap of his thighs against mine echoes around me while I cry out and struggle to breathe. His body blankets mine as he pulls me back to him, and I anchor myself by grabbing his forearm.

"Tell me if it's too much." He whispers in my ear. "Are you okay?"

"Y-yes. Don't stop."

He's not taking it slow or easy. He's fucking me like I almost begged him for, and I'm boneless in his arms.

"Jerk yourself, counsellor. I want to feel you squeeze my cock while you come."

"Not...gonna...take long," I pant and do as he says. Hunter doesn't relent. It's like we're two animals in heat, unable to do anything else except fuck. Harsh breaths and dirty moans accompany the slapping of skin. Sweat beads on my forehead, and I'm hovering in a state of bliss that I never want to end.

Hunter's lips brush next to my ear. "C'mon, baby. Let me see you unravel." What is it about his voice that flips all my switches? My body tenses, and I spill over into my fist with a long moan, dragging out the orgasm high for as long as I can. Hunter's rhythm falters before he pulls out and shoves me forward.

Hands dangling over the back of the couch, I crane my head back and watch him as he unloads across my ass with a filthy moan that I know I'll want to hear again and again. His chest heaves and glistens with a sheen of sweat that brings a smirk to my lips.

"Looks like I made you work for it."

Hunter laughs. It's a breathless laugh as he works to return his breathing to normal. "Nothing I can't handle." He hands me a shirt from the floor to wipe my hand with. "You good?" With another article of discarded clothing, he wipes my ass off and gives it an appreciative slap.

"This whole casual sex thing will work just fine, Gabe. I'm going to shower and probably fall asleep. See you in the morning."

Just like that, he leaves me naked in the living room and smelling like cum. I pad to the small half bath to clean up while I wait for him to finish in the shower and look at myself in the mirror.

"Yeah, I'm good. Thanks for asking, at least." My skin still has the flushed pink of sex, and my knees are red from the friction on the couch. "I hope you know what you're doing," I say to my reflection. "He doesn't want more. It's best to remember that."

Eight
Hunter

"How's married life, sugar?"

Diamond sets my slice of cheesecake in front of me with a sparkling smile.

"Glad to see the town still shares information better than a manure spreader at full speed."

Diamond takes that as an invitation to sit with me for a moment. I say nothing as he grins and taps a well-manicured finger on the table.

"So it's true. You and Hottie McLawyer tied the knot?"

"Do you call him that to his face?"

"Nah. I call him Mr. Handsome to his face." Diamond winks, and despite my reluctance to talk about Gabe, I confirm details.

"Yes, we're married." When Diamond doesn't leave, I dig into my cheesecake and shove a forkful into my mouth. "If you're looking for anything else, you won't get it."

He heaves an exaggerated sigh and stands. "Fine. Be all broody about it and not talk. I'll just ask someone else...like Mr. Handsome himself." Diamond struts back to the coffee counter, and I shake my head.

It's what we wanted. What I wanted. For the town to know and make sure the information that Gabe was putting down roots here spread, but it's not like me to talk about someone the way people in love often do. I don't wax on about how amazing he is or how we met, because there's no story to tell.

Unless it's considered socially acceptable to brag about how great of a fuck your husband is. Because the sex is fucking amazing. The one perk for the year so far is that, at least.

"Well, hello, Mr. Handsome!" Diamond's voice rings out, and I look up to see Gabe enter the Thirsty Cow. He took my advice and stopped wearing a suit to the office this week. Instead, he's dressed in jeans and a button-down shirt with the sleeves rolled up. He still has the shiny-as-fuck dress shoes, but it's a start.

I watch as Diamond shamelessly flirts with him, and Gabe laughs along with it. Diamond moves off to fix his order, and Gabe turns around. His gaze immediately lands on me, and a brilliant smile fills his face. He says something to Diamond and then strides across the café towards me.

"I didn't think you'd be here until later. I was coming by to have an early coffee." He leans down and kisses me quickly on the lips. My head jerks back as he pulls away. "It's common to kiss your spouse in public," he murmurs as he sits across from me, and I nod.

"Yeah, yes…I just wasn't expecting it." *Understatement.* It wasn't even on my list of things to expect from this arrangement. "So, public affection is okay with you?"

Gabe leans back into the chair across from me and crosses his arms behind his head. His biceps strain against the fabric bunched there. For an office worker, he's kept himself fit.

"Yeah, Hunter. I'm fine with it. But if you're not, don't force it, and I won't make you uncomfortable."

"No, it's okay. I'm just...not used to it, I guess."

There's no '*I guess*' about it. I'm not used to it. Full stop.

I hid from my grandfather for so long, it became second nature to keep my hands to myself where anyone could see. Kissing someone publicly was something I always wanted, but the anxiety constantly simmered below the surface.

In bars with alcohol flowing, I could drown that out easier, but here in Kissing Ridge, it felt like the judgmental eyes of my grandfather were everywhere...even with him dead.

"Here you go Mr. Handsome." Diamond sets a mug in front of Gabe with a wink my way, and Gabe's warm laughter draws my attention to him.

"Maybe you shouldn't call me that anymore, Diamond. Or at least not in front of my husband." Gabe's foot touches mine under the table.

"It's fine. He *is* handsome, so it's a suitable name. Just don't get any ideas about putting the moves on him. He's spoken for."

Before I can second-guess what I'm doing, my hand reaches out and grabs his, bringing it to my lips for a kiss. Gabe's lips part with a small breath, and Diamond coos before leaving us alone.

"Well, you didn't waste time on trying out the public affection." Gabe pulls his hand back and sips his coffee.

"You said husbands do that. Just seemed like the right time."

Gabe huffs a small laugh. "The right time to get a bit possessive in front of the barista and town gossip. Well played, Hunter." Gabe brushes it off and changes the subject to what we have to do in an hour, but I wonder if it's something Gabe likes and wants more of.

"So, this 4-H meeting thing...tell me why it's helpful. Is there something I should do or say? People to pay attention to?"

"Well...all of them are important, Gabe. Even the kids, because they will probably grow up and remember how you treated them. But the adults here are people with established farms and businesses. They often need financing for various things. While you don't give them financial advice, they need lawyers to take care of registering property liens, severing lots, even selling off milk quotas."

Gabe nods along, and I know he's nervous about this. Considering how he'd never even heard of 4-H before he moved here. My crash course one night over dinner helped, but he wasn't kidding when he said he knew little about raising animals.

"Okay. Right. So be nice to everyone and hope they think of me when they need stuff." He nods firmly. "I can do this."

His words are confident, but his body isn't, and I reach over to squeeze his hand.

"Gabe, I promise this will be okay. Just be yourself."

He snorts and shoots me a skeptical look. "I'm afraid of a groundhog, Hunter. How can I be okay around farm animals in the first five minutes?"

"This is about animals, then?"

He shrugs and looks away, and it's so unlike his usual demeanour. The cocky confidence and professional attitude have disappeared, and he's like a child scared to enter kindergarten for the first time because maybe someone will laugh at him.

"I made a change in my career, Hunter. I took a huge chance to come here and I've...I've never failed. What if this is the first time?"

I shouldn't care, but I know how he feels. It's scary to cross into something you know little about, but I know he'll be a hit. He's a man most will like easily. A few people in town won't warm to him, but they're the minority.

"Come on. Once you meet Margie, you'll feel better about this."

Gabe stands with me. "Who's Margie?"

"She's the best," I say with a giant smile, because there isn't any other way to describe her to do her justice. "Trust me, okay?"

He puffs out a breath as we walk to my truck. "I don't have much choice, do I?"

"Nope." Opening the door, I pull out a shopping bag and pass it to Gabe. "Try these on. I guessed your size, so here's hoping they fit."

He peers inside the bag and pulls out one of the generic black rubber boots with an orange sole.

"Good guess. I'm a twelve, so these work." When he moves to put them on the floor, still in the bag, I laugh.

"Put them on, Gabe. Those shoes won't hold up in a barn. That's our first stop."

"I guess that makes sense." He puffs another breath and rubs his neck. "So, ah, do you tuck the pants inside or leave them out?"

The peal of laughter comes out before I can stop it, and thankfully, Gabe joins in.

"Tuck them in, counsellor. We'll make you a country boy yet."

"Hunter Burke, why have you been a stranger!?"

Margie grabs at my ear like she used to when I was a boy, and I let her give me shit. I deserve it. After she tugs my ear, she pokes me with her cane and smiles. "I've missed you."

My throat swells as I bend to hug the tiny woman. My grandmother's best friend and the one to whom I came when she died. I owe my life to Margie, and for the last few years I've been absent for reasons I'm sure she's aware of, but it's no excuse for me to stay away from the woman who was and still is a huge part of my life.

"I've missed you, too, Margie." Glancing behind me, Gabe waits with a nervous smile, and I lower my voice again. "Don't get mad, but I'll explain later."

Straightening, I motion for Gabe and wrap an arm around his waist. "Margie, I'd like you to meet my husband, Gabe."

A mix of emotions swirls across Margie's wrinkled face, and I know she's trying not to curse me out and cry.

Gabe extends a hand to her. "It's nice to meet you, Margie."

She bats his hand away and motions for him to hug, and Gabe does so easily. My heart lurches along when I imagine what she must think of me for not keeping her in the loop and introducing my husband while we were dating.

"I've always hoped Hunter would find someone who could put up with all his bullshit."

Gabe barks out a laugh while Margie genuinely seems pleased. "I wouldn't call it bullshit. He's a little grouchy and likes his kitchen to be just right. I can't fault him too much for that."

"Gabe is the new lawyer in town, and he's not familiar with 4-H or much of the country life. I brought him to meet people."

Margie points her cane at me. "We will talk later, young man. I'll see you under the tent after." She then smiles at Gabe, who, of course, returns the full Gabe dimpled grin. "You're in excellent hands, Gabe."

After she leaves, I puff my cheeks with a breath. "Well...that could have been worse."

"She loves you. You're close," Gabe murmurs as I watch Margie exit outside. "Who is she?"

"She was my grandmother's best friend, although she hated who Gram married. Margie was the only friend to stick by my gram and put up with him. When she got sick, Margie dropped everything for her...and for me. The two of us got through a hard time together."

The sound of voices interrupts us, and we both turn to find the kids and their parents arriving. Gabe steps closer to me and wipes his palms along his jeans. He smiles and nods as people greet me and get their kids settled. Part of me wants to push him into the crowd and tell him to figure it out, much like my grandfather would have.

But I don't want to be like him in any way and, as uncomfortable as it is for me to do this, I grab his hand and pull him along with me into the small group.

"Everyone, before I speak a little about grooming your animals, I'd like you to meet someone special." Smiling at Gabe, I wrap an arm around his waist and pull him close. "This is my husband, Gabe. He's new in town, and he's also a lawyer, so I'm shamelessly promoting his services because he's super good at what he does."

The group claps, some congratulatory wishes float to us, and Gabe's muscles relax. "You're more than welcome to chat him up while I talk to the kids. Margie has her famous cookies under the tent, too. So you can stay while I talk to the kids or mingle...whatever you like."

Gabe turns to me and lowers his voice. "Thank you."

"Just keeping up my end of the deal. See the man in the overalls? He has a massive dairy farm, and his youngest son is getting ready to take over. He's here with one of his grandkids. Go talk about baseball and slip him a card."

With a nod, he slips away in his new rubber boots and chats with Mr. Bruce before they both head out to the tent.

Clapping my hands together, I wait for the kids to focus on me.

"Okay, gang. Listen up. Today, I'm showing you the different brushes and what they do and why it's important to keep your animals brushed. Could be a calf or a rabbit, but they all need it. You ready?"

A chorus of yeses sounds, and for the first time in a very long time, I'm excited to be back in this meeting space and remember some of the best times of my childhood.

"Mr. Bruce is a die-hard Blue Jays fan. You should've warned me." Gabe chuckles as he clears the table after our late dinner.

"I told you to talk baseball. That was your warning."

"He thinks Bo Bichette isn't good anymore because his hair was his secret. Like Sampson cutting his locks." Gabe snort-laughs again while he loads the dishwasher. "I sort of agree with him and good news...he said he wants to discuss changes to his will and severing property."

He snaps the dishwasher closed and beams a smile at me. "I owe you, Hunter. He seems like a well-connected guy. This could lead to more business."

"You don't owe me anything. In fact, I got the first advance from the trust today. So I guess they felt we met all the conditions of a genuine marriage."

"That's great news!"

"It is. Jackson and I are going to move forward with renovating the barn for rodeo clinics now that the property is settled. I can finally get this business started and do something with my life."

Not that I've been a failure. Far from it, but I'll always regret choosing to tie myself to my grandfather's money rather than making my own way sooner. Rodeo was the only thing truly my own, but it wasn't a huge money earner. I had plans, and those plans needed more than seasonal income and a mediocre rodeo stock-breeding business.

But this place…fuck, I couldn't walk away.

Gabe remains silent as the water drains after I washed the dishes. I've enjoyed his company tonight. Dinner conversation wasn't something I'd thought I'd crave, but it seems like I've missed it.

"Do you want to join me on the porch for a bit?"

I don't want the evening to end, which is an odd feeling for me to have. Thankfully, Gabe agrees, and I don't feel like an idiot for asking. The night is pleasantly warm, and even though the sun has set, there's just something peaceful on the porch at night.

Gabe settles next to me on the porch swing, and we both laugh when the chains groan under our weight.

"Is this going to hold two grown men?" He laughs.

"I hope so."

I replaced the cushions last summer, so they offer more padding to encourage a person to relax. To stay and enjoy the night sounds without getting a sore ass.

"You were good with the kids today," Gabe offers. "I didn't know brushing animals was so important." He doesn't laugh. He states it simply as a fact he didn't know, while he stares out into the darkness. "Maybe it's a good thing I never had a pet growing up. I'd only want to give it treats and sleep with it."

Gabe pushes the swing with his foot, so we have a lazy sway, and I glance over at his profile. His gaze seems far away, like he's lost in his own memories. I don't want to intrude, but it seems when I'm around Gabe, he makes me do a lot of things I've never done before.

"My grandfather said no pets inside. If an animal couldn't be useful on the farm, then it was useless. We had a few barn cats to catch mice, but nothing could ever come into the house." He was so insistent on that, I was afraid to push the envelope in case he hurt something I'd become attached to. "I joined the 4-H club when Margie suggested it. I think I was ten. She let me keep a rabbit at her place, and I loved every minute of taking care of that rabbit."

"What was its name?" Gabe turns to face me, and the single porch light illuminates his face. Behind those wire-rimmed glasses are eyes full of an understanding I've never met before.

"Bugs." We both laugh. "Unoriginal, but it was the first thing I could think of."

"It's cute," Gabe murmurs, turning back to the darkness. "I wanted a cat. A stray was around our apartment building all the time, and she was the sweetest thing. I called her Blackie." Gabe smiles as I chuckle. "She had the best purr. I wanted to bring her inside so badly, but my mom said pets weren't allowed in our building and she couldn't afford cat food."

He sighs and pushes the swing again with his foot. "That's as close to owning a pet as I ever got. One day Blackie disappeared and never came back. I was heartbroken. My mom died about a year later."

"Gabe...I'm sorry."

An image of a sad young Gabe grips me, but I don't know how to comfort someone. I've been on the receiving end enough, but I struggle to reciprocate.

"Life isn't always full of rainbows." He shrugs a shoulder. "Anyway, I thought you did a great job with the kids, and I learned a lot. You have the gift of teaching."

He turns towards me again, and there's a sincerity not just to his words but in his expression. I invited him to sit with me so I wouldn't be alone, but I didn't think it would lead to this charged moment.

"Thank you," I manage. He smiles a small smile, like he knows how hard words are to come by at moments like this. His hands rest on his thighs as we rock lazily in the swing while the chains squeak.

My heart is thumping so hard in my chest, it feels like it might snap a rib.

I've enjoyed this evening more than anything in recent memory. A lightness I've missed has returned, and I know it's partly because of Gabe. I can't let him sit here by himself when he's lost in sad thoughts.

Reaching over, I grab his hand and thread my fingers through his. Gabe inhales sharply and squeezes my fingers with his before he slides a little closer, leaning his head on my shoulder.

Nine
Gabe

"**G**ood morning, Diamond."

The adorable barista at The Thirsty Cow bats his eyelashes my way before reaching for my thermal mug. I don't need to give him my order. I've been coming here enough that he knows it without asking.

Diamond is one of those people who makes your day brighter just by being in it. Mostly because he's a wicked flirt, but he's so effervescent it's hard not to be drawn to him.

"Good morning, Mr. Handsome," Diamond says in his flirty tone, and I smile. He's a cute little thing with his short platinum-blond hair and megawatt smile. My gaze sweeps down to his long lean legs in cutoff jean shorts and cowboy boots.

"How many hearts are you breaking today, sweetheart?"

Diamond smiles into the coffee cup as he adds a shot of hazelnut flavour. "I'm not into breaking hearts, sugar." He shakes a delicious powder on the top of my coffee before sliding it over to me with the lid on the side. A heart shape sits on top, and I quirk an eyebrow.

"Are we talking sugar hearts or real hearts now?"

"There's no time in my day to waste breaking hearts. I'd rather hold out for the right one." Diamond winks as he leans on the counter towards me. "But what about you? Mr. Fine in his suit and perfectly scruffy jaw. You break hearts when you leave a room, and somehow, you snagged Kissing Ridge's most eligible bachelor from right under our noses. What's your secret?"

With a small laugh, I duck my head. Diamond isn't one to be subtle. I already know that, but I also know I can't say too much.

"Sometimes you just get lucky...and I got lucky."

Diamond purses his lips, and for a moment I think he knows the truth.

"Seeing him on the sly and locked it down before he changed his mind?"

"Something like that."

"Well, I can't say I blame you, Mr. Handsome. He's one fine-looking man, and the two of you look good together. The way you were smiling at each other the other day seems like you have a connection that most people wish they had."

Diamond passes the payment terminal my way, and I tap my card.

"Do you think so?"

"Of course I do. I never say anything unless I mean it. I might not know you as well as the other guys yet, but I will. You and Hunter just have this..." He motions towards me with his hands. "You have this vibe."

He leans closer to me and lowers his voice. "If I could be a fly on the wall in your bedroom, I bet I'd die from the heat."

Coughing out a laugh at his forwardness, I place the lid on my coffee. "Some things aren't up for discussion, Diamond. Have a good day."

He booms a laugh. "You didn't deny it! See you later, Mr. Handsome!"

After leaving the Thirsty Cow, it's back to the office for work. The 4-H event Hunter took me to was a lifesaver. New business was gained, and Mr. Bruce became a new friend. Already, the older man came by twice with an album of old baseball cards while we talked about the game and discussed a complex will at the same time.

Mr. Bruce introduced me to his banker, Shelly Nelson, whom he trusts implicitly, and recommended that she use me for her real estate deals going forward. We exchanged cards and have sent each other new business already.

In a few short weeks, I went from wondering if I'd made a huge mistake with this new venture to feeling like I could conquer the world. I wouldn't fail, and I owed that to the handsome and mysterious man I call my husband.

The ring on my finger still takes me by surprise. We're a few short months into this, and it's still odd seeing Hunter in a softer light, but I think when the end finally comes, we can at least call ourselves friends.

"Good morning, Mr. Davis."

Penny, my legal aide, greets me and I nod with a smile. "Hello, Penny. How was your evening?"

"Amazing!" she gushes and I can't hold back the laugh.

"What happened?"

"My friend and I went to the Happy Badger. It's like a country dance bar place, and I learned how to dance from the cutest guy! I'm still floating about it."

Penny is twenty-three and freshly out of college with the energy of someone who survives on Red Bull. When I bought the business and learned the old legal aid was retiring as well, I thought I'd be well and truly fucked. But Riley's assistant knew Penny and sent her my way.

We interact more like siblings than a boss and coworker, and I should probably change that, but unless Penny feels uncomfortable, I won't.

"What kind of country dance is this? Are we talking about square dancing? Because Penny, I'm not a fan."

She follows me into my office with a stack of files. "Two-stepping and line dancing, Mr. Davis! You need to try it. Hunter can teach you."

Pausing, I turn to her. "Does he dance like that?"

"Mr. Davis...I know you haven't been here long, but if he doesn't dance, I'd eat my shoe. His grandmother owned the dance studio in town for years. She probably taught half of this town at one point."

Well...this is interesting.

"I don't know why that never occurred to me," I lie, but thankfully Penny keeps chatting away and doesn't notice my distraction. "I'll have to ask him to take me one night."

"You must. It's so much fun."

After Penny leaves me an itinerary and a list of tasks for the day, I check my schedule and do something I've never done in my life.

"Penny, could you please reschedule the last appointment at 3 PM? I'm leaving early today."

You'll need to torture me to admit I came home early to get a glimpse of Hunter on a horse. I didn't *need* to leave early to ask him to go dancing with me. That could have been accomplished after working my full day, but part of me was curious about how this rodeo clinic operated, too.

With his first advance from the trust, he dove into the planning with Jackson to continue what they started. He wanted a rodeo school. He called it teaching clinics, but that's what it was. A school, and it was perfect for him.

There was a change in his morning attitude now that he had fresh purpose. His surliness before coffee and chores was replaced with a boyish excitement to get to the clinic. Smiles came sooner and more often.

Maybe I'm just optimistic, but it feels like his life has turned a corner and I want to be a part of his growth.

Six cowboys I don't know and don't capture my attention are there with Jackson when I arrive. None of them are on horses, and there's no sign of Hunter.

I give Jackson a nod, and the group returns to the barn as I approach the ranch house. Thinking I'd missed my chance to see Hunter in action, I turn my thoughts to this evening instead.

A roar of hooting and cheering rings out from the barn as I reach the front door. Too curious to stay away, I abruptly turn and head to the barn, hoping the commotion is for my missing cowboy husband.

I stand in the shadows of the barn entrance and watch as Hunter and another cowboy talk from atop their horses before heading to the chutes. Then I watched a fantasy unfold before my eyes.

Hunter, atop his gorgeous horse, a fierce line set to his jaw as he swung a fucking rope over his head like the sexiest western hero to have ever lived. He and his partner worked together to rope a steer, and it was my new favourite thing to watch. Actually, no. My favourite thing was the absolute joy on his face.

Hunter was already a breathtaking man, but this was...it was next level. He handled a horse and a rope at the same time with so much confidence it made my dick hard just watching it. This was what he was meant for, and I don't know what it means right now, but I hope he returns to competing.

I'd done a little snooping online about Hunter, and I know Jackson wasn't always his rodeo partner. He used to be a roper, and by the looks of things, he was damn good at it, too.

"He looks good, doesn't he?" Jackson stands next to me at the barn entrance, and I glance his way.

"Are you referring to something about the way he can throw that rope, or is that a general statement about the man himself?"

Jackson laughs softly. "Sounds like you might have a crush on my best friend, Gabe."

Looking on, Hunter laughs with the other man, and an animated conversation occurs. It's the most real I've seen him since I've known him and that hat...fuck. He needs to wear that more often.

"A crush on my husband." Jackson might be a little too observant. "What if I say, maybe?"

Jackson nods and shoves his hands in his jeans while he rocks back on his heels. "I'd say there are worse men you could be infatuated with. But I'd also tell you to tread carefully." Jackson faces me and steps closer. "I love him like the brother I never had. I know you two might have a hard time playing along with this for so long, but I don't want either of you getting hurt."

"I can handle myself, Jackson. If the infatuation wears off, I'll pick up the pieces just fine."

Jackson cocks his head and studies me. He's just as much of a romantic as Riley, and I imagine he doesn't like to think about the possibility of things ending between me and his best friend.

"You might, but he won't."

Jackson's expression remains blank, and the simple statement makes me pause.

"Wait. You think...do you think he likes me back?" Shit, I sound like I'm twelve, and Jackson holds in a laugh.

"Just be careful, Gabe. Don't break his heart."

He pats my arm and returns to the barn. With a last glance at Hunter on his horse, I head back to the ranch house with Jackson's words. If anyone's heart gets broken with this arrangement, it's mine.

Hunter has been more than clear about this being a casual arrangement. There isn't an agenda to make it more for him. Maybe not with me either, but I've never tried to hide my attraction to him. We have the physical sparks perfected, and so what if I have a tiny crush on the man?

I know what I'm getting into and despite Jackson's warning…I'm asking my husband out on a date.

Hunter comes in after I'm dressed and showered, and I meet him at the door with a cold beer. He raises an eyebrow but accepts the drink with a murmured thank you.

"You're home early," he says before he drinks from the bottle. After swallowing, he gives me a once-over. "You going somewhere?"

"Hopefully somewhere with you. I'd like to ask you to come to the Happy Badger with me tonight. Dinner and dancing."

Hunter walks into the kitchen and leans against the counter. He's dusty and sweaty from the work today. He pulls his T-shirt up to wipe at his face with the end, and I don't hide my appreciation of the view.

"This sounds a lot like a date, Gabe."

Yep. It sure does, and that's what I want it to be.

"Let's call it a celebration. It looked like you were having fun, and the day was a success."

Hunter studies me in that quiet way again. Like he's not sure how to react or what to say, and maybe he's never met anyone like me. Maybe he's still trying to figure me out and I'm okay with that, too.

"It was a definite success. I'm trying out a new roping partner and getting back into it. Into roping, I mean. We need to work out the rodeo schedule, but I'm making a comeback."

His almost-shy smile does me in. Hunter wants to shout about this to anyone. It's right there, and he's holding back on expressing the joy. I want him to celebrate this. With me. Tonight. He should smile and shout, and tell me how excited he is to be back in rodeo.

"I definitely think that requires a celebration. So...will you have dinner with me tonight and teach me how to dance while we mark your return to the ring?"

This time, he laughs out loud before draining the beer. He rinses the bottle and leaves it in the sink. "You think I know how to dance?"

"I know you do."

When he notices I'm not bluffing, he shakes his head. "You won't give up if I say no, will you?"

"Not a bit." I laugh.

"Give me fifteen then. I'll get cleaned up, but I'm driving."

He disappears up the stairs, pulling off his shirt on the way, and I fan my face. Lord, it's almost a crime to look that good.

And he didn't say no.

"Spill it," Hunter says as he pops a fry in his mouth. "How do you know so much about me that I haven't told you?"

After arriving at the Happy Badger, you'd think the king himself had entered. So many people fawned over Hunter, and it had been confusing at first. Until I saw the photos on the back wall of a much younger version of Hunter and what had to be his grandmother holding dance trophies.

"Google," I say with a laugh. "But mostly Penny. She was the one who told me about this and dancing." Knowing how close he was with his grandmother, and seeing so many patrons greet him like they haven't seen him for a decade, I wonder if I crossed a line, and he's just being polite. "Was it wrong to ask you here?"

Hunter wipes his mouth with a napkin and leans back in the booth.

"Not at all. It was probably the kick in the ass I needed." He turns his head to the wall of photos and smiles. "My grandma was an amazing dancer, and my grandfather hated it. It was the one thing she defied his wishes on. She taught dance of all kinds, and when this place opened up, offering a place to dance casually, then had a competition...well, she was all over it as much as possible."

Hunter drops his chin for a moment and tears at the napkin. "Since she accepted me as I am, I went with her a lot. Dancing was fun when I couldn't be at a rodeo. It let me just...be, you know?" Hunter's gaze shifts to a wall of photos near us. "We won three competitions here before she got sick. I was her main man." His smile returns and holy shit, Jackson was right. I'm crushing so hard on this man with a million layers, like some sort of sexy stacking Russian doll.

The music turns up, and couples flood the dance floor. Hunter's smile returns as he watches the couples dance. His body moves to the music subtly, like he's only waiting for me to signal I'm ready.

"I'm two left feet. Think you can teach me all those moves, cowboy?"

"I'm a little rusty, but I'll give it a go if you promise not to step on my boots."

"I somehow doubt you're as rusty as you say. You don't rope anymore, and from what I saw today, you looked pretty good. I think dancing will come just as easily."

Yeah, I like to talk big and I'm usually good at it, but watching the couples on the dance floor move as one and look so graceful makes me nervous. Forget about stepping on his boots. I'm more concerned about falling on my ass.

Hunter stands and nods his head to the dance floor. "Come on, counsellor. Don't be scared. It's super easy."

Sliding out of the booth, I drain my drink and place it on the table. Hunter's deep rumble of a laugh has me shooting him a scowl.

"You asked for this, counsellor. Don't chicken out now."

Hunter takes my hand and leads me to the dance floor, where I'm hyper aware of the eyes watching the dance prodigy return home. He positions my hand on his shoulder before holding my other one to the side.

"Quick, quick, slow, slow, Gabe. Just do that and feel where my body leads you. No fancy spins or dips."

With a shaky breath, I nod. "Okay. Let's do this."

He leads me in a series of steps, and he steps on my foot twice while I try to fall into the rhythm.

"Don't look at your feet," Hunter murmurs. "Look at me, Gabe."

And that's the game changer. My nervous laughter dissipates as I watch Hunter's face, and through some miracle, I don't stop moving my feet as he leads us around the room.

"Look at that, counsellor. You're doing it just fine," Hunter whispers, and I immediately look down at my feet and stumble into him. His arms wrap around me, bringing me next to his body, while we both laugh and regain our balance.

"I won't be bringing home any trophies soon, but thank you. This was fun."

Hunter pushes my glasses up and allows his fingertips to drift across my cheek. "It was my pleasure...Can I show you one more?"

My nod to agree is automatic.

"Since you're so close to me, we can do the same steps like this." His fingers splay across the small of my back as he holds me so close our chests touch. "Our legs are closer, but just keep the same quick, quick, slow, slow. Same thing, just closer." His breath skates across my skin, and I flex my hand in his.

Hunter leads us in the close dance. Even though the music is faster than our steps, I don't feel like we're out of place on the dance floor. But I feel out of sorts. This has been the perfect date. We've laughed, gotten to know each other better, and he shared a little about his grandmother.

Hunter has been a dream. Right now, as the one in his arms on the dance floor, I don't want the dream to end. But as they say, everything has an ending. The music fades, and Hunter pulls me closer.

"Thank you for this, Gabe."

Hunter's gaze dips to my lips, and I lick mine in response.

"We should probably go," I breathe.

His gaze searches my face, and I swear there's a tenderness there he didn't have before.

"Yeah. We should. Big day tomorrow."

It's late when we get home and neither of us says a word as we step inside the dark house. Hunter flicks on the light in the hallway, and after our shoes are off, we both move to the stairs to our bedrooms.

I'm not imagining the heat between us. After being so close to him and in his company for hours with his hand on me dancing, I'm a willing bed partner, but...something feels off.

"Well...thank you for tonight, Hunter. I had a lot of fun."

Hunter licks his lips. "Me too." He drifts closer, and I've never wanted a kiss so badly in my life. I get one, but not where I want it. His lips brush over my cheek and hover next to my ear. "It's late and I have an early morning. Thank you for inviting me out and celebrating with me, Gabe." He doesn't step back immediately. It's like there's a fragile soap bubble around us, both of us unsure of what to do to keep it intact.

"Maybe we can do this again sometime?" I whisper, placing a hand on his chest. "Maybe when you don't have an early morning?"

"Maybe." His voice is thick, and I wish he'd just... "Good night, Gabe."

The fragile bubble bursts.

He moves away without another glance and enters his bedroom, closing his door softly behind him. I stand in place for a few minutes, replaying the way his breath felt next to my ear.

Finally, I enter my bedroom.

Alone...and wondering what the fuck just happened.

Ten
Hunter

“Do you want to keep practicing?”

Levi, my new roping partner’s voice, is somewhere in the background, but thoughts of Gabe keep distracting me. It’s only been a week since we went dancing, and for the first time since my grandmother died, I felt comfortable back in the Happy Badger.

I’d avoided it for so long because I convinced myself it would be too hard. The memories would swamp me with grief, and I never wanted to return. But it wasn’t like that at all.

Happy times with my grandmother exploded, and I shared them with Gabe over dinner. Patrons who danced when I was still a young boy were there, so pleased that I was back. The feelings of belonging surfaced for the first time since she died, and it wasn’t the grief-filled journey I thought it would be.

All because Gabe simply asked me on a date so I could teach him to dance.

“I’m not on my game today, Levi. Sorry about that.” I pull up my horse next to him, and his youthful face gives no hint of disappointment.

“Shit, don’t be sorry. I’m not at my best either, but I will be by the time rodeo day hits.” He practically bounces in his saddle. “I know I've said it before, but I can't believe you agreed to partner with me. I'm so fucking amped for this weekend."

"I'm still just a guy, Levi."

He shakes his head. "No, you're not. You're a legend, Hunter. This is your chance, and mine too, to come out on top."

I don't want to kill his enthusiasm, but he's gotta know a single rodeo doesn't get an invitation to the national finals. "Levi...it's one rodeo. Kissing Ridge is big, and the money can be decent, but it won't vault you to finals. You need to collect points for that."

"Yeah, I know, but this is still amazing, Hunter. I grew up watching you. You're a legend."

"Ugh, don't make me feel so old."

He snort-laughs and leads his horse out of the ring. "You're only as old as you feel! But I'm fine ending for the day. Text me if you want one last round before tomorrow."

After acknowledging that, Levi gets to work cooling down his horse, and I cast another glance at the house. Gabe's car is there, and I wonder if he'd like to step out of his comfort zone again and enjoy a bit of the country?

I've replayed that dance date in my mind far too many times, and I know I want to return the gesture somehow. It might not be romantic, but I think he'd like it.

Hitching Dixie to the fence, I promise to be back in a few and jog over to the house. I find Gabe inside with a book and his feet up in the living room. Despite it being late summer, he has a blanket across his legs and a mug nearby of what I assume is a warm beverage. He looks good here, like this, in my home.

"Hey, done for the day?" Gabe asks as he sets his book aside.

"That bit I am. I was…" Oh god. I'm actually asking him on a date, aren't I? I should have thought more about this before waltzing over here without a solid plan.

"You were…?" Gabe prompts.

"Would you like to ride me? With me! Fuck." Running a hand over my face, I stare at the ceiling while I recover from my slip-up. Maybe I should have taken him to bed after that dance night instead of keeping my distance. I wanted to, but Gabe had me feeling off-centre that night, and even though I wanted nothing more than to come so hard I'd forget my name, I paused and went to bed alone.

That's not like me, and it's all Gabe's doing.

"You want me to take a ride with you? Sure. Where to?"

"On a horse. Do you want to ride a horse with me?"

Gabe's eyes widen. "Uh…so…I've never been on a horse. Shocking, I know." His throat bobs as he stands and walks closer to me. "But if you think I can handle it and will be there in case I'm in trouble, then yes. I'll ride with you."

A thrill mixed with something else I can't name courses through me, and I nod.

"Cool. Yeah, I'll be there. You can ride Dixie, and I'll saddle Mack." I turn to leave, but Gabe calls out to stop me.

"Hunter? Do I need to wear anything…special?"

"Jeans. Boots." I pause. "Do you have a hat?"

"I have some ball caps."

"Bring one of those then and meet me up at the barn in about fifteen minutes."

Gabe acknowledges, and I return to the barn just as quickly as I left. Levi is just pulling away with his horse and trailer, and I breathe a sigh of relief that he doesn't see me acting like a bumbling idiot around the man whom I already call my husband.

Mack comes easily to the barn with a promise of a carrot, and once she's secure, I throw myself into getting her saddled while trying not to think of the man inside who has somehow made me consider what it would be like to be married for real.

I can't deny that I enjoy having someone here. Sharing meals, brewing extra coffee in case he wants to take a mug to work, and even answering my random questions when I'm stuck with my crossword puzzle. Gabe just fit right in, even when I didn't want a roommate.

I'd be lying if I said I didn't like the guy. But Gabe makes me think too much about the what ifs for the future, and that scares the fuck out of me. I want to keep him around, but what happens after a year? We're just friends with benefits? Would the benefits even continue? Because as much as I've wanted more of him after our first few months of fake married bliss...I wanted more of him away from that.

"Can I help?"

Gabe's soft voice draws me from my thoughts, and when I turn, he stands in the doorway looking like the most delicious of country boys I've ever seen. If he couldn't see me, I'd bite my knuckle over his level of hotness.

Gabe has the best brand of boots. I can tell just by looking at them, and I'm happy he spent wisely. His jeans are still so blue they'll probably bleed in the wash, and his shirt is a faded red with the image of a hot sauce bottle on it and the phrase, *'Hot Stuff,'* stretched across his chest. Which I agree with because the ball cap alone suits Gabe more than any custom-tailored suit could.

"You bought a pair of boots. How do you like them?"

Smooth. Compliment his boots. I'm such a jackass.

"I haven't worn them much, but I got the rounded toe ones because they looked more comfortable? I think?"

"They're very comfortable." I clear my throat and motion for him to say hello to Mack. Gabe's soft smile as he cautiously approaches Mack is everything, and he seems more comfortable than last time. Mack even stretches out to him with a soft nicker, and I raise an eyebrow.

"I don't have anything today, Mack. Can we still be friends?" Gabe pets her head with a fond smile.

What the hell?

"Is there something you're keeping from me, counsellor?"

Gabe pats Mack like he's been around horses forever, and he's definitely not as nervous as the first time. "Since you showed me where the carrots were, I come out every day and visit them. Even Lewis." When I remain silent, he rushes on. "Is that okay? It's not bad for them to have a carrot a day, is it?"

"Uh, yeah. I mean no. It's all fine. It's...when do you do this that I don't see you?"

I'm literally out here whenever he could be. How has he done this without me knowing?

He shrugs. "When you're inside. Usually in the shower or when you're out at Jackson's. It's always different, and you're never here."

I honestly don't know what to think about him doing this. I'm definitely impressed, but I'm also confused and rather than grill him about it right now, I just lead Mack out to where Dixie waits.

After tying Mack, I motion for Gabe to come to the side of Dixie. She does the same thing as Mack and greets him with a snuffle that puts the biggest smile on his face. You can give me gifts, cook me dinner, and any number of things most people would consider a gift, but to love my horse and she shows affection back? There's nothing to top that.

"You trying to steal my girl, Gabe?"

Gabe dips his head, and Jesus Christ, his neck turns a pinkish shade right there in front of me. What the actual fuck?

"I'd never, Hunter. I just wanted to get comfortable around the animals you spend most of your time with. You said they're your family, and that's important. I never thought I'd get to ride one."

The warmth in my chest has to be because of the late-summer temperature and a lack of water intake. That's all it is.

"You can't be married to a cowboy, live at a ranch, and never ride a horse. That's just not possible."

Tapping his leg, I point to the stirrup. "Put this foot in the stirrup, grab the horn, then push up and swing your other leg over."

Gabe nods and tries it. He wobbles a little the first time, but sits in Dixie's saddle, proud as a peacock in the middle of its harem.

"This is so cool! Can we run? I bet that's amazing!"

Chuckling, I shake my head. "You need to walk and control a horse before you run with it, Gabe. Let's work up to that."

I show him how to hold the reins and explain how to get Dixie to stop or to speed up. "She also knows verbal commands."

After mounting Mack, I look over at Gabe. He'll be so sore tomorrow, but judging by his smile, he'll think it's worth it.

"You ready?"

"You bet!"

"Here's the first command Dixie knows." I click my tongue. "Let's go."

Gabe laughs as Dixie moves forward, and he grabs onto the saddle horn. We walk side by side since Mac seems to want to be near him, and I lead us down the side of the main pasture towards the larger field at the back of the property.

Gabe remains quiet with a giant grin on his face, and I don't know why that just gets me, but it does.

"It's beautiful out here," Gabe says the closer we get to the mountains. "I can see why you love it here."

"It is beautiful. As shitty as the family life was, this was and still is the place that settles all my troubles, you know? When you can find a peaceful place, sometimes it drowns out all the loud noises inside."

We ride in silence for a few minutes, and I feel Gabe's gaze on me. I turn to find him watching me. "What happened to have you raised by your grandparents? Can I ask you that? Is that part of your noise?"

With a long sigh, I remove my hat and wipe my forearm across my forehead while I choose my words. "My parents died in a car accident on their way home from a Christmas party one night. I was sleeping over here that night as I often did, and there was a knock on the door after midnight. I should have been asleep, but my grandmother's cries woke me. They both died at the scene. I was only six."

"Hunter..."

Gabe wants to rush to console me. I know he does. Everyone does, and in some way, that makes it easier to tell this story on horseback. I can keep my distance and still share my shitty story.

"My dad and my grandfather often argued. Dad was leaving the ranch to be with my mom, you see. My mom was wicked smart and had a scholarship to a big university. My dad was the captain of the local hockey team, with scouts watching him. They could have been anything they wanted, but they became parents to me instead."

"Teenage pregnancy?" Gabe whispers.

"Yep. So they gave it all up to have me. My dad was never drafted, anyway, and I think my grandfather liked to blame that on me. *'You can't be a great hockey player when you're being a dad to a newborn.'*" Lord knows I heard the line of how disappointed he was about that far too often. "But I think my grandfather saw me as the reason his son died instead of a way his son could live on. He wanted his son and instead got me. A gay grandson who didn't live up to anything he wanted from his son."

Gabe says nothing right away, and I appreciate that. Most people only know my parents died, and my grandparents kept me because they were all I had. They don't know the words spoken inside the house, and they sure as hell don't know how much I struggled between winning my grandfather's love and doing things I enjoyed.

Or even just discovering who I was. Not just sexually, but on a much deeper level. I wanted to please him, honour my father and be a boy living the dream on a ranch. But nothing ever satisfied him.

We arrive at a gate on the fence in our far field, and I bring Mack to a stop. Dixie automatically waits because she knows where we're going and what to do. After dismounting and opening the gate, Gabe rides Dixie through, and I lead Mack before closing the gate behind us.

"This is crown land now. I keep a gate so I can ride here when I want, but also to keep others out and signal that it's private property." Swinging back up onto Mack, I feel Gabe's soft gaze on me, so I turn to him before moving the horses forward.

"I've never been on a horse before, or spent much time in the outdoors, Hunter. I have noise to deal with too, and I just want to say thank you for showing me this."

I'm not used to letting people in like this. Jackson is probably the one who has come the closest. Nobody gets to visit my sanctuary, and I've led Gabe here almost without a second thought. It should bother me, but I feel a connection I haven't felt in years. Like he's a kindred spirit.

"You're welcome." We ride along, side by side, in the open meadow behind the ranch boundaries. Dixie has been here countless times and easily takes Gabe along the smoother path, like she's aware he's a greenhorn but also needs to protect him.

Since Mack needs more training with commands, I part a little farther away from Gabe and Dixie and practice working with Mack on commands. Stopping and listening, and the subtle tug on the reins to turn her head and focus. Mack is from the same breeding line as Dixie, sharing a common father but years apart, so I'm not surprised Mack takes to the new commands as well as Dixie ever did.

Finally, we reach the creek that cuts through the meadow, and Dixie stops at the edge.

"Thank god your horse is on autopilot. I wasn't sure if she'd listen to me if I yelled stop if she got too close to the water." Gabe laughs with a hint of nerves, and I dismount from Mack.

Tapping his leg again, I motion for him to dismount. "Just do it backwards to get down. Same way you got on."

Gabe does, and when his feet are firmly on the ground, he breathes out in relief. "Seriously, Hunter. If she went into the water, I might have had a panic attack." He stretches his back and shakes out his legs with a groan. "Lord...how long does it take to get used to being in a saddle like that? I do yoga, but this is intense."

I chuckle as he massages his ass. The newbies are always a little fun. Gabe is no exception, but there's something extra I love about this. Maybe it's him on my horse, or the fact he bought boots without my telling him to. Whatever it is, it's moving into dangerous territory for my heart.

"It can take a while. You're okay, though?"

Gabe nods and steps close to me with a hooded gaze. He takes one of my hands and plants it squarely on one ass cheek. "I'd be better if someone else wanted to massage me. A capable hand to take the tightness away."

Jesus.

My breath catches and my brain moves my other hand to his ass, hauling him close to my body. "You're a dangerous man, counsellor." He moans softly when I squeeze his ass.

"I wouldn't hurt a fly," he whispers.

No, I doubt he would, but he could hurt me and probably doesn't even know it.

His hands creep up to my chest, and the heat of his palms presses into my skin through my shirt. "It's not the time for this, Gabe." My fingers flex on his ass, completely disagreeing with my statement.

"I'm going to go with it's only because we're outside with horses and not something else. Don't shoot me down again, cowboy. My ego might not recover." Gabe's voice wavers, but his gaze doesn't.

Despite the swirl of mixed emotions, my voice remains firm as I squeeze his ass one last time before gripping his chin firmly. His pretty lips part, and I resist running a thumb across them. "I'm not shooting you down. You do things to me, Gabe, and I need to wrap my head around what it means."

"I have time." Gabe grips my wrist and pulls my hand from his chin. He feathers a kiss on my wrist that makes my knees quake. "I'll wait for you."

Then he drops my wrist and spins away so quickly I'm left rooted to the spot while I watch his broad back retreat to Dixie.

Wait for me? I'm not sure what he means, but I hope I can figure it out.

Eleven
Gabe

This is my third time at Kissing Ridge Rodeo, and it might just be my favourite.

Is it because I'm here with my fake husband, being paraded around like a show pony? Probably.

It's the most attention Hunter has shown me since he took me on my first-ever horseback ride last week. What I wouldn't have done to have him fuck me against a tree right then, but something profound shifted with him that day. Maybe in me, too, but there was no way I'd push him to do something he didn't want.

I meant it when I said I'd wait.

Hunter is worth waiting for. I might die of blue balls waiting, but I'm willing to take the risk.

"This man is Neill Dunn. He sponsors the rodeo. I'll talk you up," Hunter whispers near my ear, and I want to tell him I can promote myself now, but it's too late.

"Mr. Burke! I heard a rumour you tied the knot. Is this the lucky gentleman?"

Sparkling blue eyes set on me as Hunter laughs. "Ropers can't tie knots, Mr. Dunn. Unless it's a quick release. But yes, you heard right." Hunter slides his palm to the small of my back. "This is my husband, Gabe Davis. He's a lawyer here and one of the best."

I extend a hand to the man, who shakes it with a warm smile. "Pleasure to meet you, sir. I'd say I'm the lucky one, though. Lawyers can be hard to live with."

He laughs and smiles at my joke. "I'll let you two debate on who is luckier, but I think it's a draw. I don't mean to talk business at a fun event, but I need to when the opportunity is right in front of me. If you have a business card, Gabe, I'd love to chat with you about some rodeo things. If you're married to this man, it's part of your life now, so you'll understand."

Fishing into my pocket, I pull out my wallet for a card and hand it to him. "Business happens everywhere, and I'd love to help, Mr. Dunn."

He tucks my business card into his front pocket, still with a friendly smile, and I one-hundred percent like the guy.

"Good luck today, Hunter. I'm looking forward to seeing you roping again. Young Levi needs a mentor, and you're just the man for it."

Hunter dips his head with a murmured thank you, and Mr. Dunn squeezes his shoulder before leaving us be.

"I can't wait to watch you today," I say and tug on his belt loop.

Hunter turns his smouldering gaze on me, and my heart rate jumps under his attention.

"Is that right? What if I fuck it all up?"

"You won't. But if you did..." Boldly, I tug him closer to me. Close enough to lean in and kiss, which I want to do badly. "If you did, you'd still be a champion to me."

His gaze flicks to my mouth, and his tongue peeks out to wet his lips. "Good to know, counsellor. Maybe you should kiss me for good luck."

"Just for luck? Or something else?"

Hunter doesn't reply. Instead, he presses his lips to mine, and I melt into him. My body moulds to his as my arms go around his neck, and I'm lost in everything that's Hunter Burke. Hunter's kiss differs from before. While there's still desire there, this has something else, and it feels like I've earned something I didn't know I was competing for.

When he finally releases me, I playfully pluck his hat from his head and set it on mine. He chuckles and holds me tight with one arm while taking his hat back with a wicked smile.

"Do you know what the cowboy hat rule is, counsellor?"

Laughing, I step back from him when the announcer's voice sounds over the speakers.

"Never touch a cowboy's hat?"

His lips twitch as he bends down next to my ear. "In the land of flirting with cowboys, the hat is a symbol of who you belong to." Hunter slides his hands around to my ass and pulls me closer to him. "If I put my hat on you, it means I'm interested. You're mine." His hot breath is a brand on my skin, and I swallow hard. "But Gabe..." Hunter nuzzles his nose under my ear, and my knees quiver. "If you take my hat, that's a proposition. You take a cowboy's hat...you take the cowboy to bed and ride him until the sun comes up."

"Jesus fucking...." I can't breathe because Hunter just sucked all the air from my lungs with that sexy history lesson.

Hunter steps back, tips his hat with a wink and...walks away. Leaving me with my jaw on the ground, a half-hard dick and a whole new appreciation for cowboy hats.

"G-Good luck!" I shout after he's too far away to hear me because that's how long it took me to find words to reply that weren't curses or gibberish.

I walk back to the stands for my seat with Jackson's parents and Riley, completely stuck in the charged conversation I just had with Hunter. How the hell am I supposed to just watch a rodeo with that playing on repeat in my head?

"Hey, Gabe!" Riley calls out as I bound up the steps. "You look far too concentrated to enjoy a rodeo. Did something happen?"

"Maybe?" Pulling out my phone, I google the cowboy hat rule while telling Riley what happened. He gently takes my phone out of my hand.

"Gabe, don't look it up. It's true, and if he said that to you..." He whistles low. "He's got it bad."

Riley waggles his eyebrows, and, despite feeling very out of sorts, a smile lifts my lips.

"You think so?"

My heart races again at the thought that maybe this might mean something to Hunter and not just be a convenience. It's been very lucrative for me so far with all his contacts in town, and he's received his first advance from the trust, but Jackson was right when he said I had a crush on the guy.

I did before I married him, and while it was purely physical initially, now...now I'm not really sure what it is.

The rodeo announcer carries on, and I listen with half an ear, but it's enough to know Hunter rides with Jackson in the first half and Levi after the break.

Riley bumps my shoulder with his. "What's going on, Gabe? Something is off with you. Is it this thing with Hunter?"

Jackson's parents whoop and yell, so I glance out to the rodeo ring along with Riley. He stands and wolf whistles with his fingers and yells out to Jackson, who waves with a smile and a wink at Riley. Hunter's gaze locks with mine, and a flush of heat runs through my body. He tips his hat and winks, and I honest to god feel like my entire body is blushing.

"There *is* something with you, isn't there?" Riley lowers his voice. "Something that's not pretend?"

With a quick glance towards Jackson's parents, who are chatting with a few others, I bend closer to Riley in my seat.

"I don't know what's going on with us, Rye, but...there's something. He's...he's not like the Hunter I met two years ago or even six months ago. He says and does things with me he wouldn't with anyone else."

"He's never had a relationship since Jackson has been friends with him, Gabe. Nothing long-term." Riley murmurs, and I hear the concern in his voice. "Do you want this to not be fake?"

"Yes? Maybe? I don't know." I sigh and run a hand over my face as the first competitors get ready. "He does something to me, and I can't ignore it. That's as specific as I can get." A saddle bronc rider bursts from the gate, and we pause our conversation for a moment. "He took me for a horseback ride last week, and it was heaven, Riley. He taught me what to do, he showed me the fields behind the ranch and he...he told me a lot about his parents and grandparents. Something shifted, and I feel it, Riley."

My best friend studies me closely and squeezes my hand. "I don't know if he's that kind of guy, Gabe. He loves Jackson and guards their friendship closely, and he's accepted me, but...he's never given me a reason to believe he wants a relationship." Riley gives me a small smile. "I don't want you to get hurt."

Another bronc rider rides, and the crowd roars around us. I know Riley means well, but I don't want to admit to him it might already be too late for me being hurt. I'm already too attached to the guy.

"Let's just watch our men. Don't worry about me."

"If you change your mind..."

Riley always wants to be my support, and I love him for it, but it's not the right time to raise my fears.

"I'll come to you. Let's have fun."

Riley nods, picking up on my tone that I no longer want to talk about it, and we turn our attention to the action in the ring.

After the saddle bronc and bareback riders finish, the steer wrestling teams move into position at the other end of the ring. Riley is wound tight. I'm afraid to talk to him in case he shatters in his seat.

"He's so fucking hot when he does this, Gabe. I never want him to quit steer wrestling. Just gimme one rodeo a year and I'll die a happy man."

Riley keeps his eyes glued to the chutes, and while I laugh inside at how manic he is over Jackson and his event, I understand a lot more now.

"Oh my god. They're up." He inches to the edge of his seat while the crowd claps for the local team. Jackson's head nods, and a single, *'yep!'* carries out. Hunter and Jackson burst from the chutes chasing down the steer, and I view Hunter in a totally different light.

I don't keep watching Jackson to see if he wrestles the steer. Instead, my attention is on Hunter as he guides his horse to Jackson's with a single glance over his shoulder to see how his partner did. He rides Dixie up to Jackson's horse, and his lips move as he pats the horse on the neck.

There's no doubt in my mind he's used to being out of the spotlight when competing with Jackson. His motions are all from the heart because the attention from the crowd is on the man in the ring wrestling a steer. There's a fleeting moment of tenderness between Hunter and the horses as he gathers the reins of Jackson's horse and leads her back.

Riley whoops in his seat next to me, but my attention remains on Hunter. Hunter's gaze lifts and immediately locks with mine. The corner of his mouth lifts in a half smile, and he taps his hat.

Damn.

Even that tap makes me hot all over.

And he still has to get in the ring and do the whole sexy rope-throwing thing. I just might die. If I knew cowboys were so damn sexy, I'd have gone to rodeos years ago.

The other events pass in a blur, and when there's a break in the rodeo action, I finally join in the conversation with Jackson's parents and others in the stands.

"It's Gabe, right? You're Riley's friend?"

An older man greets me, and I remember him as the dad of one of the other cowboys.

"Yes, that's right. You're Jamieson's dad, right? Charlie?"

"Griff's dad. You're close." He chuckles and I try to hide my surprise but fail. "I know. I look a lot different from the first time we met." He pats his stomach. "I've gained loads of weight, and I'm not a walking skeleton anymore. Those boys feed me well."

"I'm happy to hear that. It's almost their turn."

"It is, but I was hoping I could ask you something. A legal question if that's okay? I know this is out of office hours, but Griff said you were very helpful when he needed."

Griff took me up on my offer to draft a power of attorney while his dad was in rehab, and clearly, rehab is doing wonders for the man.

"I'm always available for questions. How can I help?"

"Well...I don't have a will, and I need to make sure I make things easy for Griff. He's done so much for me, and I want to do this for him, but I don't know where to start."

"I'd be happy to help, Charlie. Do you want to call me and make an appointment, or would you prefer if I come to the house?" I normally wouldn't offer that, but it turns out many of the ranchers and farmers appreciate me going to them. Their days are often weather-dependent or full from before sunrise to sunset. Something else Hunter has taught me since moving here. I'm not a guy in a suit in an air-conditioned office anymore. I wear jeans and cowboy boots with button-down shirts and do business next to tractors or over quick lunches along the fence.

Visiting Charlie's home seems like a normal extension to that.

His face lights up. "Would you come to the house? I can make it to the office, but the house would be great."

Pulling out a business card, I pass it to him. "Call me and we can pick a day."

"Thanks so much, Gabe. I super appreciate this."

He pockets the card, and the genuine sincerity in his voice warms me so much that if he doesn't call me, I'll call him first.

When we settle back into our seats and the action starts again, my heart thumps hard in my chest listening to the announcer.

"Ladies and gentlemen, you are in for something special tonight. Young Levi D'Amour is starting his team roping career in Kissing Ridge with none other than Hunter Burke, our hometown hero. You might remember, though it's been many years now, that Hunter and his previous roping partner were top dogs."

The crowd cheers, and I look at Riley, who is just as excited as the rest of the crowd.

"Jackson said he was thinking about it! I didn't realize he said yes!"

"He did. He's been practicing, and he's nervous, but I think he'll do great."

Levi and Hunter wave to the crowd, and Levi's smile is so big it barely fits on his face. Hunter is stoic as usual, but his gaze darts to mine quickly, and I smile softly with a nod.

A few teams go out before they do with mixed results, and then it's Hunter and a new partner lining up in the chutes. Hunter's game face gives nothing away, and I hold my breath while the barriers are secured and a plucky steer loads the chute. Levi calls out his signal, and the two of them race out after the steer.

Hunter's arm swings the lasso and quickly releases it, catching the steer clean on the neck and turning his horse to give Levi a clear throw for the feet. He catches one foot, and the steer falls, while they remain on their horses until the flag drops.

Hunter's smile is the only thing I notice. Levi releases the steer and remounts his horse while Hunter winds up his rope, and I don't even need to be close to him to know he's excited.

"Young Mr. D'amour and his roping mentor just ran their first rodeo event together, folks. It's a five-second penalty for only one foot, but what a great start for this young buck! Why don't you stand up and tell him how much you want to see them again?"

I jump to my feet with the rest of the fans and holler, "Hell, yes!"

My husband, fake or not, deserves this and just did an amazing thing. If he wants to do more amazing things, I'm all for it. Especially when he smiles and laughs like that, and I can almost picture the weight of his stress flying off with every passing moment.

After returning to my seat, Riley cocks his head and I know that look.

"Don't make me say it out loud, Rye."

He snort-laughs and shakes his head. "Giddy up, Gabe. I think there's a cowboy waiting for a ride." He snickers.

"If you aren't turned on by competent men working a rope, can you even call yourself a fan?"

"It's gonna be a long night waiting to get home," Riley sighs with a pout.

Good thing I'm used to waiting.

"Gabe!"

Jackson claps my shoulder before he slides next to Riley at our table. "Hunter should be here shortly. He was right behind me." He lays a kiss on Riley with the dopiest grin, and I can't help but smile.

"He said he'd meet me here." I shrug. He didn't say when. I know he has a lot of responsibilities after a rodeo. Especially one where he re-entered roping with a huge welcome and a new partner.

"I think he caught the roping bug again. He worked well with Levi, and I wouldn't be surprised if he returns to the circuit full time." Jackson sips from his glass while watching me.

"What about your rodeo clinics? Isn't that supposed to be your plan?" I ask.

Jackson shrugs a shoulder. "Yeah, but I have enough going on that if he doesn't want to do it full time next year, it's fine. Besides...I think he needs this. He loved roping, and it was taken from him too soon." Jackson screws up his nose and, if he's thinking about Hunter's grandfather, I agree with the scrunched nose.

A commotion near the entrance draws our attention and my breath catches as Hunter moves into the bar with Levi. Cowboys, young and old, clap them on the back with affection, and a swell of pride fills my chest for this rough-edged but tender man.

I'm not the only one with eyes for the man of the hour, though. It's easy to spot the buckle fans as they approach the ring of suitors or simply wait for a break in the circle to get close.

The last time I watched Hunter in a bar, he went to a corner on his own and turned everyone down—including me. He might have followed me to the parking lot that night, but he still never gave me what I wanted.

A cute man at least ten years younger, possibly more, if I'm judging by the baby face and lack of facial hair, steps in front of Hunter and boldly grabs at his hat. I suck in an audible breath, angry that another man touched his hat and on edge, wondering if Hunter will tell the man the same thing he told me.

His eyes flash with anger, and his hand darts out quickly to snatch his hat back and place it on his head. When it looks like the man won't leave his personal space, my feet move on their own and somewhere behind me I hear Riley's mutter of, *oh shit,* as I walk towards Hunter and his admirer without a clue of what I might do when I get there.

"Come on, Hunter. Let me buy you a drink instead. We can get to know each other."

"Excuse me." The man turns to me, clearly angry I'm interrupting, but I don't give a shit. "My husband doesn't just let anyone take his hat, and honestly, that was rude. If you want to take a buckle home tonight, maybe you should work on your game."

Hunter cough-laughs while the man decides if I'm telling the truth or not.

"You're married? For real?"

Both of us hold up our ringed fingers, and the man's shoulders deflate. "Hall pass?" he asks me hopefully.

"Not on your life."

Twelve
Hunter

Gabe pissed off and proprietary is hot as fuck.

I never would've taken that guy home even if I were single. He's much too young for me, and grabbing my hat was an instant strike. I only wear my hat to bars after events because it's definitely a better magnet for sex than belt buckles, but tonight was different.

Gabe would be here, and I laid a pretty strong promise for him. This hat was his, and honestly, I didn't even want to come to the bar tonight.

"The nerve of that kid. He can't be more than twenty-five. Who just grabs a guy's hat like that?" Gabe seethes as he watches the man's back.

"You did the exact thing earlier, counsellor," I remind him with a raised eyebrow, but Gabe doesn't roll over.

"I have certain privileges as a husband, Hunter. That rule doesn't apply to me."

He's so sure of himself and fiery as he moves closer to stake his claim. "Oh? I wasn't aware that was a husband rule. What else?"

He leans close to whisper next to my ear. "No extra-marital sex. We agreed, Hunter."

"I wasn't going home with anyone but you, Gabe. We already agreed on no outside sex," I murmur back, and he nods sharply, like we just agreed on eggs for breakfast and not about being exclusive during this arrangement.

"I want you to take me home," he says, and all the hair on my arms stands with the lust that drips from his every word.

"Now?"

He huffs in annoyance, and it's the cutest thing when he pushes up his glasses and glares at me.

"I want to ride the fucking cowboy, and don't you dare change your mind. Not after everything you did and said tonight. Not to mention over the last week. I can't..." he trails off and smashes his lips against mine. My arms immediately wrap around him and pull him closer as he kisses me right there in the busy bar.

When he finally allows us to breathe, I have to agree with him.

"Home sounds good. Let's go."

Taking his hand, I spin on my heel and lead us out of the bar. Once in the parking lot, we run to my truck, laughing, and it feels amazing. When have I ever run from a bar laughing, horny, and so into someone before?

Never. I've never felt like this and it's scaring the fucking hell out of me, but I don't want to stop either. Gabe makes me feel alive in every part of my being.

When we reach the truck, he doesn't let go of my hand and instead pushes me against the driver's side door.

"You know I need to drive to get us home," I say with a laugh.

Gabe's hands roam and cup my balls through my jeans. "I've never wanted someone like I want you right now. I just need a little something to make it home." He kisses me again and rubs at my crotch while he presses his against my thigh. "God...Hunter..." he whispers, and the coarse want in his voice grips me like a vise, and I rip my mouth from his.

"Get in the truck, Gabe. Buckle up. I'm breaking speed limits."

With a last kiss to my neck and a nip to the flesh for good measure, he does as I ask.

I get behind the wheel, focus enough to start the damn truck, and somehow drive home with Gabe next to me breathing so heavily I'd be concerned for his health if I wasn't doing the same thing.

It's a tense fifteen-minute drive, and when I finally pull into the ranch, I need to stretch my fingers out after gripping the steering wheel so tight the entire way home.

Gabe unbuckles and is out before I am. Instead of heading to the house or waiting for me, he meets me at the front of the truck and pulls me to him roughly. He kisses me again, urgent and possessive and...hot. So bloody hot. His fingers work my shirt buttons as I steer us towards the house.

"Someone is impatient. I guess the wild animals aren't a concern when you're about to get laid?"

Gabe pauses. "Wild animals?" He punches me hard on the shoulder. "Don't fucking joke about that now, you asshole." I bark a laugh, but he cuts me off with his hot mouth on mine and a hand down my pants. "The only thing wild right now is me, Hunter."

"I see that," I groan as he palms my dick through my boxers and licks at a peaked nipple. "I'd like to make it in the house, counsellor."

"Fine." He turns to walk the remaining steps to the ranch, but doesn't let my hand go. My shirt tails flutter behind me, and my belt buckle slaps against my thigh. If I gave him more time, my cock would probably be hanging out, too.

Gabe steps inside, and as soon as the door closes, he moves towards me, and while I'm not opposed to being mauled, I don't want Gabe to feel like this is one-sided. I may be restrained on the outside, but inside I'm a fucking tornado in a trailer park.

"Gabe."

He pauses, and I grip his chin before feathering a kiss to his lips. "Turn around and put your hands on the wall."

Gabe does as I ask and doesn't question me. With his hands high on the wall, I cover his wrists with my hand and whisper near his ear. "Keep them there like a good lawyer for me."

"Yesss...."

With my free hand, I reach around and flip open the button of his jeans and carefully lower his zipper. He rests his head back against my shoulder with a moan.

"Look at you leaking for me so much. Damn..."

The front of Gabe's boxers is soaked with precum, and I brush my thumb over it. He widens his stance and turns his head towards me. I can't deny the silent request for a kiss and take his plush lips with mine. His intensity has dialled back some, but still simmers there, ready to explode.

"Keep your hands to yourself, counsellor."

"I-I will."

Swiftly, my hands dive into his jeans, and I tug everything down to his ankles. His bare ass is a gorgeous sight, and I drop to my knees behind him. His breath hitches and he clunks his forehead to the wall when my lips touch his ass.

He sticks his ass out when I squeeze his cheeks, drawing a dirty chuckle from my lips.

"Hunter," he clips in a hoarse voice. "Don't tease m—"

His complaint is cut off when I bury my face in his ass and give him what he wants. His palms smack the wall, but he doesn't take his arms down. Gabe uses the wall to push back and ride my face standing up, which is...impressive.

His moans and mutters, and little huffed curses as my tongue works him over, set me on fire. As much as I want to make him come right here like this, I want what I promised more. Hell, I want it more than my next breath.

When I pull away, Gabe struggles to catch his breath as I make him step out of his pants before standing up.

"You can put your arms down, counsellor." Massaging his shoulders, I lean in and kiss his neck. He still carries some of his distinct scent. Fresh lemon and something spicy that makes me want to lick his entire body so I can put a taste to the scent. "I wasn't kidding about the cowboy hat rule. If that's what you want, I —"

"I fucking want, Hunter." He turns and pushes the shirt off my shoulders before kissing me soundly. "I've never wanted anything more," he breathes, and my skin prickles with anticipation. Gabe's hands are in my pants, pushing them down while we stumble towards the living room.

His desire and urgency are heady as fuck, and I kick the coffee table out of the way before pulling him to the floor with me.

"There's more room on the floor than on the couch." Gabe peels my boxers off and pushes me back, and I'm completely at his mercy.

Our roles switched as he presses a firm hand to my chest and wraps his lips around my cock.

I could watch him swallow me all day long. He's a beautiful man, but there's just something about watching him please me that makes him seem more beautiful. I've always been drawn to his lips. Maybe it's that. Or maybe it's the way he's so confident in what he wants from me.

But now isn't the time for me to be doing...whatever the hell I'm doing while this man captures my attention like no other. He pops off my cock with a satisfied sigh and swings a leg over my hips. He lines himself up and sinks slowly onto my dick and it's fucking torture at how slowly he's moving.

"If you need lube, we can go upstairs." I smooth my hands up his thighs, and little goose bumps chase after them.

"No, it's not that. You seem bigger than last time."

"Pretty sure my dick didn't grow bigger from a few weeks ago, Gabe."

"Try months. You've not fucked me since three weeks after we got married. I've been waiting to do this, so don't..." He sinks lower, bottoming out, and his ass touches my thighs. "Don't talk. Enjoy it."

Gabe rides me like he wished, but not like a wild stallion. He's slow, almost sensual as he moans and swivels his hips. I can't stop watching him and touching him everywhere. Wrapping my hand around his cock, I stroke him as he finally lets go and rides me like it's the last time he'll ever have a chance.

"Fuck...Hunter...." he pants. "Don't stop."

Gabe seats himself fully and throws his head back with a loud guttural moan. His dick swells in my hand as he rocks his hips.

"Fuck...Hunter..." My name sounds reverent on his lips, and when my gaze shifts from his release, now spilling down my hand to his face, my orgasm hits me without warning. Sheer, white heat runs up my spine as I come and gasp for a breath.

"Gabe...shit, Gabe."

His lips are on mine, feather soft. "I'm here, doll. I got you," he whispers, and my body has so many aftershocks you'd think there was an earthquake.

"Sorry, I didn't warn you. I hope that was okay." We've had the talk before about no condoms, but it just seems polite to ask if he wants a load in his ass or not.

His sex-blissed smile squeezes my heart, and a crack of panic seeps in.

"It was totally okay. Do you want to get cleaned up and call it a night? You must be exhausted." Gabe's gentle caress across my chest should be welcome, but my brain says otherwise. Taking his hand away, I squeeze it.

"Why don't you hit the shower first?"

He's silent for a moment as his gaze roams my face, and I hope he doesn't see what I'm trying my best to hide.

"Okay. If that's what you want. Will I see you after?"

The guarded hope in his voice is almost too much for me. I know what he wants, but I can't do that.

"If not tonight, then in the morning."

He sets his lips together and I feel like a huge asshole, but I can't share a bed with him. Sex is one thing, but having him in my arms all night and rubbing his scent all over my sheets? I'm not ready for that.

And I don't know if I'll ever be.

He gracefully exits and doesn't bother gathering his clothes, walking upstairs naked and leaving me on the living room floor, wondering if I just fucked everything up.

Margie's old beagle waddles off the porch of her farmhouse to greet me. She's had a beagle ever since I've met her. When one dies, she mourns, then gets another one. She just loves beagles.

"Hey girl. It's just me." I crouch down for the dog to sniff me, so she stops barking. Her eyes aren't that good, the cataracts visible, but she wags and thumps down for a belly rub once she recognizes my voice.

While I scratch her belly, the porch door squeaks open, and Margie wastes no time busting my chops.

"It's about time you showed up here, boy. Are you planning to stay and visit?"

Standing, I walk to the porch with a broken heart for not being here for her. "I'm here for as long as it takes to get you to forgive me."

"Hunter, there's nothing to forgive, but there's lots for you to fill in. Come on in and help me finish cooking for the youth group. We'll talk."

Bending down, I wrap my arms around her and hug. Her shaking arms return it, and she smells like she's been baking apple pies, Gabe's favourite.

"I'll always love you, my boy. Don't think I stopped because you vanished for a bit," she whispers in my ear, and I blink back the wetness.

"Thank you. I love you, too."

We return to the house, and just like I did a million times growing up, I kick off my boots and grab a pair of slippers by the door. When I enter the kitchen, I find a familiar setup. A giant country table covered with pies, bread, and vegetables. Her stove has two giant pots on the go with hearty soups.

"Who are you feeding today, Margie?"

She checks her paper on the fridge and reads out, "Youth group at the cathedral and the Big Brothers and Sisters." She returns the reading glasses to her head. "And, of course, the soup kitchen."

Margie's mission in life is to feed everyone who needs it. Her husband died very young, and they never had children. They both dreamed of filling this house with kids and their friends, and being a beacon for young people. When he died, she kept on without him, but never wanted to date again.

"You're a good woman. Anyone boarding with you?"

"Not right now." She tosses some salt into one of the pots and hands me a spoon. "Keep stirring those for a few more minutes, then we can package them." By the table, she has boxes labelled for each location that contain packaging materials. We fill them up with the food she makes and then deliver it. I've done this since I was ten years old, and nothing has changed.

But I came here with a purpose other than reconnecting with Margie.

"So, ah, did you like Gabe?"

Margie's small smile signals I've come to the right person, and I quietly puff a breath.

"He seems lovely. Very charming and devilishly handsome. How long have you been married?"

The soup I'm stirring is done, and I carry it to the large table to cool. She smiles, happy that I've fallen into her process again so easily.

"We just passed four months and..."

I stir the other pot while Margie perches on the stool next to me. "I've heard some rumours, Hunter. When he died, I tried calling you to warn you, but you were just as stubborn as he was."

"I'm not like him," I bite out, and Margie pats my arm.

"I know, dear, but you ran and asked nobody for help. I expected you to turn up here, but you never did."

Not a fact I'm proud of, but self-preservation was my default. I wasn't sad that my grandfather died. I was scared about my future and angry at myself for letting it get to this.

"I'm sorry. I was a prick. I should have come to you, but...I was embarrassed and, fuck...I didn't want anyone to know he practically excluded me from the will. It's humiliating."

Fuck, that felt like spitting shards of glass to say out loud, but it's the truth.

"Fair enough, but I'd never judge. So what did the son of a bitch do?"

Despite myself, I laugh at Margie's candor. "God, I love you." I smile at the grey-haired spitfire, and not for the first time wonder how many years I have left with her. When everyone in your life dies or leaves, that's your default mode of thinking. How much longer, and how badly will it hurt this time?

"I almost bankrupted myself trying to keep the ranch bills paid because he left the property in a trust. I'm allowed to live there for as long as I want, but his lawyers failed to add me as someone who could access the trust to pay for things. After I fought them for almost two years, my attorney made some progress. It was stressful."

"I should've known he'd make you work twice as hard for it as anyone else. He was always too hard on you, Hunter. So many times I wanted to grab the nearest fry pan and smack him in the face."

"Margie!" I gasp, but she laughs.

"It's true. You were just a boy when your life was torn apart. Your gram could only do so much to keep the peace. That's why she brought you here so often. So you could be yourself and be a kid."

Some of my happiest memories were here, and yet I clung to the ones on the ranch instead. My entire life to this point has been a series of poor judgment and mistakes. Maybe this is another one.

"Gabe is a marriage of convenience, Margie." I hate referring to him like that, but it's true. "If I weren't married, I couldn't access the residual, and if I never married, his money would go to an anti-LGBTQ+ organization. I couldn't let that happen."

"So...he's not really your husband?"

The second pot of soup is finished, and I carry it over to cool with the other pot. "We made a deal."

Margie remains quiet for a moment before easing off her stool and opening the fridge. She rattles around and pulls out a bottle that she raises towards me. "Grab us two glasses. We're sitting and drinking this out."

"It's barely 9 AM."

"So? You're not gonna spill it all unless that tongue relaxes, so come on then. You didn't come here to beat around the bush, and I have meals to finish."

Grabbing two short glasses, I follow her to the front porch where the beagle snores. She sets the bottle on the small wrought-iron table, and I pick it up to pour us two glasses of the maple liqueur she had hidden in her fridge.

"What kind of deal did you make with the handsome devil?" She sips the liqueur and sighs. "This is straight from Quebec. They do maple the best."

I don't recognize the label, but I wouldn't doubt Margie would special order to support the cause of a memorial park for a late husband who's listed on the label. That's just who Margie is.

"He's a new lawyer here. Real city boy. He was wearing suits to the office." Margie makes the appropriate scoff of disbelief, and I nod. "Right? So he's more casual now, and I've introduced him to a lot of the big ranchers. The business is picking up, and he should be successful now."

Gabe has made major progress, and I'm proud of how well he's fit in with the farmers. He may still be green around the animals and such, but he's built trust with the community because he respects their job. Which, in the beginning, they were uncertain if he did.

"And what do you get from this deal, my boy?" She takes another drink while I down my entire glass in one go.

"Money," I grunt. "If I'm married, I get advances at certain points." I pour myself another glass, and Margie holds out hers for a top-up. "The first advance was when I showed the marriage licence. The next one is soon. I get the rest after a year."

She nods and sips. "And after a year? What then?" she asks gently, and I swirl the creamy liquid in my glass before downing a large gulp.

"Then's he's free to leave."

My throat burns with the words, and Margie says nothing for several beats.

"Do you want that?"

She was right about my tongue loosening with a little liquor. The words to speak pile up right there, but I can't get them out. Instead, I shake my head no.

"Does he?" she asks, and that's the question that breaks the dam, and my fears come pouring out.

"He looks at me like nobody ever has, and when he touches me, it's...it's not only about sex. He...he..." I trail off, not sure what else to say because I've not asked Gabe outright if he'd consider not leaving, but when he was so tender and called me doll, I freaked out.

"It sounds like you have a chance to build something real with this man, Hunter."

"I could fall for him so easily, Margie. I'm keeping him at a distance because I know it will hurt when he leaves."

Margie clucks her tongue. "You're so sure he'll leave, and you haven't asked him yet."

"They always leave!" I clutch the glass and take another swallow. "If they don't leave, they die, and I don't want him to be another one to break my heart. I just can't."

We sit on the porch for a few moments. Margie still sips from her glass, and I have a slight buzz from all the liqueur I've downed in a short time. The beagle snores, and I let myself imagine what it would be like if this were Gabe and me and the pet he always wanted instead. Could we make something work?

Will he break my heart, or will he finally mend it if I give him a chance?

"Let's finish packaging the food before it gets too late, yeah?" Margie stands and grabs the bottle from the table. "Thanks for not letting me drink alone. This stuff was too good not to share."

"Yeah. Thanks...for everything."

She pauses and rubs my shoulder, squeezing just enough to make me look at her.

"You'll figure it out, Hunter. You always do, but if you need advice, mine is to take the chance. If you found love, don't let it walk away. Do something that makes you happy. He's not here to judge you anymore."

With a last pat on my arm, Margie enters the house, and I take a minute longer to finish my glass.

He may not be here to judge me, but I do a damn good job of doing that myself.

Thirteen
Gabe

It's no surprise I'm in the kitchen alone—again.

Ever since our attraction boiled over to the hottest sex ever, Hunter has been distant. I wish I could say it doesn't bother me, but I'd be lying. I want to talk things out, but he finds creative ways to dodge the subject constantly.

Going to bed alone never hurt as much as it did that night. I thought we were on the same page, and turns out we weren't even reading the same fucking book. With a sigh, I pour a coffee and head out to the porch swing on the back deck.

Since Hunter first showed me this swing, I come out often. With fall closing in, the mornings are chilly, and I've taken to bringing a blanket out with me. After wrapping it around me, I settle on the swing and let the gentle squeaks accompany me on a day just as grey as my mood.

I miss my sisters today. Both of them gone too soon, and it's always the fall when I miss them most. Karina died on a rainy Saturday night in September at the hands of a drunk driver, and Katia took her own life the following October. Since that October day, the only family I've had is the one I make myself.

Riley is the best one I found, and through him, I've found Jackson and a group of cowboys to befriend. Diamond, the barista at the Thirsty Cow, would probably be a great friend, too, if I allow it. My work friends were just that, friends through work, and while they helped me each time while I grieved my sisters, they didn't remain close friends in the way you sometimes need.

This thing with Hunter wasn't supposed to be complicated. It was the means to an end for both of us, but somewhere along the way, I let it mean more to me.

A light patter of rain hits the tin roof of the porch, and I wrap the blanket around me tighter while I dip into the melancholy that sneaks up on me around this time. I'm not sure how long I sit there, stewing in my sadness, but when the patio door opens, my heart lifts when Hunter steps out.

"Hey." He shoves his hands in his pockets. "Can I join you?"

"It's your porch. Go ahead."

I don't mean to sound so caustic, but I've barely seen him for two weeks. I'm allowed to be a little pissy about it even while I hate doing it.

He settles next to me, and his warmth is welcome on the chilly day. He smells good too, like he's been baking pie or something.

"Listen...Gabe..." He releases a long sigh, and I turn towards him. "I'm sorry for being such a prick that night. It...I didn't know what to do." His throats bobs and he keeps his gaze on his hands. Hands that set me on fire with a single touch, but keep their distance when things get too difficult. "I'm, ah, not good at this sort of thing, and I didn't mean to hurt you."

He means it. I know he does, but I need more than words.

"You did, though. Whether you meant to or not."

"I'm sorry." He swallows again, and I turn to stare out into the back pasture. After a moment, a warmth settles on my thigh, and I glance down to find Hunter's hand, palm up. When I turn to him, his gaze is open, and the soft vulnerability that he's shared with me a few times before is back.

I'm not sure if I should accept his offering and allow myself to keep getting closer to a man who pushes me away every time things move to a deep level, but I could use a friend right now. Maybe it's wrong for me to use him for comfort, but right now, he's offering, so I'm taking.

Sliding my hand in his, I shift, and Hunter pulls me closer as the rain increases its intensity. It's hard to see the individual rain drops now as the rain intensifies, but the patter on the roof has an odd comfort. His arm moves and settles around my shoulders, and I rest my head against him.

A calloused thumb wipes the wetness from my cheek. "Why are you sad, counsellor?" His gentle voice is like another blanket around me, and despite being angry with him, I talk.

"I miss my sisters today. Sometimes I get sad—depressed, actually—in the fall, around the days of their deaths. This is one of those days."

"Do you want to talk about them? Or...anything that might help?"

"Not today. I just want to feel it for a while."

Hunter says nothing, but his thumb keeps wiping the odd tear from my cheeks, and it shouldn't make me feel better that he's seeing me like this, and sitting with me, but it does. His quiet presence helps, and as much as I wish I could remain angry with him...I can't.

"I'll sit here and feel it with you, Gabe. For as long as you need."

And he does.

"Mr. Davis?"

Penny pokes her head through my office door.

"Yes?"

"You have a delivery."

"You can sign for anything. You know that." I turn back to my screen, researching how to include intellectual property into a will for a rancher who has a secret pen name and writes romance novels. It's an odd thing to know about a big, burly guy with a goat farm.

It's also a distraction from the man whom I call husband in name only. Thoughts of him and his multiple layers keep invading my mind. It's unsettling that I'm letting a man take over my thoughts so much, but Hunter Burke is a puzzle I can't seem to walk away from.

"Not this delivery," Penny states.

Pushing away from my desk, annoyed more than I should be, I brush by her and walk to the front of my office, where I pause in front of a man dressed as a giant teddy bear.

"Gabe Davis?"

"That's me, yes."

He passes me a stuffed bear that looks a lot like his outfit, and then hands me a bouquet of teal-coloured carnations. He blows into a little harmonica thing, then unfolds a sheet of paper that he sings from. Badly.

"You can't say no to a teddy bear. Please join me at the Happy Badger tonight and don't be square."

It sounds like a jingle from an old television commercial.

"Don't be square? Who even says that anymore?"

The bear shrugs and hands me an envelope. "The one who hired me to say it, I guess. Have a great day."

The envelope is thick, and with my arms full of flowers and teddy bear, I turn to find Penny about ready to burst.

"Go on. Get it out," I sigh as she bounces around behind me.

"The bear has tiny glasses like yours and ohmygod this is the sweetest thing ever."

I turn the bear around and notice the tiny glasses that are indeed just like mine, and this can only be from one person. Since he sat with me on the porch and witnessed me at my lowest, there's been a different tension between us. We're walking on eggshells, and I hate it.

Maybe this is his way of taking a step to move us past this and, dare I hope...build something more than the strange situation we put ourselves in.

"Is it from Hunter? It must be!"

Suddenly feeling overly emotional, I don't want to share this with Penny right now.

"If I have a secret admirer, I'll let you know."

Rushing back to my office, I close the door and lean against it. The bear's glasses are cute, I have to admit, and my mood softens as I inspect the bouquet of carnations.

He remembered my favourite colour, and yeah, he gets bonus points for that.

My hands shake as I set the flowers on my desk and peel open the thick envelope to remove the single-folded sheet of paper inside.

Gabe,

I know I'm shitty about saying the right thing and I want to apologize again. Properly.

Please meet me at the Happy Badger, 7 PM tonight. Give me the chance to be good for you and wear your dancing boots.

Hunter

Is there any way I won't fall for this guy? A handwritten note for a date to apologize is not what I expected. In fact, I thought his attempt at an apology was what happened on the porch swing.

This feels like a spark of hope.

He asked for a confirmation at the end of the note, and I'm mid-text before I stop and just call him instead.

"Gabe?"

"You asked me to confirm the date, so I thought I'd call you."

"Oh, right...Did you, ah, like it?"

The uncertainty in his tone thaws my mood.

"I did." My fingers brush over the cute bear. "But I have to say, I didn't expect this from you. A teddy bear and flowers from a singing bear are pretty sentimental."

"The teddy bear had glasses like you," he says quietly. "I wanted to show you that you're on my mind a lot."

"You remembered my favourite colour, too," I whisper.

"I remember a lot about that day, Gabe."

I don't know why that shocks me, but it does. Our wedding day was so rushed and not at all romantic, and yet...Hunter is doing his best to make it that way.

"I'll meet you tonight. I can't wait."

"Me neither, Gabe. Have a great day, and I'll see you soon."

"Bye, cowboy."

"Bye, counsellor."

I'm not sure how I'll concentrate on the rest of my day now, knowing what awaits me tonight.

Once I arrived home, I changed into a red button-down shirt I know looks great on me, and my most comfortable jeans that make my ass look incredible. If he's putting in the effort to get me there, I'm putting in the effort to showcase the goods.

With a smile, I slip on my cowboy boots. They're surprisingly comfortable, and I started wearing them to work when I have farm visits scheduled.

For a city guy, I'm at least looking like the locals now. As I head to my car, Lewis chirps, and I change course. It's been a while since I've visited the little dude.

"Hey buddy. I haven't been out to see you for a few days. Let me get you a carrot."

Jogging into the barn, I locate the treat bucket and pull out a small carrot for Lewis. As I'm about to leave the barn, heavy panting and stall boards rattling stop me in my tracks.

I tentatively enter the row of horse stalls, the carrot clutched in my hand in front of me like a weapon. If it's a wild animal, I could poke it in the eye with the root vegetable if it doesn't like carrots. That would work, wouldn't it?

Dixie pokes her head out of a stall, but she's not the one making the ruckus. She nickers, but not the usual way when I'm bringing her a treat. This one sounds...stressed. stall boards rattle next to her—Mack.

The carrot drops from my hand as I jog down the barn aisle to her stall. Mack is not okay.

Her coat is shiny, like she just ran a marathon under the August sun, but she's been in the barn for a few hours already. I know that because Hunter said he brings them in earlier in the fall, while the bears do their last-minute foraging for hibernation. That wasn't news I liked to hear, but he insisted that in all his years here, he's only had a bear in the pasture once.

That's one time too many, if you ask me.

Mack paws at the ground, then stretches her neck and body out before kicking a back foot at her belly. She lies down, then immediately gets up with a low groan I've not heard from her before. Her expressive eyes, the ones that I sometimes feel are smiling at me, plead for me to help, but I don't know what's wrong.

She walks in a few circles in her stall, lies down and immediately gets back up—again—and in my gut, I know something is very wrong. I don't need to be a horse guy to know that.

With a shaky hand, I pull out my cell and call Hunter right away.

"Hey, counsellor. Are you on your way?"

"No. I'm in the barn." Mack's panting intensifies and my panic bubbles over into my voice. "There's something wrong with Mack!"

"What's going on?" Hunter asks, calm and measured while I work at tamping down the panic.

"She's all wet, like she's sweating, and she's pawing at things, lying down and getting up. She looks like she's in pain."

Hunter curses, then takes charge. "Gabe, I'm calling the vet. His name is Jonah. Mack will probably be okay, but Jonah will get there faster than me. Can I ask you to do something?"

My shoulders relax with his steady voice and latch on to the words that Mack will be okay. If I keep thinking that, it will happen, right?

"Yes, of course. Tell me what to do."

"In the tack room, Mack has a hook. There's a halter on it. That's like a bridle with no bit for her mouth. Do you remember when I showed you?"

"Yes." I walk towards the tack room as he continues. "Put it on her and clip the lead rope to the side. Walk her around slowly until Jonah gets there. Do you think you can get a halter on her by yourself?"

"I-I don't know, but I'll try."

"Just read her movements. It slips on easily and she's used to it. I'll be there as a soon as I can."

"Okay. Please hurry." My voice cracks. "I don't like her like this, Hunter."

"I know Gabe." Hunter's voice is soft as he does his best to comfort me. "I'll be there soon."

After pocketing the phone, I find Mack's halter and the lead and try valiantly to remember what Hunter taught me all those weeks ago. Halters, bridles, bits, saddles, and brushes. It was a lot for a newbie to digest, but if I wanted to ride with him again, he said I needed to learn all these things.

Returning to Mack with the halter in hand, I find her still lying down, but she raises her head when I open the stall door. Her breaths are still harsh pants, and I try to channel Hunter's calm.

"Hey, girl. Your dad said to put this on you, okay?"

Mack's eyes are so expressive. Over the weeks that I snuck her carrots and talked to her without Hunter knowing, I believe we bonded. I didn't know horses had personalities that were as unique as humans. Her eyes are my favourite part and over time I learned to read her looks. It probably seems silly to think it, but sometimes I wonder if she's so good with me because she knows I'm new to horses.

I think she knows I'm here to help now, even though my hands are shaking and I'm sweating as bad as she is. Mack allows me to slip the halter on and buckle it, and that simple task feels like a massive victory. But it doesn't make anything better.

She lays her head back down, and I'm unsure what to do, so I call Hunter again.

"Gabe?"

"I got the harness on but she's laying down and just huffing. Should I get her up?"

"If she seems comfortable, that's okay. Just stay with her. I'm almost there. Try not to panic. You okay?"

"Yeah. I think so."

"You're doing great, Gabe. I'm ten minutes out."

Hunter hangs up, and I get comfortable in the stall next to Mack's head.

"I don't know what's going on with you, Mack, but whatever it is, you're going to get better." She puffs as I pet her ears. "I only just went for my first ride with you and your dad, and it won't be our last, okay? I know I'm not a horse guy, but I really like you, and I think you might have made me a horse guy."

I've never felt so helpless in my life. How do people manage it with sick pets? She's not even mine, and I'm on the verge of an emotional meltdown.

A male voice I don't recognize calls out in the barn. "Hello?"

"In the stall with Mack!"

Footsteps sound down the barn aisle, and the man, who must be the vet, pokes his head over the door.

"You must be Gabe. I'm Jonah. Hunter should be here soon. I was nearby when he called. Sounds like Mack is colicing, but I need to check her out to be sure."

"Is that bad?"

Jonah moves into the stall with me and kneels next to Mack. "Sometimes it can be, but if you catch it early—" He listens to Mack's heart, lungs, and belly. "—which it seems like you did, the chances of full recovery are much better." He hangs the stethoscope around his neck and stands. "Her gut sounds are pretty quiet. I need to do a rectal exam. Do you think you can help me?"

"Ah...in what way?"

A familiar low chuckle sounds as Hunter shows up at Mack's stall. "Not the way you think, counsellor." Hunter stands in the aisle, dressed in jeans that have never seen the inside of a barn. The blue button-down shirt is one I haven't seen before, but damn, does it ever look amazing on him. He's definitely dressed to impress his date, and it takes a moment for me to pick up my jaw. I'm still sitting in the stall with Mack's head partially on my lap when he leans down to plant a soft kiss on my lips. "We need to get Mack on her feet for the doc."

"Oh." Petting Mack one last time, I whisper she's a good girl and to be brave before sliding out from under her head. "I'd like to help."

"The more hands, the merrier," Jonah says as he pulls on a pair of gloves that go up to his shoulder.

Hunter bends to speak to Mack, and the horse nickers at his voice before slowly pushing up to stand with Hunter at her side. He walks Mack out of the stall, and Jonah motions for me to join him.

"Stand off to the side and mind her legs. She might try to bring one up like she's scratching, and you want to avoid a kick. Hold her tail out of the way for me and just stand like that."

Hunter and Jonah share a few words I don't understand before Jonah slathers one arm with lube and works it into Mack's butt. Remind me never to complain about a prostate exam again. Mack barely moves with the intrusion, but her panting continues.

"There's a large mass of fecal matter here. I'll run the nasogastric tube and try the mineral oil. If it works, then we avoid surgery." Hunter's eyes close with a sigh as he presses a kiss to Mack's head.

Jonah removes his arm along with a bunch of dry poop and pulls off the glove. "That's good, right? To not have surgery?" I ask, and both men nod.

"We've had a cold fall season, and she's likely not getting enough moisture with the grass dying so soon. It happens, but I'm confident we'll have her feeling better in no time." Jonah nods, confident in his findings, and pulls a huge rubber hose from his bag. While Jonah places a coating of lubricant on the hose, Hunter moves Mack close to a hook on the wall and clips it to one side of her halter. He keeps the lead short on the wall side while holding her halter with his hand on the other side. I can't imagine it feels good getting a tube down her nose while she's awake, but she's barely fighting it.

Hunter works with Jonah, stroking Mack's throat for her to swallow. Jonah places his mouth on the tube and sucks...which absolutely grosses me out. Both men quietly cheer when Jonah removes his lips, and a rush of gurgling sounds from the tube. Mack stomps once, but Jonah moves fast. From his oversized coat pocket, he produces a giant syringe filled with mineral oil. Hunter holds the tube while Jonah slowly injects the oil. When he's finished, he removes the tube, and Hunter moves to unhook Mack from the wall.

"We released a lot of gas, and some of the impacted feces came out with my exam. The mineral oil I just gave her should help soften the stool. Walk her around for a bit. You know the drill. How about if I come back at midnight? If she's not improving, I'll reevaluate."

"Thanks, Jonah. We'll be here. I'd appreciate you coming back to check on her."

"She's hopefully out of danger. Gabe caught it early." He packs up his things and pats Hunter's arm. "Watch for poop. Call me if you need me sooner. I'll wash up, then be back in a few hours."

Jonah disappears, and Hunter again closes his eyes, taking a deep breath before turning to me.

"Walk with us?"

"I was going to, even without an invitation."

The moon lights the pasture as Hunter opens the gate, and we step out with Mack. A definite chill is settling in, and frost is likely at this temp. Hunter holds Mack's lead and runs a hand down her neck several times. It might be dark out, but I notice the shine in his eyes as he watches Mack.

"This is pretty common, Gabe. If I were here, I'd have given her something myself and called Jonah to keep him updated, but I knew you needed some reassurance before I got here."

"You weren't worried about Mack?"

"I was, but you were scared, and I figured if the vet was here, you'd feel better."

I let his words sit with me for a moment. He wanted to ease my mind about a horse I was becoming attached to. He didn't need to do that, but I'm grateful he did.

"I'd never have found her if it wasn't for Lewis. I went to get him a carrot and heard Mack." Poor guy never got his carrot. I'll have to give him a bigger one next time.

Hunter bumps his shoulder against mine as we walk. "You're a softie for the animals now. You screamed when you first met Lewis." There's a smile in his voice, and while it's true I screamed, I'm also a softie like he says, and I'm not even embarrassed.

"They grow on you," I answer. "Kind of like their owner."

Hunter doesn't respond. Which is okay. I know how hard it was for him to invite me on a date, and apologies...well, sometimes people can't say the words, but actions mean just as much.

We don't talk for a while. It's just us, the crisp night that verges on me needing an extra sweater and the soundtrack of Mack passing gas like a champion. Even with that less-than-romantic ambient sound, it feels like the best quality time we've spent together.

Mack stops and lifts her tail.

"Do you have your phone? Can you shine your flashlight on her crap?"

I feel like I should make a joke about bodily functions, but from what I've learned tonight, maybe that's not wise. After finding the fresh pile, Hunter pushes at the solid shiny mass with the toe of his boot.

"Good. Looks like the mineral oil is working. That one is still hard, though." We keep walking in the moonlit pasture, following the fence line, then across to the barn and back. "I'm sorry our date didn't happen."

Hunter's gaze meets mine, and if we weren't walking Mack, I'd grab him and kiss him until we ran out of breath.

"The date you *planned* didn't happen. This is still a date. We're already dressed for it, so we'll just do it differently."

Hunter pauses the walk and stares at me. His lips parted like he wants to say something, but he remains silent for several beats until Mack huffs and we walk some more.

Hunter's hand finds mine, and, with a shaky breath, he brings my hand to his lips.

Fourteen
Hunter

Mack will definitely be fine.

After several hours, she's already perkier and far more comfortable. She's passed a normal stool, and it's only then that I decide we can rest and put Mack in her stall to monitor.

Me, though? I'm not fine.

Hearing Gabe's panic over the phone with Mack did me in. I broke the speed limit to get here because, while I was concerned for Mack, I wanted to protect Gabe from the worst if it happened. Without being there to see Mack myself, I didn't know how bad she was. If she died with him...I don't think he'd recover for a very long time, and he didn't need that on his plate.

Seeing him in the stall with my horse, her head lying on his lap while he didn't care about his clothes and only had eyes for Mack...it took all my willpower to keep it together. He stole my heart at that moment, and I didn't want it back.

I was already walking a tight line with falling for him. Tonight, I wanted to step forward and genuinely try not to just be here for a charade of a marriage and casual sex. I wanted to make this work and show Gabe he could trust me.

For a guy who spent his whole life pushing people away because whenever I loved someone, they left, Gabe makes me want to be better. I want to break this stupid pattern of mine. He makes me want to hold on tight and take a risk.

After walking Mack and holding Gabe's hand the entire time, I was determined not to let this night be a total loss.

"Do you mind if I make us some sandwiches and bring them out? It's nothing fancy, but neither of us has eaten, and I think you want to be close to watch Mack."

That's it. He's perfect. If I still wanted to fight this connection with Gabe, the option to push him away just fled like a racehorse with no jockey.

"I'd love that, actually. Could you bring something warm to drink, too? I have some blankets and lawn chairs in the tack room. I'll get those set up while you're gone."

"Of course. Give me a few and I'll see what I can come up with."

Gabe disappears, and I hang over the edge of Mack's stall once I've led her back to the barn. She's drunk some water from her trough, and her tail swishes as she stands and blinks at me.

"I can't decide if your timing is impeccable or shit right now, Mack." Reaching out, she steps forward, and I pet her nose. "You like him, too, don't deny it. I saw you with your head in his lap." Mack snorts, and I laugh. "I'm keeping an eye on you, missy. Just let me get a chair."

In the tack room, I grab two folding lawn chairs and an old, dusty blanket. It's days like today that I'm grateful for upgrading the horse barn all those years ago. No more muddy floors and space heaters. Setting up the chairs on the cement pad across from the horse stalls, I shake out the blanket and place it next to me before taking a seat and watching Mack.

I have a camera system I could use and watch while inside, but I never liked that. I prefer to be out here and listen to every snort and snuffle. To be steps away in case a sick animal needs me. Something else my grandfather always hated. Animals were just that to him. A purpose and not a living, breathing thing with a heart that you loved.

They lived and died, and life went on, even when his best quarter horse broke her leg. The vet put her down while he walked away, and never once looked back.

Gabe would, though. I could see it in his gaze as he petted Mack's head. If Mack didn't make it, Gabe would come unravelled. We're not just spending our date tonight in the barn for my peace of mind, but his. He's lost family he loves, and while that doesn't include four-legged family for him, I know he'd carry that same grief for these horses.

Ever since that day on the porch in the rain, I've known Gabe has a tenderness to him I don't want to keep bruising. I want to nurture him, even if it means working through my own fears.

Margie said it's emotional maturity or some shit. I'm not a fan, but I can't deny how much I want Gabe to stay.

The barn door opens with a squeak, and Gabe appears in a quilted flannel jacket he must have found in the hall closet. He has a thermos, and two cups balanced on a cutting board over a giant mixing bowl.

I stand to help. "Oh, thank you. I made you that lemon tea you like. You're almost out, by the way." He sets the covered bowl down near the chairs. "I hope you don't mind me wearing this. I found it in the closet. It's freezing out here, and I wasn't sure what you had for blankets."

"No, not at all." My brain is still stuck on him, noticing I like lemon tea. "What were you able to find for us to eat?"

"Well, prepare to be dazzled," Gabe says as he laughs and lifts the cutting board off the bowl. Inside, he has several small plastic containers of meats, cheese, and pickles. He has a box of crackers, a single apple, and the remainder of a loaf of bread.

"Is this charcuterie by Gabe?" I laugh as I place the items on the cutting board that Gabe balances over the arms of the chairs.

"Uh, it's neither of us has done groceries, and the fridge was kind of bare."

"That works. I've been meaning to go, but I keep forgetting."

"I hear you. Life takes over and things get forgotten." He pops a pickle in his mouth and glances at Mack's stall. "Is she still okay?"

"Yeah, no worse, and that's a good thing. She's tired, though."

Gabe smiles as he chews and gazes at Mack's stall. "You can still go over and visit with her," I add when Gabe doesn't immediately sit.

"She wouldn't mind?" Gabe is already walking over before I reply.

"No. She'd probably like it."

I can't make out what Gabe murmurs to Mack, but I hear the happy nickers from the horse. I've eaten most of the pickles by the time Gabe returns, but after he sits, he surprises me by asking about horses in depth.

How much does a horse's feed cost? How often do they get vet visits? Is it hard to train a horse? And my personal favourite, have I ever brought a horse into the house?

It passes the time, and we chat effortlessly, each of us taking turns to check on Mack. Just before Jonah returns at midnight, we both take Mack for a walk in the yard. Since the clouds have moved in and it's far too dark to walk in the pasture.

Gabe gets his flashlight out without me asking, and when I notice Mack's droppings are mostly normal, the remaining tension in my shoulders bleeds out. Jonah pulls in just after that and confirms.

"You two have had a long night already." He listens to Mack's heart, lungs, and gut and nods with a smile. "Lots of good noises in there, and she's already perked up." He reaches up to pat Mack's head. "Monitor her water and gradual feed. You know the routine, Hunter. Call me if anything changes."

Jonah hops in his truck, and we take Mack back to her stall. I measure her water and give her a small amount of hay.

"So...what do we do now?" Gabe asks.

"We clean up here and go to bed. You must have work tomorrow?"

"Yeah, but nothing caffeine can't fix. If you need company, I'm here." He offers that like it's second nature, and maybe it is for Gabe, but for me, it's more than that.

"I wouldn't mind some company." Gabe gathers our mugs and dishes while I return the chairs and blankets, and when I turn to find him waiting with everything in his arms while wearing that overstuffed farm work coat because he's cold, I'm overcome with an emotion so thick I almost can't speak.

Gabe doesn't seem to notice, thankfully, and I open the door for him as we walk across the yard. Just before we reach the porch, Gabe stops.

"Is it snowing?"

We both peer up at the giant yard light and, sure enough, a few flakes float across the light beam.

"Seems like we have an early winter coming."

Once inside, Gabe dumps the bowl of dishes on the counter and hangs the jacket up in the closet. It's a shame I didn't have him on my arm tonight, dancing, but somehow, having him involved with my life on the ranch is infinitely better.

"I'm going to shower and get some sleep. I'll see you in the morning?" Gabe asks, and I shake my head no. No more keeping him out.

"Stay with me tonight? Please?" I ask softly and step closer. "I couldn't control what happened earlier, but I can still end the night how I want if you'll let me."

Gabe's lips part as his hand comes to my chest. "How do you want it to end?"

Drawing Gabe's body next to mine, I bring my lips to his. "With you naked in my arms. I don't want to go to bed alone anymore."

Gabe's body heat sears through my clothes as he kisses me. His movements are slow, and his lips are always so sensual. Having them on me is possibly the best thing I've ever felt.

"I told you I'd keep you company, and I think that sounds like a great way to end the night."

How can a single man move me to a lust that burns so hot one moment and then make me ache to hold him in my arms and wake up with him the next? Gabe and I kiss in the hallway, both of us moving to undress the other without the urgency of the last time, and it hits me like the ground when I'm bucked off a horse—I'm falling in love with this man.

That should make me break out in hives, but I pull him closer instead.

"It's warmer upstairs," I murmur against his neck. "Warmer still in the shower with me, counsellor."

"I like the sound of that," Gabe purrs.

Talking Gabe by the hand, I lead him up the stairs to the bathroom, and there's something about this moment as I close the bathroom door behind us that feels like it was a long time coming. Maybe not for Gabe, but definitely for me. Now isn't the time to analyze all my previous one-nighters and pushing people away, but I can't help but wonder if Gabe entered my life when I needed him most.

He's been patient with my moods and put up with far more than anyone should. He married me at the drop of a hat when we didn't even know much about each other. Most importantly, though, he fits here.

With me, with the ranch, with rodeo. With my entire life.

Our hands and lips roam while more clothing hits the floor, and our want for each other never falters. Reaching into the walk-in shower, I step away from Gabe long enough to run the water and get steam forming in the stall before pulling him in with me.

He holds up a finger and places his glasses on the counter before stepping into the shower fully with me. Water runs down his face, and it's odd not to see him with glasses like this. His long lashes clump together, and his hair sticks to his head under the spray, and I bring my mouth to his, desperate to keep tasting him for as long as I'm awake.

"Hunter...are we getting off in the shower?" His lips brush mine as he speaks. "I'm fine if we are. I just don't want to get caught under a cold spray."

"You're right. The hot water doesn't last that long." My hands slide down his arms as I take a small step back. "Clean up and we'll take this to my bed."

"I won't say no to that," he says, and quickly reaches for the soap. We both laugh like kids and race through a shower to avoid the blast of cold water when my aging hot water tank runs out. We fight over the soap and tease each other until I force myself to just stop touching him for the next five minutes, not because I know the hot water will run out, but because I don't want him to be cold.

He hates being cold.

We dry off in the steam-warmed bathroom, and Gabe rubs a towel over his hair while I stare. I should be embarrassed at how I'm ogling him, but he's too fucking gorgeous to not. Broad shoulders, lean build, and defined arms all catch my attention. He has the most adorable soft belly, with a sparse sprinkling of hair that's not a typical straight line treasure trail. It's more like a beacon towards the entire beach, throwing light in a wide swath to encourage you to find all his sensitive spots and not just one.

When Gabe stops drying his hair and catches me drinking him up, he licks his lips. Those plump lips that stretch so well around my cock I leak just thinking about it.

He lets the towel around his hips drop to the floor.

"If you keep looking at me like that, we won't make it to the bed, doll."

I suck in a breath. There's that name again. Why does it sound so good from his lips? "Would that be so bad?" I ask, my voice hoarse, and Gabe shakes his head.

"Not really, but Hunter...I don't just want sex. I want you."

He's next to me in a few steps, sliding his hands up my chest and wrapping his arms around my neck. "I want all of you. Sex, tears, broken promises with awkward apologies, and long days where you forget to come inside and eat. Your quirky cleanliness in the kitchen and the way you're looking at me right now." He presses a kiss to my throat. "I want all of you, not just these bits you think I want."

"I...I want to hold you all night and never let you go." The admission scares me, but once I've said it out loud, I wish I'd have done it sooner.

Gabe hums and presses a kiss to my lips. "That sounds like heaven."

"But I want to make us come first," I add with a laugh, and Gabe laughs, too.

"Thank fuck, because this hard on is gonna kill me if it's not taken care of soon."

With a final kiss to my lips, Gabe turns and takes off across the hall to my bedroom, leaving the warmth of the bathroom behind. I'm hot on his trail, and he's under my blanket in seconds.

"I have a hard time warming up once I get cold." He burrows further into my blankets, and I think I might like the winter just a little more this year if I have a snuggler in bed with me.

"How am I supposed to get close to you like that?" I ask from the side of the bed.

Gabe laughs and holds up a tiny corner of the blanket. "Get in quick."

I jump in next to him and immediately pull him against me. "How are you so warm? You just had a shower, and it's cold out, but you're like...a human furnace."

"I guess I run hot." I laugh, but Gabe falls silent.

"At the risk of killing the mood," Gabe whispers. "You are hot. But Hunter, I..." Gabe swallows hard and runs a finger over my right eyebrow. "I really like you. Whatever happens tonight or tomorrow or three months from now...I won't regret a single thing."

I don't know what to say to that, so I kiss him instead and hope he understands my feelings are bigger than anything I've ever known. Our legs tangle and hands explore in new ways. Not with the passion-driven lust we're used to, but something closer to the intimacy of knowing how to touch a lover that reaches their heart. A well-placed caress to commit to memory and the soft sighs of pleasure to go with it.

I could spend hours mapping every inch of his skin with my fingers and watching each reaction he gives. Gabe has woken something in me I've never experienced before. At one time, I thought I knew what it was like to care for someone, but this is something new and exciting.

More freeing than confining, and that's another barrier he's blown away.

Gabe frees a hand and pushes the cover down after several minutes of us making out. "Now I'm too hot."

I blanket my body over him, bracing myself on my arms. "I bet I can make you hotter," I whisper, and Gabe lifts his hips, grazing our cocks together.

"I know you can," he breathes, and I slide down his body, pushing his legs back so I can eat his ass. "Oh, fuck..."

I laugh softly at his exclamation and nip at his ass cheek. His fingers curl into my sheets at his side, and I don't know why that's such a turn-on, but it is. To know Gabe loses his refinement with my mouth on him is headier than any drug.

"Jesus, Hunter..." he pants as I spread his cheeks wider and tongue his hole. The moans he makes...damn. "Gimme more, please..."

"More what, counsellor?" Lifting my chest, I bring a finger to his entrance and trace a circle as Gabe's chest heaves. His hand goes to his dick when I push my finger inside, and he arches his head back into the pillow with a sigh. "That. More. You." He gasps each word on an exhale, and when his gaze finds mine, the world stops spinning.

If a single glance could brand my skin, this was it. Gabe wants more, and it's not just the action between the sheets.

Crawling up his body, I reach over to the nightstand for the lube. Gabe pulls my neck down to kiss me before I can slick myself up, and he sidetracks me with more deep kisses. While I'm under the spell of his tongue in my mouth, he's taken the lube from me and now strokes me with a slippery hand.

"Counsellor...you're sneaky," I mumble against his lips.

"Just wanted to help," he says as he lies back, and the air in the room crackles as I settle back over him. "Hunter..."

He reaches for my shoulders as I press into him. His fingers dig into my flesh as he puffs out a long breath. "Fuck...." His heels dig into my ass, holding me in place, and I'm okay with that. My lips find his neck, and Gabe releases his grip enough for me to rock my hips. "God, yes..." he moans, and allows me a little more room to move.

Sex has never felt this charged for me. I thought the first time with Gabe was a fluke. Both of us were just horny and up in our heads. But that's not it at all. His legs wrapped around me as his leaking cock slides across my stomach is like a key fitting the lock you thought you'd never open. Maybe it's love, or maybe it's just because he's a wildly attractive man, but whatever's making this feel so much more grips me in a way I can't ignore.

"I want to come in you." I breathe across his ear and snap my hips harder.

"Fuck...yes." His hands grab my ass cheeks and urge me forward, harder but not faster. Gabe wants this slow, and he deserves it. "Let me feel you, doll." He stretches his head up for a kiss, and I can't resist those plush lips. "Get lost in me, Hunter."

Pressing down into him, I chase his lips and try to do just that. Our bodies, now slick with sweat, slide together as I keep the pace Gabe wants. His fingers dance over my back before sliding into my hair.

"Hunter..." Gabe tugs on my hair and kisses me. It's a kiss that feels like home.

And then my orgasm hits me unprepared. "Fuck, Gabe..." A hot flash of pleasure surges over me.

I unload into him so hard and fast I'm panting for breath. How can his kiss be what sends me over the edge like that? It takes me a moment to realize he's still hard as a rock between us and I'm crushing him into the mattress with my full weight. My arms gave out with that kiss. When I pull away, he brings his hand to his dick, but I grasp his wrist with a shake of my head.

"Let me," I whisper as I kneel between his legs and spread him wider. Gabe's breathing is so fast, I'm afraid he might hyperventilate if I don't finish him quickly. "You're close?"

He nods with a swallow and raises his hips. I get it. Sliding two fingers in his ass, his eyes roll back. "I'm right there, doll. Fuck…" My other hand wraps around his leaking cock as I find his sweet spot. Gabe arches off the bed with a silent scream as he comes over my fist. He's fucking beautiful like this. A thin layer of sweat coats his skin, and his entire body glows.

There's an intensity right now between us that takes my breath away. His body relaxes fully into my mattress, and he closes his eyes with a sweet smile as I lower myself next to him.

Placing a kiss on his shoulder, I tell him I'll be right back. Once in the bathroom, I wet a few washcloths with warm water to clean Gabe up. When I return, he's snoring softly, and I can't wipe the big, stupid grin off my face.

This man is the one for me.

But how do I know if I'm the one for him?

Fifteen
Gabe

The howling wind outside draws me from my restful sleep.

The bone-tired exhaustion that hit me like a tonne of bricks after Hunter rocked my world slowly slides away, and I recount the happenings of last night. His strong arm rests across my chest, and I let my fingers trail across his skin. I'm snuggled up to the man as the little spoon and I wiggle my ass back into him, perfectly content in this cocoon of post-sex bliss.

The bedroom still carries the scent of our recent passion, and his arm, heavy around my body, is the only thing that makes me believe I'm actually sharing Hunter's bed with him.

Last night was scary with Mack, but what happened in this room, hell, even in the barn, breathes new hope into this turning out how I want.

His arm tightens around my chest, and sleepy words leave his lips in the stillness of the dark room.

"Counsellor...do you need something?"

I didn't before, but now that his warm breath caresses my skin and his arm flexes across my chest, I want him again with a longing that feels displaced since he's right next to me.

"Can you fuck me like this?" My voice sounds hoarse and unused. "Just...slow?"

His hand moves under the blankets to my ass with a soft caress. Hunter's hands are capable of great strength, but when he puts them on me, there's nothing but a gentleness that makes my heart ache. "You're not sore?" The blankets rustle in the darkness. "I'm getting hard just thinking about it."

Hunter's voice is rough with sleep, but his fingers at my entrance are tender as he tests my request.

"I'm okay," I whisper. The warmth of his body twists away from me briefly. The click of the lube cap sounds, and I moan with anticipation.

Neither of us says anything else. Like we've practiced this under-the-covers dance for years, he slicks himself and my ass and positions himself with a gentle kiss to the back of my neck. I push back into him, ignoring the discomfort of going too fast, and take him all the way. Harsh breaths sound in my ear as he pulls me into his chest again. Hunter kisses my shoulder as we do this wordlessly in the dark.

He's remarkably tender. So much so that I need to swallow the emotions building in my chest. This is what I've wanted from him. This isn't just sex on the living room floor that leaves me craving his arms around me during the night. He's careful and holding me like I'm the most precious piece of treasure in the universe. Waking up in his arms, I felt cherished and now I feel...fuck, like maybe we could make his thing work.

Hunter slides his hand up my throat and grips my chin. "Gabe..." his hot breath on my ear sends a shiver through my body. "You bring me to the edge so fucking fast, baby. Jerk yourself to get there." He twists my neck and contorts his upper half to kiss me, and I'm gone. Floating on a cloud of the most incredible bliss.

I gasp into his mouth as I spill over my hand, and Hunter groans into my neck as he fills me for the second time tonight.

"You sure know how to wake a guy up," Hunter pants before dropping a kiss to my shoulder.

"It can't be morning yet," I groan.

"Not for you, but it is for me. I need to deal with the horses and check on Mack before meeting the lawyer this morning."

My stomach drops at the mention of the lawyer. A reminder that this arrangement still has an end date, despite my hope for it to be real. "Is there something wrong? Do you need me there?" The silence stretches too long for my liking, and I ease away from him under the covers. "It's not my business to ask. Sorry. I'll get cleaned up and try to sleep a little longer before work."

"Gabe, it's not —"

"It's okay, Hunter. I trust you to tell me if there's anything I need to know."

I don't let him answer and head to the bathroom. If he doesn't tell me, then I won't know. If I don't know, it won't break my heart either, and I can continue living with the man I'm one hundred percent in love with.

What's a bit of denial alongside all the pretending?

"Hey, beautiful girl."

It's been several weeks since Mack's scare with colic, but I still can't bring myself to stop checking on her every night. With the winter weather closing in far too quickly, Hunter closed the gates, and the horses now have a much smaller pasture to roam during the day. They stay closer to shelter, and I like it because it's faster to see them, and I can have my visits in the barn and out of the biting cold winds.

There's one thing about Alberta I despise, and it's the icy winds that just show up to piss you off when you forget a hat.

Mack trots towards me. At least I think that's what you call it, and I reach out to pet her. It's funny how when I got here, I didn't think I could do the whole animal thing. Lewis hibernates, and I almost cried when Hunter told me he's gone until the spring...if he survives. He rushed on to assure me that constantly feeding him vegetables helped him prepare, so he was confident Lewis would be back.

I had to tell him to warn a guy next time before he dumps that kind of information. I never got to give Lewis that one last carrot, and if I lose that chance, it might break my heart.

Now I'm talking to horses daily and mentally preparing myself that this might not be my life forever, as much as I want it to be.

"If you see your dad, tell him...Well, I don't know." Mack headbutts me, searching for more carrots. "But be good for him."

Hunter dropped the info that he was meeting with his lawyer the night I felt like our relationship shifted, and I never gave him a chance to explain. Despite feeling like we were closer, I couldn't bear hearing anything negative. I ignored the information, and neither of us has brought it up since.

But it's festering, and I need to be an adult and face the music.

With a final pat to my favourite horse, I pull my coat tight around me and head to my car. Snow arrived by Halloween, and with it, the cold Alberta winds I despise. I've always hated winter. It's hard for me to shake a chill once it sets in, and I spend the entire season wrapped in sweaters and scarves, feeling like a coloured marshmallow with legs.

My car doesn't like the country roads to the ranch either. Winter has only just begun, and I've had to find the ruts until the plows finally showed up more than once. I've already called Hunter once when I got stuck at the end of the driveway, too.

He just kissed me on the cheek, got his tractor, and pulled me out before cleaning the end of the driveway in a few quick passes. Until then, I didn't know I liked a man who knew how to operate heavy equipment so expertly. Not that I need to be rescued, but it was nice to watch all the same.

No snow at the end of the driveway to get stuck in this time as I make my way to the Thirsty Cow for a long overdue meet up with Riley. Just me stuck in my head about why Hunter hasn't talked about the lawyer, and I need a best friend rant.

After parking and cursing the bitter wind because it's what I do, I stomp into the Thirsty Cow, and my slightly sour mood disappears when the bubbly Diamond greets me.

"Mr. Handsome!" he shouts, and I can't help the smile that forms. "You've come back!" He looks behind me with a raised eyebrow. "No hunky husband today?"

"No, just me. Sorry to disappoint."

He clicks his tongue. "Not a disappointment at all. One tall, dark, and handsome is better than none." He points to the corner. "Riley is who you're meeting, I presume?"

"You presume right. Could you —"

"Bring you an Americano with hazelnut and a slice of apple crumble?"

Diamond smiles because he knows my weakness is apple anything and it sounds perfect.

"Oh, man...you have crumble today?"

"Sure do, sugar. Go sit and I'll get that to you in a jiff."

Riley stands when I reach him in the cozy corner at the back, and we share a long hug. Summer was busy for us both, and we didn't get together as much as I hoped.

"Still not liking cold weather, I see." Riley laughs as he returns to his seat, and I remove a few layers.

"It's the fucking worst. And the dryness! Static and dry skin." I flop onto the couch next to him. "Sometimes I wonder why I live in Canada. Then I remember I don't like poisonous animals, and I feel better about it."

Seriously. I'd rather deal with dry skin and a wardrobe of sweaters than worry about the spider in my bathroom trying to kill me.

"Do you have plans for Christmas?" Riley asks.

"Shit. I haven't thought about it much. What are you doing?"

Riley and I have spent many holidays together, often with his Aunt Agnes. We missed a few years when I worked, but since my sisters died, Christmas was just another day. I like the food and, of course, I loved giving gifts to Riley and Agnes, but other than that, it was never top of mind.

Riley bites at his lip, and I pat his knee.

"Say it, Rye. I get it if you and Jackson want to be on your own."

"Are you sure, Gabe? I hate not being with you over the holidays."

"I'm an adult. Maybe I'll see what Agnes is up to."

"Yeah... she's got plans, too. Me and Jackson are going to his parents' in Arizona this year. The dogs are coming, too, and Aunt Agnes has a '*friend*.'" He uses air quotes and rolls his eyes. "She's spending Christmas Day with this friend. They met at the retirement home, and there's some kind of party going on."

I laugh, thinking of the party at the old folks' home, but happy Agnes has found someone to fill that void for her.

"I'll be okay, Riley. Honestly."

"Hunter doesn't have family either..."

I meet Riley's gaze and just as I'm about to open my mouth, Diamond shows up with my coffee and apple crumble and perches on the arm of the couch.

"So, tell me, Mr. Handsome, have you and the husband been back to the Happy Badger since you set the place on fire?"

Riley smacks my arm as I chuckle. "You two went dancing? Shit, we are long overdue to catch up."

"No, we haven't been back. We were supposed to, but then one of the horses got sick and...yeah. Not yet."

"They're having a big New Year's Eve Party. With dancing. You two should go. From what I hear, you're a natural." Diamond pushes off the sofa with a sigh. "I also want to watch." Laughing, he struts away, and I shake my head.

"Gabe...you clearly have a lot to tell me. Are things working with you and Hunter more than you thought?"

Scooping a mouthful of crumble into my mouth to delay answering his question, I think about how to reply. There are no secrets between me and Riley, and it's why I wanted to meet with him today. I need an outside perspective. One I can trust.

"A lot has happened, Riley. We went dancing because I learned his grandmother used to take him. It was the most incredible evening, but I went to bed alone. When we planned to go again, Mack got sick. We've..." I trail off, thinking about how it's been me avoiding Hunter lately instead of the other way around because I'm too afraid to hear bad news.

"Oh my god, Gabe," Riley whispers. "You really like him, don't you?"

"I think I do."

I know I fucking do. We may have spent a few evenings together since that last epic night, but Hunter still hasn't spoken about what he went to the lawyer for. Probably because I keep changing the subject. We're only six months into this fake marriage, and we agreed to a year, but my mind keeps telling me he's got what he wanted and he's just waiting to let me down gently.

My eyes burn, and I blink it away quickly. I don't want to miss seeing him or Mack every day, and I need to be there in the spring to see that stupid groundhog.

Riley's hand appears with a tissue, and it's only then that I notice the wetness on my cheeks.

"Sorry. I'm sitting here crying over a man. How fucking pathetic."

"It's not pathetic. You care, Gabe. He probably does too, but neither of you wants to take the first step and admit you have feelings."

That's half true. I did tell Hunter that night I really liked him. Just like any middle school kid would. Lord, I'm a love-sick loser.

"About six weeks ago, I found Mack sick. She had colic." Riley grimaces and reaches for his cup. "I was supposed to meet him for dancing that night. He sent me a teddygram to work and everything, Riley. I almost called you to see if he asked what to do."

"He sent you a teddygram? Like the singing one?" I nod, and Riley's eyes would have cartoon hearts if it were humanly possible.

Reaching for my crumble, I smile as I remember the little bear with glasses I still keep in my office. "He did. But then I found Mack and panicked, and we spent the night in the barn eating snacks and just talking about everything while we monitored Mack. When we finally went inside, it was...fuck, it was intense."

"I don't say this enough about Hunter, because he prefers people think he's an ass, but the man has a heart of gold, Gabe. He doesn't show that to many, but it sounds like you've seen it several times now."

"I just wish he'd tell me exactly how he feels, you know? He brought up the lawyer, and when I asked if he needed me there, he took so long to answer, I assumed the worst. I've been stuck in a negative space ever since."

Riley sits back with his coffee, comfortable like its own living room, as he tucks a foot under him. "If his meeting was to start the divorce, and he serves you...Will you fight him on it?"

Divorce.

I've drawn dozens, no, probably hundreds, of divorce agreements during my time as a lawyer. I've listened to the initiating spouse, and not once did I consider how the receiving spouse would feel. Families broken and spouses blindsided, all because one of them was no longer happy with the union. Now I feel sick and set my apple crumble down with a shaky hand.

"Technically, we agreed it would end after a year, and I'd be an ass to fight it if he wants it sooner."

"But you weren't in love when you agreed to that."

Riley's words roll off his tongue easier than they do mine, and I turn my head towards my extremely perceptive best friend.

"No, I wasn't." Which is as close as I'll get to saying those words to someone other than Hunter since I've not even told him that.

"You need to tell him, Gabe."

"It wasn't supposed to be like this, Rye. This was just helping a friend. He scratched mine, and I scratched his." Puffing out a breath, I lean back on the sofa and turn towards Riley again. The smile on his face is soft, and his eyes carry hurt for me.

"Sometimes people come into our lives when we think we don't need them, only to learn that they make our lives better by being there." He shifts forward and grabs my hand. "Look, Gabe, you know I'm a romantic at heart, and I'd love nothing more than to plan a real wedding for you one day, but I've never seen you like this. Don't keep this to yourself."

"What if he says he doesn't feel the same way?"

"Do you really think that?"

"No. I think he cares." My body still remembers how it felt that night. How he lit me up and how he kissed me. The way it felt to wake up his arms. "He feels something. I just don't know how much."

My phone pings with a text, and I suck in a breath.

> **Hunter:** Hey, counsellor. Just wondering where you are. A clipper is supposed to move in soon, and I don't want you stranded somewhere in that shitty car. Let me know when you're coming home, please?

Turning the phone towards Riley, he pulls his phone out when it pings and laughs.

"Jackson sent something similar. We should probably get going to keep these two from worrying themselves to death."

Riley gathers our cups and plates, and I end up finishing the last bit of crumble after all. It seems like most patrons have the same idea to split because the Thirsty Cow is so empty you could bowl in it.

"You two drive safe, okay?" Diamond tucks a phone in his pocket. "I just called my staff for the evening to stay home, and I think I'll head home early, too. It's getting nasty out there."

"Do you need us to help with anything to get you out of here faster?" Riley asks, but Diamond shakes his head.

"Thanks, sugar, but I won't be long. I just need to shut things down and lock up. I don't live far either."

"As long as you're sure?" I say and share a glance with Riley.

"Get yourself gone, Mr. Handsome. I'm more than capable."

Diamond pushes us towards the doors, and after zipping up, Riley and I hug once more outside.

"Text me when you're home!" He calls out.

"I will! Drive safe."

Fucking Alberta clippers. An entire season of snow dumped in an hour or two. Something else I hate but will choose over snakes in my bathtub any day.

After driving for ten excruciating minutes in the heavy snow, I'm finally making the turn onto the first country road to the ranch. As an Albertan, I know how to drive in the snow, and I'm well aware of how fast the snow accumulates in one of these storms. But I'm also not used to driving in these conditions in the dark on back roads.

I lived in the city all my life and snow removal follows different rules there.

My knuckles ache along with my jaw as I slowly creep forward along the road and keep to the centre to avoid any chance of accidentally hitting the ditch. It feels like ages have passed when I finally reach the stop sign to turn for the last stretch to the ranch.

"Okay. I'm almost there," I mutter as I pull out onto the road and pray to god I'm actually still on it. Tire marks disappear too quickly in the country with the reduced traffic, and the only thing guiding me is the GPS diagram showing me I'm still on the road.

But I have no frame of reference for how far I am from the ranch. Familiar markers are invisible, and I've resigned myself to just keep looking for the light at the end of the driveway. My shoulders are tight, and I'm leaning so far forward against the steering wheel to see better, my nose could touch the windshield.

The wipers work triple time, and if I go any slower, I'm afraid I might get stuck.

"Come on, come on. Please let me see the light pole for the ranch soon." I mutter to my empty car. Time seems to stand still, and I focus on my deep breathing to stay calm.

Finally, the light of the ranch shines through the snow, and I give the car more gas to make the turn...and get caught at the end of the driveway. After streaming curses, it could be worse. I could be in a ditch somewhere.

After I kill the engine, I check my coat zipper is completely closed, pull my hat lower, and begin the walk up the lane towards the house, instantly regretting not grabbing a warmer hat to cover my ears before I left.

When I finally reach the door of the ranch and step inside, I feel like an icicle and press my back against the door while wiping the melting snow from my eyelashes.

"Gabe! Are you okay? I was just about to go look for you!"

Hunter rushes towards me, and finally, the stress bleeds out of my body. My teeth chatter from the cold, and Hunter rushes to help remove my snowy clothes.

"I-I got s-stuck at the end of the d-driveway."

"You walked up the driveway? No wonder you're freezing. I started a fire already. Take off everything that's wet, and I'll grab another blanket."

Hunter almost runs into the wall in his haste to get a blanket, while I still shiver and shake with cold. God, I could never pass a wilderness survival test. I'd die from hypothermia in June, for god's sake.

My pants are soaked through, and I kick them off at the door along with my underpants and socks, but I leave my sweater on since it's the only article that's dry. Hunter returns with a blanket and wraps it around me, leading me away from the cold and wet pile of garments.

The warmth of the fire in the living room is heavenly, and the wall of heat smacks into me. "Oh god, it's so warm. You're a lifesaver."

He places me on the couch and instantly sits next to me with his arm around my shoulders to pull me closer.

"You need a better vehicle if you're staying here, counsellor," he says, and his voice hitches. "I tried to track your location, but the internet is shit with the storm, and it never updated since you left town."

"W-were you actually going to look for me?"

"Yes. And I wasn't coming home until I found you."

Riley's words echo in my head, and I turn to look at Hunter. "We n-need to t-talk," I chatter, and Hunter nods slowly.

"Yeah, we do, counsellor." He brushes his knuckles over my cheek. "But let's get you warm first, okay? We have a lot to work out."

He hugs me closer, and I burrow into the blanket and his side while I cautiously hope we're on the same page.

Sixteen

Hunter

Gabe's shivering has finally stopped, and he's curled into my side like a contented cat. The fire crackles and pops, and it's times like right now that I'm happy I kept the old wood-burning fireplace.

There's nothing like a wood fire to shake the chill from your bones.

Along with Gabe's shivering, my heart rate is back to normal. The longer it took for me to hear from him, the more I panicked that I'd lost my chance, and something terrible had happened. Sudden snowstorms here are fairly normal, and I know he's a capable driver, but that car of his isn't suitable for winter on the back roads.

I could kid myself and say that's all it was, concern over him driving in a snowstorm, but I kicked my own ass and admitted it was because I was afraid I'd lost yet another person I loved.

It's been decades since the night I lost my parents in a car accident during a snowstorm. The longer it took for him to arrive, the louder the thoughts of *'not again'* grew.

Just because I've accepted I'm in love with this man doesn't make it easier for me to put all my feelings into words, though. Too many years of staying quiet and never expressing my feelings is a hard habit to break. But things are finally turning around for me in my life. The will has been mostly sorted. I'm not hovering near bankruptcy, and the business Jackson and I have discussed for years is coming to fruition.

I even have a new beginning in rodeo lined up with Levi.

But I'm missing something I never allowed myself to wish for.

What's missing is someone to laugh with and share stories on the porch swing. A person to talk through crossword clues with. Someone who loves this country life like I do and puts up with my moods, not because they have to, but because they know it's just how I am.

And hugs.

Since I met Gabe, I wasn't aware of how much I missed hugs. Sure, I bro hug my friends, and now that I'm back to visiting Margie, I get her mom hugs, too, but nothing can replace that feeling of warmth and love when a person hugs you simply because they want you in their arms and love you.

That's how Gabe hugs me. Like he never wants to let go.

"You're awfully quiet." Gabe murmurs. "What's on your mind?"

"You, actually."

Gabe lifts his head from my shoulder and shifts around his blanket cocoon. "Oh?"

Okay. I can do this. I said we'd talk, and I've avoided this for too long. He deserves to know how I feel. Reaching over, I run my thumb over the plush lips I love so much.

"I want a divorce," I whisper.

Gabe's lip quivers, and he shifts away from me. "You're the king of mixed signals, Hunter." He clears his throat. "I refuse. I more than refuse, in fact. Would you like to know why?"

His voice grows louder until he stands and drops the blanket while he paces in front of the fire completely bare-assed except for the soft, green sweater.

"I love you. Okay?" He throws his hands in the air. "I didn't think I would, but I do. I love it when you leave me unfinished crosswords, and you hold me when I'm sad. I love the way you call me counsellor, and I love how you make me feel." He pauses and turns towards me, dick bouncing against his thigh as his agitation grows. "I love the man that you are, Hunter. I refuse to believe you want to walk away from us and forfeit money to an organization that hates people like us for existing. If you want a divorce, at least wait until then, but know that I don't want to leave."

His chest heaves, and a single tear slides down his cheek, breaking my heart. Further proof I'm not good at this kind of thing. I didn't mean to make him cry.

"I love you, too, Gabe." Standing, I reach to wipe the tear from his cheek as confusion fills his handsome face.

"What?"

"I probably should have led with that." Grimacing, I reach for his hand. "I'm not good at...feelings and shit, but I fell for you, Gabe. Harder than I ever thought was possible."

"Why do you want a divorce, then?"

Puffing out a breath, I lead him back to the couch and pull the blanket over his nakedness. This is hard enough to say without him flashing me. "It's hard to concentrate when you're showing me the goods." Gabe forces a smile, and I need to make this right.

"I went to the lawyer a few weeks ago and did something I'm not proud of." Gabe stills, and I guess I just need to blurt it out. "I blackmailed the lawyer, I think?"

"What!? Jesus Hunter..."

"No, it's okay! Mostly. I already have three of the four payments, and it's a substantial amount of money. I wanted to know if I walked away, how much the Broken Rainbow would actually get. Would the sum be something significant for them, or did I need to wait it out?"

"Any sum is significant," Gabe spits, and I understand his anger, but I needed to know, and I needed to bend this in our favour.

"I agree, but I had a hunch and did some digging." Based on a profile I saw on a hook-up app, and a bit of catfishing is what I should say, but I'll keep that to myself for now. Is it dishonourable? Of course it is, but my grandfather never played by the rules, and as the frequent target of his outbursts, I felt it was okay to cash in on this just once.

It's also why I didn't want to tell Gabe anything when he asked. As a lawyer himself, I didn't want to put him in an awkward position. "The lawyer is in the closet, Gabe. I might have threatened him a little to bend the rules for me."

Gabe runs a hand over his face and mutters something about legal ethics that I pretend not to understand.

"Hunter...that's gross. I mean, the guy is a prick, but I don't condone outing someone like that."

It didn't sit well with my conscience, either. As soon as I hefted the threat at him, I regretted it. But once it was said, I couldn't take it back.

"I know. It wasn't my finest moment, and nobody knows. Just him and me and now you. That's how it will remain. But...I don't want to be married to you because I was forced to. I want to be married to you because I love you."

Gabe shakes his head. "I don't understand."

"When we said our vows that day in a courthouse, it was because I hated my grandfather and needed money. I didn't want to do it. There was no love in that room, Gabe." Swallowing hard, I push on and hope I might get this last bit right since I've caused him enough heartache tonight. "I don't want to celebrate that day on a calendar. It doesn't stand for what you are to me. I want to celebrate a day we chose because we want to spend the rest of our lives together. Because the love I have for you is so big, counsellor, that I've struggled to accept it was possible for me to feel this way."

Gabe's gaze softens, and I reach for his hand, dusting a kiss across his knuckles. "That's why I want a divorce. So we can do this over and take happy pictures celebrating with our friends. Do all the things that people do when they celebrate being married. I want our day to be filled with love. This shouldn't be a tainted day, and it needs to be ours alone. You deserve that."

Gabe bites his lip. "You want a divorce so we can re-marry for love?"

His voice is so soft, I have to lean closer to hear him.

"Um, yeah. I guess that's it in a lot fewer words."

"Your words mean everything." Gabe's hand on my cheek is warm, and I'd walk away from every dollar of my family's money if it meant I'd get to spend more nights with him like this. "What about the money and the lawyer if we divorce now? Does it still go to that organization?"

"Oh! Right...I asked him if the wording was open to interpretation, and he agreed it was. He'll still pay the remaining amount to me after a year based on the initial marriage date. I know I came at him wrong with the threat to out his little secret, but Gabe, I think he was relieved he had someone to talk to. We had a very...honest discussion." The man knew my grandfather would turn on him if he discovered his sexuality, which I completely agreed with. He felt sick drafting all the conditions Jeremiah told him to, and while I wish he would've used his position to do good, I know it's not always as simple as that. "I think the guilt of this will and keeping a secret from his family is getting to him. So the Broken Rainbow won't see a dime, but a different charity will."

"You won't keep it?"

Money has played a huge part in how my life turned out this way. I lost a man I cared deeply for because I put money before him. It took far too many years to move past that decision, and I didn't want to repeat the past.

"I thought about it, but you've taught me some things these past months, and I don't need it. But there are people who do. Like the people Margie feeds every week, and the homeless shelter. The 4-H club could use some help for the kids who can't travel to shows. There's no shortage of people in need in this community, Gabe. I've always known that, but I've done nothing about it."

Gabe tilts his head as he absorbs all this.

"What did I teach you to draw this conclusion?"

I huff a laugh. "To be cliché, money doesn't buy happiness. You came here in your expensive car and fancy suits, and I immediately pegged you as a snobby rich guy. But then I got to know you and learned you weren't a trust-fund kid and perhaps lacked the love I always craved as a kid, too. You and me...I think we're a lot alike."

Gabe remains quiet for a moment and it's enough time for me to wonder if I fucked it all up and he's thinking of ways to tell me to fuck off. Maybe all this sneaking around, gathering information, and making decisions without him might not have been the brilliant idea I thought it was.

"You have such an enormous heart, Hunter. It takes a while for others to see it because you keep yourself locked up so tight. But this town knows you're good, and your friends know you're amazing." Gabe moves the blanket and comes closer, swinging a leg over and sitting on my lap. "I know you and I are meant to be. I don't love that you played dirty with this lawyer, but I understand." He kisses me softly. "It will break my heart to sign divorce papers, doll. It really will."

"I just don't want our day connected to him, babe. I want it to be ours."

Gabe kisses me again, and I clutch him closer. It always scares me how much I want him, not just like this, but here with me. Sleeping or awake, naked or clothed, I crave him within reach, and to know he feels the same about me is possibly better than winning the national finals.

"I'll do it if that's what you want. I'll let my heart break the day I sign because I know you'll pick up the pieces. It's the only way I'll do it."

Gabe's voice wavers, and I place a hand over his heart. "I promise I won't leave you broken."

A gust of wind rattles the porch windows, and the lights flicker before finally going out. In the fire's glow, Gabe's eyes widen.

"Will the horses be okay out there?"

I huff a laugh and smooth my hands down his back. "They have shelter in a heated barn with food and water. They're safe."

He opens his mouth and snaps it shut. I laugh out loud again because I know where his mind went.

"Gabe...they don't need to come in the house, and they will never come in the house. The barn has a generator if they need it."

"Yeah, but what if—"

I pull his mouth to mine and kiss him so thoroughly we don't need a fire to keep warm. "No what-ifs and no discussion on house horses. But I will lay you in front of this fire and see how many times I can make you come to pass the time until the power comes back."

"Oh...well...when you put it that way, then yeah. No house horses."

I kept my promise and made Gabe come three times before he just couldn't keep going, and we fell asleep on the floor next to the fire. I added more logs during the night, and when the lights flickered back on, we both woke up with an exhausted groan.

"Five AM should *not* be a time to wake up at," Gabe mutters and pulls a blanket over his head.

"Get used to it, sunshine." I laugh and whip the blankets off him.

"Hunter! Give those back, goddammit!"

He's like a cat in a bathtub, flailing around for blankets and downright screeching at me. Of course, I relent because that's not the response I expected, and I roll my naked self on top of him.

"Are you trying to trick me into not being mad because you're like a sexy weighted blanket?" Despite the sex marathon of last night, he presses his hips to mine with a hum. "A hard weighted blanket." His fingers bury into my hair and tug my head back. "Let me suck you off and I won't hold the blanket theft against you."

"That doesn't really sound like a negotiation, but I'll take it."

Flipping us over with me now on my back, I grab the closest blanket from our cocoon and throw it over him.

"Totally works for me. I didn't get to taste you last night." Gabe slides down my body and settles himself between my legs. He pulls the blanket up over his shoulders as I expected he would and smiles up at me as he tongues the tip of my cock.

He flits his mouth in barely there touches, and despite my frustration, I huff a small laugh. "This is payback for the blanket stealing, isn't it?"

Gabe chuckles and puffs a short breath across my balls. "Maybe just a little, but I really do want to taste you, doll."

A small moan escapes my lips. "I like it when you call me that." He runs his tongue over my shaft in one heavy lick, and I lift my hips up off the floor to follow his tongue. "I'll beg, Gabe. Wrap those lips around me, please. I wanna see you swallow me."

Pushing up on my elbows, I stare at Gabe as he stretches his lips over my cock and winks. He fucking winks before taking me to the back of his throat like it's a walk in the park.

Those lips slide over me, red and spit slicked, and a trickle of drool hangs from his chin.

"Fuck...Gabe..."

If my arms weren't already shaking, I'd grab his head and hold him there, maybe even take a photo if he'd let me because he's a wet dream with those lips.

"Where do you want it, baby? I'm close." Gabe's eyes meet mine, and he hollows his cheeks. "God...you're so fucking perfect," I pant, and Gabe tries to smile with my dick in his throat, which makes me laugh.

Then he does this thing with his throat and his tongue, and it's over. My body flushes hot with pleasure as I come down his throat.

"Fuck Gabe...fuck..." He never takes his mouth off me, but he can't swallow it all at once. Cum leaks out the edge of his mouth and he finally pops off with a satisfied smile as I collapse back to the floor.

Gabe crawls up my body and hovers over my face. His flushed cheeks and puffy lips make him more beautiful than before. Maybe that's just the orgasm talking, but he really is gorgeous.

"Kiss me," I murmur as I pull him to my lips. My taste still in his mouth makes my fingers grip his neck tighter. "You're everything to me, counsellor. Never doubt that," I whisper across his lips.

His shaky sigh caresses my skin, and I wish I could stay like this with him forever.

"Never, doll. Never." Gabe's warm gaze searches mine and I hope he sees that I'll never do him wrong again.

Seventeen
Gabe

For two full days, Hunter worked around the clock clearing snow.

First, he dug us out, and then the barn. Then he showed me how to feed the horses and make sure their water doesn't freeze and said he'd be back late. Stupidly, I let him go alone, not realizing he was visiting farms in the area with older couples who might need help after the snow. If I'd known that, I would have gone with him to help, too.

Our road is long and rural. With storms like these, Hunter said, it takes several days sometimes for plows to get this far. After pulling out my car and cleaning the driveway, he made his first non-negotiable rule as a husband.

"You're getting something bigger, with 4x4 capabilities to drive in the winter, Gabe. I don't feel comfortable with you driving this. I know you love your car, but I'm going to have an ulcer if I know you're out in the snow driving this. This probably sounds bossy, but —"

"Okay. I'll look for something to take in the winter."

His mouth drops. "Just like that? You're going to get a new car because I said so?"

Chuckling, I throw my feet onto his lap as he sets his crossword aside. "No, not because you said so. Because I don't want you to always worry about me. If that's what it takes to save you from an ulcer, then I'll do it."

Clearly not used to this kind of discussion, he nods and picks up his crossword book again. I suppress my smile and return to my book, the crackle of the fire in the background something I've grown to love in this far too early cold snap.

"Hunter?"

"Hmm?"

"Relationships work when you communicate. I'm not offended and you're not being an ass. I love you, and if you worry, I'll help you worry less."

He squeezes my foot, and I return to my book. "What if I worry you'll never suck me off like you did the other morning again? Will you fix that right away, too?"

This time, when I put my book down, Hunter's eyes sparkle with laughter and my heart skips. As a man who always wears a serious mask, seeing him with a playful smile like this will always have me count my blessings. "I'll take it into consideration and assure you that won't be the last time."

"So not a man of immediate action, then. Got it."

A few beats pass and he moves my foot to his crotch, so it touches his semi-hard cock. "Do you need something, doll?"

He clears his throat and hides a smile as I press my foot into his bulge.

"Yeah, actually. I need an eleven-letter word that refers to buttocks. Starts with a C."

"Are you being serious, or is this your way of getting me on my knees?"

"Depends if it's working, I guess."

I snort-laugh and sit up, motioning for him to show me the clue. After a moment, the word comes to me.

"Try callipygian. It's a Greek word. Basically, it means nice ass."

I spell it out, and Hunter raises an eyebrow. "Are you bullshitting right now? How do you know that?"

Moving my foot along his dick, I chuckle. "I dated a guy who was super into art and Greek mythology. It was a word he always used to say, and I've never forgotten it."

Hunter sets his crossword aside, and his eyes darken. "Just how did this guy use it?"

"Are you jealous because someone told me I was a very callipygian guy?" My smile is full-blown as he moves my feet and kneels over me on the couch. Unzipping his pants, his cock springs free before his hands move to my sweatpants.

"I'm not jealous. I'm...territorial."

He manhandles me, but I let him, and he shoves my pants down enough to take both our lengths together in his hand. "Callipygian," he mutters as I slide my hands into the back of his pants to squeeze his ass.

"*Mhm*...do you have a better word?" I pant.

Hunter spits in his palm before resuming his strokes. "Husband," he groans and bends to smash his lips to mine. I arch into his hand and let him consume me in whatever way he wants. Whatever words or actions he needs, because I'm the lucky one here.

He strokes us together, hard and frantic. Like he's afraid that if it's not over quickly, I might disappear.

"I like that word better, too. Only you can call me that, doll," I whisper against his lips, and he shatters. The warmth of his release coats my cock, and I follow him over.

He buries his face in my neck. "Sorry. I don't know where the caveman thing came from, but I never thought about you being with someone else before and it…Well, I didn't like thinking of you with another person."

Hunter sits back, and with a shrug, he whips off his shirt and wipes us up with it. He doesn't make eye contact even when he cleans me off and tucks me back in. There's a shake to his hands that causes me to sit up and grab his face, forcing him to look at me.

"Hunter…" It takes a moment, but he finally meets my gaze. "I don't want anyone else. You're stuck with me."

He puffs a shaky breath, and I wait him out. How did he go from claiming me one minute to being so hesitant the next? He's never been anything less than straightforward, and while it's stung a few times with his bluntness, he's never been so conflicted about choosing words.

"I know this is stupid…"

"No, it's not. You can say it, doll."

That gets him raising his eyes, and my lips lift in a small smile.

"I went to therapy for a while when I was younger. I kept it a secret. My grandfather would've called me weak and made me feel even worse, so I just went on my own twice a month." He swallows hard. "It was two hours each way, so when I had days off, I'd go. The woman told me…she told me I had attachment avoidance, and it was most likely caused by my childhood. I've worked at being better for years. Jackson has been...he's my best friend for a reason, you know?"

"He's a great man and friend." My thumb strokes his chin, and Hunter lets his eyes close.

"You're the first man I've allowed myself to get attached to like this. To love again since...since Alec, and I just..." He huffs, frustrated, but he's so achingly vulnerable I want to wrap him in bubble wrap and never let him leave my side. I wish he didn't have to feel like this his whole life. So many people have missed an opportunity to get to know him, and that hurts me. "I heard you talk about someone else, and it just made me scared that I'd lose you like everyone else I've ever cared about."

His voice trails off, and for a moment, I can't find words that are adequate. Do I know what that feels like? Absolutely, I do. But I never carried the same fear Hunter does. If I loved and lost, by death or break up or whatever, I grieved it and moved on until I could hide in my job. I made excuses to not look for love, not out of fear of losing, but because I blamed myself for losing them all.

If I'd have listened or lived closer, I would've seen the signs that my sister didn't want to stay on this earth. If I'd have been a better son, maybe my dad wouldn't have left, and I don't know what I did to end the few serious relationships I had. I'd likely put my job first too many times, but I was the common denominator in all the losses. Perhaps not forming more bonds would save us all from hurt. So I just kept to myself.

Until I met Hunter.

"Thank you for telling me. I'm honoured you trust me, Hunter. I know I can't predict the future entirely and say I'll never leave you, but while my heart beats, just know it beats only for you. Even after I'm gone, if you remain, it will always be yours." Bringing my forehead to his, I let my hands cradle his face. "I said it before, and I will again, forever. That's how long you have me, doll."

His arms wrap around me, and we hold each other with the fire still crackling and our hearts laid bare for one another. An unspoken promise that it's more than I love you, but an oath to cherish and protect these fragile emotions we keep buried from the world.

"I'll never stop falling for you, Gabe," he whispers before brushing his lips on my temple.

"I'll always be here to catch you, doll."

"Mr. Handsome!" Diamond greets when we enter the Thirsty Cow, and his smile grows when he notices Hunter behind me. "Oh, it's tall, dark, and hunky." Diamond fans his face. "Both of you, together again. Welcome."

"Did you have any problems getting home the other night?"

Diamond shakes his head with a sunny smile. "My legs hurt from walking through the snow, but I made it home just fine."

"You didn't offer him a ride?" Hunter shoots me a glare.

"I did, and he declined because he said he lived close."

Hunter grunts, an unimpressed noise, and I slap at his chest. We share a silent conversation over it that he seems not to want to drop. Diamond slaps the counter for our attention. "If you two keep arguing over me, I might think you care," Diamond jokes, but his cheeks flush.

"We care. In fact…" I look towards Hunter, and he nods. "You're on our guest list for the wedding. Not to cater it, but to be there as a friend if you can make it."

"I thought you were already married?" Diamond looks between us as another group sends a blast of cold air into the building behind us.

"We are. It's complicated, but…" I reach out and squeeze Diamond's hand. "You're a friend and we want you there."

"Consider me absolutely honoured, sugar." His voice hitches, and he launches himself into me for a hug before quickly doing the same with Hunter. "I'll get your usuals to you, and if you're celebrating, I'll bring a treat. Actually, I'll just bring a treat, anyway."

He bustles off, and Hunter laughs softly. "I like him. He's a good guy."

"He definitely is."

We head to the back corner where Jackson and Riley have already rearranged some seating for everyone we asked to join us later. Riley pops off the sofa as soon as Jackson nods to signal our arrival.

My best friend's gaze ping-pongs between the two of us. After I spilled my feelings to him the last time we were here, he's more than aware of what's at stake for me. Hunter reaches for my hand, and Riley engulfs me in a hug.

"You told him!? You're staying together?"

Riley steps back, and Hunter graces him with a rare, beaming smile. "Sit down, Riley, and we'll explain, but yes, after we get a divorce."

"What!?" Both Jackson and Riley say in perfect unison.

"I don't want our day tarnished by my grandfather," Hunter begins. We take seats on the sofas, and Hunter finds my hand again, holding on to it so tight it almost hurts.

"We're getting a divorce, then picking a date we want to be married on—for us," I finish.

"Why don't you just stay married and celebrate it on another day?" Jackson asks, and it's something I've thought about as well.

"I think it's important to Hunter that we make a fresh start, and I agree. It'll only hurt for a day, but we'll remarry in the spring."

"Before or after rodeo season?" Jackson laughs.

"Actually..." Hunter begins before turning to me. "We never discussed that, but could we do it early? Rodeo really picks up in July and August. How do you feel about June?"

"Did you commit to more rodeo already?" I ask. He said he would, but he never actually confirmed it.

Hunter flushes and pulls me to his side. "Uh...is it a problem? I haven't told Levi yet, but yeah, I want to do more rodeos and run the rodeo school with Jackson. I should have—"

I cut him off and cover his mouth with my hand. "Do I get to come and watch these rodeos?"

Hunter pulls my hand away. "I hoped you would."

"I'm in!"

Riley laughs in the background, and it all fades away, because nothing else matters. My husband wants to throw that rope around and be all sexy on a horse. I'd be a fool to say no.

We spend the next half hour speaking with our two closest friends about how things have changed and that we're in love for real. No faking. It's great to get it out there finally, and I'm obsessed with the way Hunter smiles now. He's so laid back and...happy. Genuinely happy to be here and talking with friends. The former standoff aura has all but disappeared as he constantly reaches out to touch me.

The rest of the group arrives, Jamieson and Griff, and a few of the guys from rodeo school who live near town. Levi greets Hunter with the same stars in his eyes as he always does, still struck to be around a legend in his sport.

Honestly, I can relate. Sometimes I think I'll never get used to having this man kiss me and call me his.

Hunter takes a moment to tell Levi he's up to returning to rodeo roping with him, and the resulting shout of joy is enough to make your eardrums ring.

The conversations carry on around me, and I drift away for a bit, wondering when my life got this full.

"Penny for your thoughts, Mr. Handsome?" Diamond holds a fresh slice of apple crumble. "Or a crumble for your thoughts?"

Riley excused himself to the restroom, and the others are talking about rodeo training and schedules. I guess I let myself zone out. I'm just soaking it all in. This group of men who have welcomed me into their mix, even this coffee shop that feels like home. Contentment has wrapped itself around me, and I just want to soak in it like a sponge for a while.

"Ah, thank you, Diamond." Taking the crumble, I motion for the empty seat next to me. "Do you want to join me?"

"I can spare a few. Luckily, the boss is a nice guy like that." He smiles warmly, and for the first time since I've been coming here, Diamond drops the effervescent mask and touches my arm lightly. "I'm truly happy to see both of you smiling and in love. He was always so distant, and you make him smile. That's special."

Diamond's tone sounds like he knows more than just the love part in his statement, but he quickly turns back on his charm. "If you ever need to talk, I'm a good listener, and I really am so happy to be included. You're not just a handsome customer...you're a friend."

"You're a friend to me, too, Diamond. Thank you for making me feel at home here."

He smiles softly. "That means everything to me, Gabe. Truly."

Hunter approaches our seats, and Diamond winks as he stands.

"Just kept the space warm for you, hunky."

Diamond struts off, his long legs taking him away from us quickly.

"Did I interrupt?" Hunter asks gently.

"No. Not at all, but if you're ready, I'd like to go home."

"Of course."

We take a few minutes to work through the goodbyes and congratulatory hugs with everyone. Griff chats about his dad with me for a moment. Charlie wants to make us dinner one night, and Jamieson promises to bring me blueberry jam the next time he drops by. Levi hugs me so hard my ribs hurt, and tells me he'll take great care of Hunter when they're on the road.

By the time we're in Hunter's truck, the silence of the cab is welcome.

"Are you okay, counsellor? You got pretty quiet."

"I'm okay. Just thinking about how much my life has changed." Hunter reaches over and clasps my mittened hand.

"In a good way?"

"In the very best way."

Eighteen
Hunter

I've never cared for Christmas.

When my parents died so close to the holidays, as a kid, it's what I always thought of first when the Christmas lights and decorations appeared in the stores. I learned pretty quickly that Santa couldn't bring my parents back.

My grandmother did her best to make it a special day for me, and we made a lot of new memories together, but there was always that black cloud that stayed. She missed her son, too.

Margie always made me fun Christmas cookies and invited my grandmother to leave me with her for some holiday fun, and in a way, that was what I loved the most about Christmas. My time with Margie in the kitchen and her animals. Singing along to silly songs and eating all the fun food while rolling around with dogs.

As I got older, my Christmas visits turned into late nights of Scrabble at the kitchen table while she tried to teach me how to make bread from scratch. The keyword is tried, but I enjoyed it all the same.

But this year it's different. So much different.

The carols on the radio pulled words from my lips, and I was throwing all the holiday snacks into the cart at the grocery store. The festive window decor made me pause and enter rather than walk by, and instead of wishing the season would pass faster, I was looking forward to it in a way I never had.

Tape zipping off a roll and paper rattling carries into the kitchen and makes the stupid grin on my face grow even larger.

Gabe told me I couldn't come into the living room until he said the coast was clear. After pouring him a glass of the amaretto he loves into the monogrammed glass I couldn't wait to give him, I wait in the kitchen, sipping my peach Crown Royal and feeling more than the warmth of liquor in my chest.

"Okay! It's all clear!"

I finish the message I was typing on my phone and hit send, promising Margie that Gabe and I will be there tomorrow at noon for Christmas lunch before shoving the phone in the pocket of my lounge pants. With my drink in hand, I saunter down the hall to the living room that Gabe and I decorated together last week.

The tree we bought stands in the corner, adorned with its multi-coloured lights and random collection of decorations I found in the storage room. Gabe was particularly charmed by one that was a photo of me on a horse when I couldn't have been more than ten years old. The photo was inside a clear plastic ball with my handprint in green paint on one side. I made it for my grandmother at school and didn't know it was still in the house.

Of course, it took up prime real estate on the tree, hanging front and centre for us to see every time we walked into the room.

Gabe stands up when I enter the living room, and I immediately burst out laughing.

"What did you do?"

He wears a Santa hat with red-and-white polka dot pyjamas that are absolutely ridiculous. Empty rolls of wrapping paper are everywhere, and there aren't enough gifts under the tree to explain all the empty rolls.

"I know it's not Christmas morning, but I'd like to propose a new tradition." After topping up his amaretto, I set the bottle on the table. Gabe sighs, then sips, and grins at me. I pluck a piece of ribbon and tape from his hat.

"You know you didn't need to go through all this trouble. Just being with you is all I need for Christmas." There's so much he's already given me. He doesn't need to wrap things or go through all this fuss.

"You say that now." He laughs with a hint of wickedness, and I narrow my eyes.

"If I don't like what you've done, I won't give you your present."

"Well, that's not fair." He pouts, but he pulls me to the couch, anyway. "When I was little and my mom and sisters were still here, we didn't have a lot, but we made it fun. Sort of like dragging the day out and making it feel full, if that makes sense."

"Sure. You wanted the day to last longer. Christmas magic and all that."

"Yeah. Kind of." He sets his glass on the table, and it's now that I notice all the empty tape rolls. Which is about as many as the wrapping paper rolls. "So...we taped all our gifts with loads of tape or put zip ties around them. Maybe ribbons or string. We wrapped everything in extra layers. Anything to make it take longer to unwrap."

I bark a laugh. "So I'm supposed to get completely pissed off on this merriest of occasions because I can't open my gift?"

"It's fun, I promise!"

I'm skeptical.

Gabe has wrapped three small gifts this way with no less than six rolls of paper and eight rolls of tape. And that's just what I see and can count.

"I didn't even wrap yours, though. This feels unfair."

"How can you not wrap gifts at all?" His face falls, and I immediately lean in to kiss him.

"I didn't say they weren't wrapped. I just said I didn't wrap them. You want to do this tonight instead of the morning?"

"Yes!" Gabe stands and cleans up the mess while motioning to my almost empty glass. "Let's refill and get started!"

His enthusiasm is infectious, and once again, since I've met Gabe, I'm smiling and loving this life again. Maybe even learning to love Christmas again. I'll reserve that judgment until after the gifts and this tape job.

But first, I disappear upstairs and retrieve the bag of gifts for Gabe. I wasn't kidding, though, when I said his gift wasn't wrapped. These are gifts, but more of a decoy for him than anything else.

When I return to the living room, I place all the pretty wrapped gifts under the tree before saving one and sitting next to Gabe.

"I just want you to know that I have zero experience gifting people I love things. I hope you're not disappointed."

Passing him the small box wrapped in shiny red paper, Gabe falters. "Shit. You went all sincere, and I went all asshole with the tape. I didn't think you'd be so..." He bites his lip. "I was actually expecting a gift bag stuffed with tissue paper."

Laughing, I sip my drink and motion for him to open it. "You're not wrong about that assumption. But my sources said if I wanted to woo you, this was the way to go."

"Woo me?" he whispers. Gabe seems more stuck on that than the tape he plastered to my gifts.

"Yeah, you see...I've never been one for romance or feelings, but you keep getting me doing all kinds of things that go against that. I love how you light up when I do something that surprises you." Gabe's gaze meets mine, and he smiles. The smile that makes my rusty heart creak and reach for the WD-40. "Just like that, counsellor," I whisper as I dust my knuckles over his cheek. Such a gorgeous man. "I love that. I bring that smile to your face and I love how you make me feel shit."

Gabe snorts. "*Feel shit*. Not quite poetry, but I'll take it."

"Like I said, this is mostly new to me, and I want to do this for you. Now open the damn present, will you?"

Yes, I'm more excited for him to open it, and that's just a part of this whole thing, isn't it? Gabe takes a long sip from his drink, and after a quick calculation of how many he's had tonight, he's probably well on his way to being drunk.

Gabe rips the paper from the box and pops open the lid while I hold my breath. He pulls out the piece of paper inside and raises an eyebrow.

"Read it, Gabe." He's not the only one playing games this Christmas.

He unfolds the paper to read the handwritten note. When his gaze meets mine, there's a shine of excitement. A guarded hope that has me reaching for his hand.

"Put the drink down. Come on."

Gabe almost misses the table, and then he speed walks down the hall. He has his feet in his boots before I reach him, and he didn't even bother with a coat.

"If this is what I think it is, I'm gonna... I don't know what I'm gonna do, but don't make me wait."

After shoving my boots on, I grab a coat for him and follow him to the barn.

"Gabe," I call, and he stops to wait for me. He shivers, but I'm not convinced it's from the cold. After holding the coat for him to shrug into, I take his hand and enter the aisle of the barn.

"Hunter...oh my god."

Mack pokes her head out of her stall when she hears us, along with Dixie. When I finished chores and the horses were in for the night, I set a stool in front of Mack's stall with a saddle I purchased second-hand from one of the trail riders in the area. It's a gorgeous black saddle that I know will fit Mack, and he should be comfortable riding with it. Gabe has made it clear he wants to ride more with me, and he's already bonded with Mack so much that she's his horse.

And that's the second part.

"Looks like Mack got you a card, too." I motion to the envelope jammed into the crack of the stall door, and Gabe laughs.

"God, Hunter. As if you had Mack get me a card." His cheeks are pink from excitement, and I bet he was the cutest little boy at Christmas. He runs a hand over the saddle. "My very first piece of horse stuff. It's gorgeous, Hunter."

His fingers open the card, and I watch him as he reads. His lip quivers, and when he turns to me, he punches me in the shoulder.

"Ow!"

"You asshole!" he chokes out as he strokes Mack's neck. "She's really mine?"

The card wasn't from Mack, of course. It's from me gifting him Mack because, as much as I love her, every man needs a horse to call their own, and she trusts him. They're a perfect fit, and he'll be in good hands with her.

"She's yours, counsellor. I'd have put a bow on her in the morning, but you were so insistent about doing this tonight."

We spend a few minutes with the girls and promise to see them in the morning before I pull Gabe back to the warmth of the house. He kicks off his boots and throws his arms around my neck.

"You got me a horse, and all I got you were new crossword books with Greek mythology themes."

"Did you just tell me what you spent an hour wrapping?"

"I get a *horse*," he says again and stares at me like he's seeing me for the first time.

"I love you, Gabe. I'll give you anything you ask for. Always."

Which is something I've realized this week. There's nothing I wouldn't give him if he asks. Even if it made my life harder, I'd make his easier without a second thought.

"You might change your mind once you start unwrapping." Gabe laughs as we settle back on the couch, and he hands me a taped-up gift.

After three minutes, I hate the taped-up present thing, but he relents and lets me use scissors because I gave him a horse, and he feels guilty.

"Okay, I'm not a fan of the tape thing. Next year, think of something else." Finally, through my first one, I remove the crossword book inside. It's not something from a store shelf. The cover is black with a gold foil title. When I flip open the book and browse the puzzles, I nearly choke on my spit. "Jesus, Gabe."

Of course, he couldn't find me a book with ranch terms or rodeo, or anything generic. This one is the karma sutra of crosswords that Gabe had personalized. Each puzzle has a sexy title, and in the background of the letter boxes, filthy black-and-white images take the place of a blank page.

"I don't know if I'll ever concentrate enough to finish one of these," I joke. Which is true. Sex-themed crosswords every night might be too much for me, especially if he's helping and spelling out filthy words. Stopping on a page, I search the clues, looking for something I don't know to ask him, and my mouth drops open. "These pictures..." I practically press my nose into the page, looking closer. "It's you." Is that me who sounds all breathless? My husband has posed for erotic pictures and put them in a themed crossword book for me.

Merry fucking Christmas to me.

"I thought you said the crosswords were Greek mythology themed?"

He smirks and sets his now-empty glass of amaretto down. "Well..." He licks his lips. "I lied. A little. Those are somewhere, too, but I thought you'd appreciate this more."

"You..." I reach over and pull him onto my lap. "Are the best thing to ever happen to me, and I love your dirty mind." It's almost hard to remember a time when I was so against even having him stay here temporarily. Now I never want him to leave. "I might have to thank Jamieson for pushing me to let you stay here. Maybe send him a lifetime supply of blueberries or something."

Gabe swivels his hips on my lap with a suggestive smirk on his lips.

"Or you could not think of Jamieson right now and turn to page twenty-seven." Gabe slides off my lap and sways, the amaretto clearly kicking in as he giggles like a child.

When I turn to page twenty-seven, I groan and close my eyes. "Gabe... goddamn, you're trying to kill me." Staring at the page and back at him, a thought occurs. "Wait a minute. Who took these pictures, and do you still have the toys?"

How did I miss this the first time? A naked Gabe with his legs in the air and a variety of sex toys spread on the floor around him fills the background for a puzzle themed for amusement parks, and honestly...it's pretty clever.

"Don't worry, I have a tripod and a camera with a timer. Nobody saw me, doll." He smirks and turns for the stairs. "Yes, I still have the toys." He takes the stairs faster while he laughs. "But they might be in the taped-up present you didn't open yet!"

Already with my foot on the stairs to follow him, I pause and glance at the tree. One large box remains.

"If he thinks I'm not using scissors to double check this box..." I mutter under my breath as I grab the box and stab at it, past not caring if I hurt the contents because my dick is hard enough it might be difficult to walk.

It feels too light to contain all the toys in that photo, but I'd hate to get upstairs and find out they were in this box and need to come back again. Finally ripping it open, I find a single note card under a pile of tissue paper, written in Gabe's neat cursive.

Merry Christmas, doll. By the time you read this, I'm already waiting for you upstairs...with everything in that picture. Gotcha :-)

With a laugh, I press on my erection and decide to take my time. If Gabe, a camera, and half a dozen sex toys are the rest of my Christmas gifts, I've been a very, *very* good boy.

But not for long.

After refilling our glasses and unplugging the tree, I make sure the fire is dying down and head up the stairs, hoping to find Gabe in bed wearing nothing but a smile.

I laugh softly at the doorway of our bedroom. Gabe is in bed, at least. Snoring and buck naked on top of the comforter. The toys from his photos sit on the night table, and I shake my head.

I can't even be mad. Instead, I grab a spare blanket off the chair in the corner and cover him with it before stripping down and sliding next to him.

"Still the best Christmas ever. I love you, counsellor. Don't ever change."

Nineteen
Gabe

"Honestly, Riley, make sure we have hot dogs. I'm fine with it."

My best friend huffs and glares at Hunter. "You can't serve only hot dogs at a wedding reception. These people will be drinking and partying with you. Don't you want something...nicer?"

Riley's tone is full of hope, and I try not to laugh, but he won't win this battle.

"You said it's our wedding and we can do what we want," Hunter says in an accusing tone. "I want hot dogs, and Gabe agrees."

Riley groans, and I finally let the laughter break free. "Rye, I told you. It's settled."

Jackson laughs along with me as he and Hunter stand. "Have fancy pickles and mustard. Will that help?" Hunter adds, and Riley sags with defeat. "Whoever did the buffet you arranged at the first wedding was great. Just do that again. I loved it."

His face softens as his gaze finds mine. The only thing we agreed to keep the same as the first wedding day was the hot dogs, because not only was it his favourite, but it was a gesture I made for him that he appreciated.

"I can't believe I'm planning a hot dog buffet for my best friend's wedding. What's next? A build-your-own poutine?"

Hunter cocks his head as he considers.

"That's actually a great idea," I say. "Let's do it."

Hunter bends for a kiss. "I knew you were the one. See you later, babe. You can make the choices and fill me in later." He kisses me again before leaving with Jackson. They have work to do in the rodeo barn now that the weather is warming up. Spring will be here soon, and I, for one, can't wait.

Riley returns Jackson's kiss and then turns his pout at me.

"Hot dogs and poutine." Riley shakes his head, but softens his gaze. "He's so damn different now, Gabe. He loves you to the moon, and while I'm relieved to know he has a heart, sometimes it's weird to see."

"He is literally my dream man, Rye. I'd do anything for him, and if it's hot dogs and poutine at a wedding, then so be it."

Riley sits back, leaving the wedding plan for a moment. "How are you doing, waiting for the divorce?"

I fucking hate hearing that word and it instantly flips my mood.

"Okay-ish. I mean, we're planning a wedding while waiting for a divorce, and technically, he still hasn't proposed properly, like he said he would." He promised he would, and I don't doubt him...but it's eating at me while I wait. "I'm excited and anxious. I'm always wondering if he's changing his mind and the divorce will be final, and he'll be gone. Wedding planning or not, it's just a stupid anxiety that I can't shake."

Shit. I shouldn't have said that out loud. Now that I have, though, I feel better getting it off my chest.

"Gabe...you don't think he'd change his mind for real, do you? He put his foot down for a hot dog and poutine dinner. That's serious."

I hate feeling insecure. It's new to me because I've never had someone like Hunter before. I don't doubt he loves me, and I can't even explain why I feel like this. It's just there gnawing at me every day.

"No, I don't think he'll change his mind. If he does, then I'm a huge fool, and he deserves to win an Oscar for Best Actor. But signing those papers for a divorce was... so fucking hard, Riley. But I did it for him, you know? He wanted to break from that day with all his grandfather's bullshit, and I understand. Honestly, I get it." In my haste to make Hunter happy, I failed to consider how this would affect me long term. Initially, I thought it would go away, but it hasn't. "I don't think I'll feel right until he slides a ring on my finger for real."

"Does he know it bothers you this much?"

"Some. I've never told him the whole thing. He already feels bad about asking for the divorce. I don't want him to coddle my insecure ass."

He's incredibly thoughtful and kind. I know my anxiety is unfounded. I know it, but I can't keep the unsettled feeling away. The closer our wedding day gets, the more excited I should be, and I can't make heads or tails of why this keeps bothering me.

"I bet if you told him how you feel, he'd make it right." Riley picks up the planning notebook. "Now that we have food settled, I can get the caterer scheduled. Is the rodeo barn still going to work, or do you want me to book a space in town? Have you thought about if it rains? Tell me all the things. If we're aiming for June, I'm running out of time to make changes."

I know Riley's change of topic is to get me back to the happy space I was just in, and I appreciate it.

Hunter and I have discussed this and agree we want to be married here with the horses and the ranch. It's where we learned our true feelings despite him insisting he had none. We've made this a happy place now, and it means so much for him to let go of the ugly memories here. By marrying here, it's like sticking our flag in a conquered country. A final middle finger to the past that made his life hell.

Even with my unfounded anxiety, I have the best memories here. He gifted me a horse here, took me on my first horseback ride, and we've shared so many evenings on the porch swing. I love it here.

"No changes, Rye. It's here. Maybe a tent for the field where we'll say our vows. Any luck on a new minister?"

Since Hunter and I aren't religious, we don't want to be married in a church or with any sort of religious overtones. Riley assured me it could be done.

"Well...yes. Sort of." He sips from his coffee cup and clears his throat. "I, uh, found a former priest who will do it."

Narrowing my eyes, I wait for more. "Former? So no bible readings or whatnot? He understands that?"

"Oh, very much so. He's a nice guy, and we spoke on the phone. He's from out of the province, but he'll totally do it. He, uh, asked for a bizarre payment, though."

"Okay..."

"Chocolate chip cookies. For his husband. I've already asked Diamond if he could bake them, and he's thrilled."

"He wants payment in cookies?"

"Said he didn't want any money." Riley passes me a printout with his bio and a photo. "Charles likes to travel with his husband, and prefers daytime ceremonies," I read aloud. "While most people prefer to pay in cash, we prefer cookies and baked goods. My husband is a foodie, and it's his goal to sample baking across Canada."

Riley bites his lip. "I know it's weird. I know...but everyone is booked or pregnant for the date. So..."

With a small laugh, I pass the paper back to Riley. "Yeah. Do it. As long as he can legally marry us, I don't care if he wants to be paid with nickels."

Riley and I review a few more details before calling it a day. There isn't a lot left except to wait for the day to arrive. Which, so far, I'm the only one nervous about.

Jackson and Hunter stomp back into the house, laughing, and it's a sound I've grown to love. Hunter's deep laugh, paired with Jackson's rumbling one, always makes me smile. We rise from the living room to greet them as Hunter hangs his jacket on the hook.

"Jackson just reminded me how busy it gets on Valentine's Day at the restaurants, and I have an idea." He removes his gear while Jackson holds Riley's coat for him. "Do you want to have an early Valentine's Day?"

"What did you have in mind?"

Hunter grins as he reaches for me. "Dancing at the Happy Badger. We never got to go back there for our missed date."

We tried to get there for a New Year's Eve Party, but it never happened. Margie invited us over for Scrabble and pie, and Hunter never said yes so fast to an invitation in his life.

"A double date, if you don't mind," Jackson adds, and I look over to find Riley absolutely beaming at this spontaneous invitation.

"I'd love to. Dinner first?"

"I thought we could give that new place in town a try. That steak place, Eat More Meat." Hunter supplies, and we all agree to meet there in a few hours.

Once Riley and Jackson have left, Hunter grabs a blanket off the couch and peeks out the porch door.

"It's a gorgeous sunny day, and the snow is melting. False spring." He chuckles. "Want to sit on the swing for a while?"

"Are you and the blanket keeping me warm?"

"Of course." He pushes his feet into a pair of slippers nearby and pulls on my hand. "Come on, counsellor. Come with me."

He bats his brown eyes with his best puppy-dog face, and I'd never say no, but that pout will always work.

"Yes, I'm coming with you."

Stepping on the back porch, he sets the blanket on the bench for me first so I can sit on a part and wrap more around myself before snuggling up to him. The sun shines warmly today for early February, and the snow drips off the porch roof. Hunter pushes a foot off so we rock slowly, the chains squeaking a rusty tune.

"Did you and Riley make progress?"

"I think so. There isn't much for us to do. He has the details. We need to get the invitations out asap. That won't take us long since it's a small wedding. I just need to buy some stamps."

Hunter hums. A contented sound, and he drops a kiss to the top of my head. "How about we get the invitations done tomorrow and send them off? We'll take a horse ride inside the ring and get you ready for the summer after that."

He promised to teach me how to ride better so I could run with Mack, and I'm excited about that almost as much as the warm weather on the horizon.

"That sounds like a perfect day."

"I agree."

We sit for a while longer and swing, the gentle motion rocking me to sleep like a baby, and I drift off to that place that's not quite sleep, but not quite awake, and my heart feels so full it might burst.

"You know, the first time I saw you, I never wanted a man as much as I wanted you then. Did I ever tell you that?" I mumble. With my eyes closed and sleepy, it's like a short movie that plays on repeat in my brain. Hunter on the back of Dixie with faded jeans, a cowboy hat, and a don't-fuck-with-me attitude.

"You mentioned something about it, I think." His arm squeezes me tighter. "You didn't say anything to me that night, though, but I saw you watching."

"I didn't approach you because I knew I couldn't just have you once and be done. Something about you..."

Hunter clears his throat. "That's why I said no that night at the bar." My eyes blink open, and I twist my head to peer up at his face. "I followed you to the parking lot."

"I saw you. It took me so long to decide to hit on you. I thought I won when I saw you under the lamppost."

We both huff a laugh, remembering the almost time we hooked up without being married first. It feels like a lifetime ago. I couldn't wait anymore and took a risk. It failed then, but perhaps it was the best thing to happen.

"Intuition? Gut feeling? Maybe the way Griff reads a bull...I just knew you would be different, and it scared the ever-loving hell out of me." Hunter's voice grows rough, and I reach up to run my fingers down his cheek. "Sometimes I'm still scared, counsellor."

Hunter bites his lip, and I sit up, pulling the blanket with me.

"I think it's normal for us to be afraid of the unknown. That's what love is, isn't it? This unknown thing we can't see that we trust exists."

"But I see you, Gabe." He cups my cheek with a calloused palm. "That look in your eyes when I stop by the office with a coffee or when I sit next to you with my crossword book. You never hide that look, and it scares me sometimes. What if I let you down?"

"I can't hide it, Hunter. I'm grateful for you and..." This seems like the best time to bring up what I told Riley earlier. Lord knows I've preached enough to him to communicate. "When we signed the divorce papers, those tears were real. Since then, I've been on edge waiting for something to happen. For you to change your mind, mostly. A lot of what-if scenarios while we wait. So I'm scared too. I don't want to lose you twice."

Hunter's lips part, and his brow furrows. "Is that why you've been so quiet? I thought it was just because you had work on your mind."

Swallowing hard, I nod. "Yeah. It's all been sort of collecting, and I'm a bit of a mess. I've never felt like this before. This...fear or insecurity is unfounded. I *know* that. I don't want to be the guy who mopes or whatever, but fuck...it's like the air keeps leaving my lungs every time I think about it."

Hunter grunts and pats my side. "Get up. I have something to show you."

I stand with the blanket, and he holds the door open for me. I don't know if he's angry or just wants to go inside. His expression remains blank as he strides down the hall to the front door. The blanket trails behind me as I follow him.

"Put your boots on and wait here for me. Give me ten minutes."

Then he's out the door while I try to catch up to what's going on. But I do as he asks and put on my boots and one of his barn coats and sit on the hall bench waiting like a kid outside the principal's office.

It feels like more than ten minutes pass, but when Hunter returns, his cheeks rosy from the nip in the air despite the warm sun, he inclines his head to follow him. Our feet slop through the melted snow and mud in the yard up to the rodeo barn. After stepping inside, it takes a moment for my eyes to adjust to the dim light of the barn.

"Stand right there."

Hunter pushes me over to the end of the fence for the indoor ring, and I laugh. "I feel like a parent being told to sit and watch a play by the kids."

"That's probably a pretty close feeling for me, too." Hunter's voice carries from the back of the barn, where another door is. It's bigger, and they load livestock through it when he runs the rodeo clinics. The door opens, and a familiar black head pokes through the door.

Hunter's low voice doesn't carry enough for me to hear each word, but I know he's talking to Mack. Hunter moves around, and gates clang while Mack keeps bending her head towards Hunter. "Would you stop that!" He chides, and Mack huffs, which makes me laugh. What the hell is he up to?

Finally, Hunter is on top of Mack without a saddle, and once they exit the chute at the end, I blink back the wetness in my eyes.

Hunter holds a single rose in his teeth as he rides Mack towards me. Mack wears a necklace of flowers that she keeps trying to eat, and I shake my head at the scene before me. He brings the horse to a stop a few feet in front of me. He slides off Mack with ease and smiles that sexy smile with a rose in his teeth.

"For you, counsellor." Hunter hands me the rose with a flourish of his hand and turns back to snag Mack by the halter before she destroys the flower necklace. "I don't care about mushy hearts and dinners and dumb gifts to show someone you love them. But what I do care about is you and how you feel. I was going to wait to do this tomorrow after the wedding invitations, but now seems like a better fit."

He pats Mack on the neck and whispers to her before turning back to me.

"I know I sent you a teddy bear, but that was me trying to apologize and figure this whole feelings thing out."

"I love that bear," I say with a smile that he returns.

"I know, but a horse is better." Hunter pats Mack once more and motions for me to come closer. "Mack has something for you."

Hunter talks low to the horse, and Mack bobs her head up and down. "Don't eat it now," Mack grumbles, a low, happy sound and bites the flower Hunter holds out. He holds her halter as she throws her head around, delighted with the flower treat.

"This isn't going how I planned," Hunter says as Mack eats the flower and looks for more.

"What was your plan?" I ask, laughing as I pet Mack and wonder if I need to bring home fresh flowers for treats now.

When I turn back to Hunter, he's dropped to one knee in the sand of the rodeo ring. "Mack was to give you this flower with a note, and after you read it, you'd turn around to find me like this." Mack tosses her head, and I pat her neck before falling to my knees in front of Hunter.

"I didn't know you felt so anxious about all this, Gabe. If you'd have said something sooner, I'd never have waited. Like a fool, I was waiting for another day on the calendar to make it perfect when any day would make it perfect." His hand reaches into his pocket, and he pulls out a black ring box.

"Gabe...until you bulldozed your way into my life, I didn't know what love really was."

"I never bulldozed. It was a convenient solution to a problem."

Hunter laughs. "It was, but it caused another problem. I wanted to keep you, and I wasn't sure what to do with that. Feelings aren't on my radar, you know? But then you showed up, and I was hoping you'd want to cuddle every night, and it doesn't hurt that you're hot as hell with an intelligent mind."

He opens the box and removes a white gold band with a row of black diamonds.

"I had this made because you're not a guy who deserves a mass-produced ring. It's one of a kind, just like you." He runs his hand through his hair, and Mack steps over to nose us, almost knocking me over. "Gabe, will you marry me again? This time, because I know what it feels like to have my heart walk outside my body, and I'd like to walk alongside it with you forever."

That's the most romantic thing he's ever said to me, and it's almost hard to believe this is happening right now.

"Hunter...that's incredibly sweet."

"I actually read it on a Valentine's card, and hoped I didn't forget when I got to this part. So...will you marry me, Gabe? I'm not perfect, but we're perfect for each other."

I snort-laugh, his honesty so entirely Hunter. "I will marry you every time you ask me. Yes, Hunter. It's a yes, and the next few months can't pass fast enough."

He slides the ring on my finger after removing the first one and places it in the box. "I love you, Gabe." He kisses me there in the sand of the ring, and I'm so happy I could burst. Anxiety can kiss my fucking ass. I kiss him back until we lose our balance and fall into the sand, breathless and laughing.

"We should probably get ready for that dinner and dancing," he whispers.

"We should."

Neither of us moves to get up, smiling at each other like two kids in love.

And I kiss him again because it's hard to stop.

"Thank you for doing this."

Hunter smiles, almost shy, and stands while helping me up.

"I'll always do whatever it takes for you, Gabe. I may not always get it right, but I'll always do it." He takes my chin in his hand. "A very intelligent man told me to communicate. Please don't let me make you feel like that again."

"I won't. I promise."

Twenty
Hunter

I can't say I'm happy to be sitting in the lawyer's office today.

I want to remain positive, but I have my doubts this visit will bring good news.

The door to his office opens, and Mason Caldwell strides in with a tight smile on his face.

"Hunter." He nods. "Thank you for coming on such short notice."

"Well, your voicemail didn't leave me any choice, Caldwell. Please tell me this isn't as bad as it is in my head."

How am I going to break any kind of bad news to Gabe?

"Hopefully not." He fidgets with the pen, and I notice a bead of sweat on his brow. "The last payment of the residual trust can't be made if we continue to file the divorce. I should've told you earlier, but I was...afraid you'd still follow through with your threat."

I feel like a total asshole for making him sweat, literally, like this. But I thought we had a good conversation last time, and he understood I'd never out him like that. Essentially, I called my bluff to ease his mind.

"Listen, Caldwell...I was out of line to threaten you like that, and I'm sorry for being the source of that stress." he nods and darts his gaze to the desk. "I promised I wouldn't make it public, and I meant it. I was just...fucking angry, okay? Living under my grandfather's thumb and being his yes man for so long, I just...fuck...I just wanted to be done with it all." Heaving a breath, resigned that this won't be as smooth as I hoped, I can only offer my regrets. "I'm sorry."

"I'm sorry, too, but thank you for that. Your grandfather paid me well, and part of this is my fault."

"I know how he was. You don't have to explain. So what happens now?"

Caldwell attempts a smile and opens the folder he carried in. "You have options. You can stay married and receive the last payment according to the trust stipulations, or you can continue with the divorce, and the funds go to the anti-LGBTQ+ organization he named. I should have called you earlier to let you know I delayed filing the divorce, but I hoped I could try to sneak it by the partners."

"I don't want that sorry excuse for a charity to get a dime. That's not an option, Caldwell." Running a hand through my hair, I huff a breath. Gabe is going to hate this. I made him sign those papers and break his heart, and it was all for nothing. God, I'm an asshole.

"You can still divorce after a year and remarry," he offers.

"I know, but..."

It's the most logical thing to do, and I went into this with such a bull attitude, determined to do this in my way because it was always his way or nothing. Foolishly, I hoped this would go my way for once.

Caldwell clears his throat. "Forgive me for offering an opinion, but giving money to that organization would bury people like me for even longer. If they gain enough ground, even your marriage could be void."

Stark truth, and I know it. I'm just disappointed in myself that I've hurt the person I care about most because of my stubbornness.

"Yeah. I'm fairly certain the divorce will wait, but I need to speak to Gabe."

Caldwell nods in understanding. "When's the wedding?" he asks.

Thinking of marrying Gabe the way we want always brings a smile to my lips. "June first at the ranch." Caldwell smiles, and I recognize that sadness in his eyes. "You should join us. Nobody needs to know, Caldwell. I invited you because you helped, or for some other reason I can think of. You'll be welcome."

"Can I think about it?"

"Absolutely." Standing, I offer my hand to him. "I know we met under shitty circumstances and both of us did some not great things, but...I'm willing to get past that if you are."

He takes my offered handshake with a squeeze. "We should support each other and not fight. You give me courage, Hunter. Thank you."

I know he means it, and he's not a bad guy. If I get the chance to start my life over, shouldn't everyone?

"I'll call you after I speak to Gabe."

After leaving the law office, I head straight to Gabe's office. There's no way this can wait until he's home. After parking on the street, I walk the block up to his office. It's a tiny wartime house nestled among all the modern business buildings, clothing stores, and boutiques. Even on a street with newer buildings, it fits in. Kind of like Gabe when he moved here.

There was a rough start as he tried to find a place, but much like his office, he's here to stay.

My attention catches on something in one of the store windows and, I immediately head inside. A little extra grovelling won't hurt, right?

With my purchase tucked into a cute little bag, if you're into that kind of thing, and I know Gabe is, I finally arrive at his office.

"Hi Penny. I don't have an appointment, but I hope Gabe is free?"

"Hi Hunter! Oh gosh, I'm sure he has time for you. He's just on a phone call, but I'll let him know you're here."

"Thanks."

Gabe's office isn't sterile, like the previous lawyer kept it. Over the past several months, he's modelled his waiting room like a living room with a matching sofa and love seat. Art on the wall is by local photographers I'm familiar with. One is a herd of Mr. Bruce's dairy cows. I'd know that barn anywhere.

A small plaque sits on a corner table, and I bend to read it.

'Thank you for supporting our 4-H club.'

That's my man.

It's nothing fancy, but it warms my insides to know he keeps attending 4-H meetings without me and providing the snacks if Margie is too busy. To think he was worried about fitting in here when he came. He's had no issue winning hearts in this town.

"This is a nice surprise." Gabe's voice has me turn around, and a smile fills my face even though it's not good news that brings me here. He steps over and we kiss softly before he motions to his office. "I have to leave for a farm visit shortly, so you caught me at the right time."

After stepping into his office, my hands suddenly feel too slick and my gift perhaps not enough of an apology.

"Hunter? Is something wrong?"

"I fucked up," I blurt, and Gabe freezes. "I didn't cheat or anything."

Gabe nods slowly. "That's...comforting. What, ah, did you do then?"

"We can't get divorced." Gabe's brow furrows, and I inhale a breath so I can deliver this to him better. "I had a call from Caldwell, and someone at his office picked up on the divorce, and he didn't file it because it —"

"Hunter, slow down. Actually, do you need to sit? You look pale."

Gabe's concern for me twists my insides, the guilt heavier than when Caldwell delivered the news.

"Babe...I made you sign divorce papers for nothing. It's not happening, and I'm so sorry I put you through that."

Gabe sits for a moment and says nothing. After a moment, he whispers, "So we're still married now? That won't end?"

"No. Not unless you want to. But then we'd have to push the wedding back longer because—"

"Hunter." Gabe grabs my chin and forces me to look at him. I'd avoided eye contact because I hate seeing his heartbreak, but he's not even sad. "I know you wanted our own day and to cut those ties, but we can still do that. Don't you get that? We aren't changing a thing except for a number on the calendar."

"You're not mad?"

"How can I be mad when I'm still your husband and I get to relive a day of making you my husband all over? We celebrate what's coming. June first is our wedding day, whether the marriage is filed on that day or not. That's the day we celebrate."

"I'm sorry I made you hurt, Gabe. I should've just paused and let this play out instead of continuing to fight a dead man, but I just wanted this to be all my own."

Gabe's gaze softens as he steps closer.

"I'm sorry, too, but I'm still in love with you and still want a wedding with hot dogs and horses and friends." He hooks his fingers into my belt loops. "I still want you. In any way I can have you."

Gabe kisses me with the same love and passion I feel every time, and I squish my eyes closed at the swamp of emotion. "Sometimes I think I don't deserve you. I've fucked up so many times and you're still here."

"Funny, I think the same thing about you."

Remembering the bag in my hand, I step back and push it into his chest. "I got this for you."

Gabe's smile is genuine as he takes the bag and sits on his desk. The pretty tissue paper lays carefully on the desk and he peeks inside the bag before gently taking the box out.

"Hunter...this is..." Gabe laughs and beams a smile. "You know I don't practice this kind of law, though, right?"

He holds the mug I bought on the spur of the moment because I didn't want to show up empty-handed with the news we weren't divorced and relive the day I broke his heart.

Printed on a white mug in black letters is the phrase, *'I put the cute in prosecute.'* It's nothing fancy, but I thought it would make him laugh, and I was right.

"Yeah, I know that's not what you do, but you *are* cute."

His cheeks flush as he sets the mug on his desk and leans his hip on the edge. "Thank you. For the compliment and the sweet gift. I love it."

"So we're good, counsellor?"

"Yeah, doll. More than good." Gabe's alarm on his computer chimes as I reach for him. "That's my warning to get over to my next client. Do you have plans tonight?"

"Hopefully with you?" I ask and place a kiss on his neck.

"I'll bring home takeout and see if Diamond has any of the cheesecake you like." He breathes against my lips before we share a soft kiss, and I step away.

"It's a date, counsellor. See you tonight."

After one more kiss and a wave to Penny, I'm back on the street, heading to my truck. One more stop to make before home. It's not one I want to make, but it's long overdue.

After the cemetery caretaker finishes and drives off, I exit my truck and walk lightly to the stone I've come here to visit.

It's a small cemetery and only four people I know and love spend their eternity here. Side by side, it's an easy visit to make. Stopping at my parents' first, I read their names and young ages before the familiar sadness creeps in.

Would I have played sports with my dad? How would they have reacted to knowing I was gay? Would my relationship with my grandfather have been different if they hadn't died?

None of the questions matter, really, but they bounce back every time I come to visit my grandmother's grave. A step to the left and I'm in front of the woman who raised me as best she could until she, too, was taken far too soon for this world.

"You would love Gabe, Gram. He'd laugh at all your jokes, I have no doubt." The lump catches in my throat as it always does. But it's not Gram that I need to talk to today.

I've not been here since they buried my grandfather next to my cherished gram that day. It wasn't even grief I felt that particularly sunny morning. It was something complicated and mixed up with hate and rage that set me on a path of self-destruction for several days before Jackson stepped in and told me it was time to settle down and let it go.

But sometimes things can't just remain unsaid. Even to the dead.

"Jeremiah, you almost won, you know. Once again, I took your bait and jumped through all your hoops like the trick pony you turned me into." A dry laugh bubbles out as I stare at his name engraved on the granite stone. "I get the last word, though. I bet you thought I'd walk away from all the money and be too scared to see any kind of relationship through. I know you thought I was worthless, but guess what? I'm not."

Heaving a breath, I pace between the two stones as the words that have sat unspoken for far too many years come flying out.

"I did everything I could to keep the ranch because I thought you didn't want me to have it. Then found out you sort of did, but you had to make me work for it. You could never just let me have a single win or anything easy. Most people would say that builds strength, but that only works when there's love with it. You never showed me love!" My shout feels out of place here, like I'm disrespecting the rest of the others, and I bring my voice back down. "When Gram died, so did any ounce of compassion you had. I lost the breeding stock to keep the ranch. Funny how the one thing I stood up for, having my name on that business, was the one thing that kept me afloat until this mess you crafted was settled."

Resigned, I kneel in front of Jeremiah Burke's headstone and say words I never thought I'd ever say to the man. "In the end, though, I have to thank you, Jeremiah. I bet you thought marriage would scare me off and make me walk away from the money so it could feed your dislike for people like me. But you underestimated me, and you gave me a gift worth far more than your money. It didn't start out that way, but Gabe became my husband because of you. He's patient and kind, smart as all get out, and he's learning to ride. Mack loves him. He has the cutest little smile when he's trying to push my buttons."

Huffing a breath and wiping at the wetness in my eyes, I continue because this notion that my grandmother is listening takes hold.

"You didn't need to make both of us miserable because she died, you know. We could have helped each other." I think I might be crying for the old bastard, and I'm not sure what that means. Or maybe I'm crying from relief that I've unloaded this to deaf ears. "I'm sorry you couldn't get over losing people in your life,

Jeremiah. I really am. Because I know how it felt, too, and I'm not walking that road anymore."

Pushing to stand, I feel lighter as I listen to the birds singing in the trees and mull over the words I just said. The one person in the world I despised pushed me together with the love of my life. Maybe it's more complicated, or maybe it's just that simple, but it still happened because of him.

"Thanks, Granddad. I wish our story could have ended differently, but it's not too late for me to write a better ending for myself."

With a last nod, I return to my truck and sit in silence a little longer. I feel like I should never forgive him for all he put me through, but a peace sits with me now, and I can't deny I feel lighter for it.

This must be the part people talk about, where you feel free after finally letting go.

Putting my truck into gear, I back out of the tiny lot without a final glance.

I'm definitely free, but maybe I should thank Gabe for that.

Twenty-One
Gabe

The ranch house is quiet when I get home.

Kicking off my boots and juggling the takeout bags, I call out for Hunter. "Hunter? I'm home!"

When no call back comes, I pull out my phone to call him. His truck is in the yard, and he knows I'm bringing dinner. It's unlike him not to keep me posted if plans change.

Just as I'm about to dial his number, I hear footsteps and a thump upstairs, followed by a curse that I know is Hunter. After leaving the food on the table, I take the stairs to investigate what my husband is up to.

Hunter exits our bedroom and almost crashes into me.

"Shit, you're home already. I lost track of the time." He bends to kiss me, and it's not a quick peck. This is a full-on make-out kiss that leaves me panting...and confused.

"Not that I'm complaining, but, uh...I brought dinner home and...why are you smiling like that?"

"Like what?" Hunter steps in front of me, blocking my way to the bedroom.

"Are you hiding something?"

"Nothing bad. I promise. But we can eat first." He closes the bedroom door behind him.

"Hunter, I won't enjoy dinner until I know why you're acting so weird."

When Hunter lets go with a genuine laugh, he's the most breathtaking man I've ever seen. His entire aura is happy, not just his facial features. Right now, he radiates happiness like the sun, and I'm directly in its path.

"Sorry. It's not weird. I'm just really fucking happy." He smooths his hands down my arms, and for a moment, he looks almost shy. "Let's have dinner and I'll explain."

Together, we go back downstairs and open the containers I brought home. It's nothing special. Hunter loves the fried chicken at the grocery store deli, so I grabbed his favourite chicken and one of the pasta salads I love. Diamond had Hunter's favourite cheesecake, so I brought that home, too, for later, along with a homemade caramel sauce that sounded too damn good to leave behind.

After dinner, it's a breeze to clean up, and Hunter suggests we have dessert and tea on the porch swing.

"I'll never say no to that."

As he makes the tea, I plate our dessert, and together we settle outside on the swing that's become one of my favourite things about this place. There's just something about the peace and togetherness of it that warms my soul in a way no vacation ever could.

"Do you think if I asked Diamond and batted my eyes real nice, he'd make me a whole cheesecake every week? I don't know what he does to make this so damn fluffy and delicious, but it's amazing."

Hunter hums and closes his eyes as he savours the cheesecake, and I laugh softly. "He calls you...what again? Mr. Hunky? Pretty sure he would if you asked."

He sets his plate on the side table and takes mine before handing me a mug of tea. Curling into his side as he pushes us gently, I let myself enjoy this moment. Once rodeo season starts, we won't have as many of these evenings together. If he's not at a rodeo with Levi, he'll be teaching at the rodeo school he and Jackson are forming, and while I'm happy he's found his footing, I'm a little sad to not have these moments as often as I'd like.

"He calls you Mr. Handsome. Maybe you should ask him for me." Hunter chuckles as he sips his tea.

"Maybe I will."

"I went to the cemetery after I left your office," Hunter says softly. "I should've done it sooner."

"Are you okay?"

He drops his head back with a sigh. "Yeah, mostly. I just wish I hadn't let him get to me the way he did all those years."

His voice is steeped with regret, and I know it's hard for him to accept that he can't change the past, but it sounds like he's ready to let it go.

"He manipulated you when you were emotionally vulnerable, Hunter. That kind of action isn't something to shake off lightly, and you shouldn't feel bad about it."

From all the stories he's shared, I'm glad I never met Jeremiah because I'd probably punch him in the face.

"I thanked him." Hunter lifts his head and cups my cheek with a gentle hand. "I thanked him for bringing me you. Without you stepping up, I'd never have married you. But I also forgave him because I think…I think the hatred I carried was affecting all my relationships. Jackson and the guys tolerated me, but the men I took to bed before you…" He trails off and slides a thumb across my lips. "They were quick replacements to lose myself in sex and avoid intimacy." Hunter's gaze searches my face, and my breath catches. This isn't the same man who left my office. "I was afraid…and then I met you."

Hunter bends and kisses me, and my free hand clutches his thigh as he kisses me much like he did at my office earlier. It's passion and love, and an unspoken promise that I always come first. But there's something different there, too, and I didn't think it was possible to be swept up into this man anymore than I already am, but he's doing it again.

"I didn't plan on this being a permanent thing, either," I whisper against his lips. "I just wanted in your pants." Hunter's chest rumbles as his hand wanders to the inside of my thigh.

"That can be arranged. Come with me?"

"I'll go anywhere with you."

He places our mugs on the table, and he pulls me into the house by the hand. He's not said a word as we walk upstairs towards the bedroom, and when we pause at the bedroom door, he holds up a finger for me to wait and slips inside.

I don't know what he's hiding in the bedroom, but I'm counting my lucky stars that it's me he's sharing it with. The door peeks open, and Hunter steps aside to let me pass.

"It's completely cliché, but after everything that happened today, Gabe, I want you to know that I'll never hurt you again. Not on purpose at least, and if I do something that breaks your heart…"

He reaches for my hand and brings it to his lips. "Please call me on it and don't just let me have what I want."

Hunter must have bought out the store's inventory of battery-operated candles. Every available surface is covered. Tea lights, pillars, and lanterns all cast the room in a romantic glow. Two giant bouquets of flowers, one on each nightstand, sit with white roses and teal carnations.

"These are the flowers we picked for the wedding," I whisper.

"They are." His fingers move to my shirt buttons, and I bring my gaze to his. "I googled romantic ideas because you know I'm not good at this shit and it said flowers and candles." His hands slide under my shirt and push it to the floor while I'm still getting my brain to catch up with everything that's happened today.

"You cared enough to do something special. I'd say you're doing all right with this shit." He huffs a laugh, and I place a kiss at the base of his throat. The vibration of his laugh against my lips dies away, replaced by a soft moan.

"I'm so gone for you, counsellor." Hunter rests his forehead on mine. Our breaths mix between us, and Hunter places his work-roughened hands on the side of my neck. His thumbs stroking my cheeks in the most tender of ways are almost too much to handle.

"Show me."

He kisses me, sweeping me farther into this love-drenched moment, while his fingers work my pants open. I want nothing more than to have his weight press me into the mattress, but Hunter's touch signals he's in no hurry to get there.

From his knees, he pushes my pants and boxers down my legs and rests his head against my thigh. Calloused fingers trail over my exposed skin, lighting every fuse in my body as my dick swells with every breath of air I take, like it's connected to my breathing and not the worship of the man in front of me.

Sex with Hunter has been hot. We fuck with unbridled passion or make out like lust-driven teenagers and even get each other off while laughing. We connect every time, and it's never disappointing, but there's a very definite shift when I grip his hair in my hands as he finally parts his lips to swallow me down.

Looking down at Hunter with his mouth full of my cock, eyes looking up at me with this...this gratitude? I've never seen him like this, and a part of me fears he thinks he has to do this to get me to forgive his actions.

"Doll..." Hunter moans around me, and I lose my train of thought for a moment, but I tug his hair and pull him off my cock. "You know you don't need to make up for anything, right? I love you just the same as I did this morning."

He kisses his way up my body until he stands again. His eyes tell me everything I need to know, no matter what his lips might say. "I love you. I love us, and we're going to make mistakes. Just love me, okay?"

"I'll love you as long as I breathe, Gabe. Probably even longer."

"That's all I need."

Hunter's body relaxes, and I know I was right. He always wants to do the right thing and hates letting people down. The divorce situation sucks. I won't deny that I wish I didn't have to experience that ache as I signed my name, but what matters to me is that he's my husband. Obviously, it's what he wants, too, and while I appreciate the romance, love it, to be honest, I want him ravishing me because he wants to and not for any other reason.

Candles flicker as we let the rest of his clothes hit the floor. His playfulness returns, and I'm once again under the spell of the hot cowboy I never thought I'd have. He pulls me onto the bed with him, our legs tangling until he hitches my leg over his hip and grins against my lips.

"Have I told you lately I love your ass?" His fingers run through my crease, and I shiver.

"I don't think so, but don't let me stop you from telling me again."

Hunter reaches up and pulls a bottle out from under the pillow. After flipping the cap, he places my hand on my ass cheek. "Pull it apart for me, beautiful." Of course I do as he asks, and he squirts a line of cold lube down my ass. "Sorry about the chill, but you'll be too hot to care in a few minutes."

He tosses the bottle behind me and, because he knows what I like, he wastes no time pushing a finger inside. My hips press into him, and he hovers his mouth over mine. "How many do you want before I have you ride me again, Gabe?"

His lips tease me with quick kisses, and I can taste the caramel sauce from his cheesecake on his tongue.

"More." It's all I can pant as he fucks me with his fingers and holds me so tight I can't even get a hand to my dick.

"I could make you come like this. Do you want that?" He pauses as he slips another inside, and we both groan. He knows all the right spots to make my body keen for more.

"Not this time," I groan. "I want to come on your cock." Hunter bites my shoulder with his fingers in my ass, and I moan in frustration. "Please..."

Hunter lingers, dusting his lips on my neck before he gently rolls me onto my back. He runs his finger through the puddle of pre-cum on my belly with a smirk. "You sure do like that, don't you? Next time, I'll remember those toys you teased me with at Christmas."

We haven't made time to have proper fun with those yet, and right now I regret it. Hunter rolls off the bed and walks to the closet, leaving me naked and needy on the mattress. The candles cast a glow on his body as he rummages in the closet.

"Picking out tomorrow's clothes already?" I joke, but it's breathless and needy, and he looks back over his shoulder.

"More like picking out your attire for the rest of the evening."

He returns with a giant white box and sets it on the bed before making himself comfortable next to me.

"Open it and put it on, counsellor. You know what to do."

Not the best time to give me a gift that's not his dick, but I won't complain. I lift the lid and my jaw drops.

"No way." Inside is a cowboy hat, and Hunter's gaze darkens as I place it on my head.

"I prefer you wearing mine, but you look damn good in a cowboy hat, Gabe. Even with clothes on." He grins as I scramble over his body. My lips press to his and I kiss him before straddling his hips.

"You are amazing. Every day. All day. I love it." Smashing my lips to his again, he smiles against them, and I slide my ass back and forth along his dick. "Gimme something to ride, doll."

He holds himself steady as I sink down on him with an appreciative moan. My fingers splay across his chest, his chest hair coarse under my palms as I adjust to him. The soft scent from the roses and the flickering of the candles couldn't be more perfect to reflect the softer side of Hunter.

"Christ, Gabe, why do you always feel so good?"

Hunter's fingers curl into the flesh of my hips, and I bite my lip and sit up. With a hand on my new hat, I roll my hips. "You were made for me, doll."

He really is.

With one hand on my hat and the other behind me on his thigh, I swivel my hips and let my head fall back as I lose myself to the pleasure that builds.

Digging my knees into the bed, I sit back with both hands on his thighs and ride him like I know he likes. No, that he *loves* because his lips part and his gaze locks on mine before his eyelids lower and he moans a long, drawn-out sound that fills the room.

"Gabe...fuck..."

His hands roam my chest and thighs, and my breath hitches when he tugs on my balls. "Yeah, counsellor, lose it for me. I want to watch you come apart so bad."

Hunter wraps his fist around my cock and strokes me with every bounce. It's so good I don't want it to end, but the best thing is, I can do it again in a few hours.

"Ah! Oh god..." Hunter wrings my orgasm from me like he wanted, and when I allow myself to open my eyes and sit up, his smirk of satisfaction just gets me.

I lean down to kiss him. My hat bumps the pillow, so I push it up out of the way and swivel my hips as I stare down at Hunter. His jaw is set tight as he grips the flesh of my hips and punches his hips up, driving himself into me. His orgasm is hard, his entire body quaking as he pants against my lips.

The candles still flicker as we pant in a sweat-slicked heap, and he brings a shaky hand to my cheek.

"Hell of a ride, counsellor," he croaks, and I laugh against his lips.

"Must have been the hat."

We extricate ourselves from each other, and before heading to the shower, I place the hat in the box and survey the room. He went to great lengths to make a romantic setting.

He didn't need candles and flowers.

He just needs to show up.

Twenty-Two
Hunter
Wedding Day

Jackson chuckles at my back.

"Hunter, if you check the time anymore, I swear the entire universe will freeze to teach you patience."

Huffing a breath, I grab my hat and button my single jacket button. "I just want to see him." I can't believe I'm missing the guy after a single night apart.

Jackson's firm hand on my shoulder turns me towards the door. "Come on, then. We can wait outside and stick to the plan."

"Is everything okay at the other end?"

Gabe wanted to spend last night with his best friend, Riley. I wanted us to dress together and greet our guests, but Gabe was a bit of a traditionalist that way, and he wanted that moment of seeing his groom. I wasn't about to deny the man, even if I didn't know what the big deal was with the '*first look*.' Although Jackson is my best friend and sitting around last night just talking and bonding more than we ever have was something truly special.

"Right as rain." Jackson smiles, but it fades when I turn to face him. Since we woke up this morning to get the horses all washed and ready, I've been a ball of emotions. Happy and sad. Hopeful and scared. This is all so new to me, but I know I need to spit it out. I've been working on that a lot, and I swear it's never going to get easier.

"Jack...I..." Puffing a breath, I try to gather the words I've played repeatedly to say to him. "I can't believe I'm already tripping over my words, and I haven't even gotten to the vows yet."

"It's an emotional day, and I'll give you a pass on it," he jokes, and his eyes crinkle at the edges when he smiles.

"You were there for me when others weren't, Jack. I just want to say...I want to thank you for being my family when I had none. I love you, and if I ever had a brother, I'd wish he were like you." Clearing my throat, I gaze into the pasture where the giant white tent sits waiting for us. I should have said this last night, but it took me all night to think of what I wanted to say.

Jackson blows out a breath and swallows. "We're doing this, are we? Okay. It's my privilege to call you my friend, and it's my honour to call you brother, Hunter. We don't need blood to say that."

Stupid allergies, making my eyes water.

"I just wanted to thank you for being here. For everything, really."

"I'll always be here for whatever you need. Always. That's what friends are for, and I know I can count on you just as much."

He pulls me into a hug, and we stay there for a moment, Jackson lending me the quiet strength he always carries.

"I can't believe I'm getting married by choice," I say with a laugh when we separate. "I keep thinking this is all a dream."

A good dream, though. It's definitely not any sort of nightmare. It's just surreal.

"Love does that. It makes reality a little more bearable that way sometimes." He pats his jacket pocket, and relief washes over him. "I thought I forgot the ring." His eyes widen. "Shit. I forgot the corsages. Be right back."

He rushes back into the ranch house, and I watch the caterers putting the finishing touches on their setup inside the large barn. Gabe and Riley's idea to rent a makeshift dance floor and have the reception here immediately after the ceremony was one I instantly loved.

Our training arena for the rodeo clinics, a building that normally has bucking bulls, horses, and men swearing when they hit the ground, has now transformed into an intimate space suitable for a celebration of love.

With a hot dog buffet. Can't forget that.

A part of me cheers, imagining my grandfather in a rage at our wedding here, but I think it's the perfect way to claim my space. People love me, and I'll do my best every day going forward to remember that.

"Riley would have my head if I forgot this," Jackson says. He opens the container with our corsages. Teal again, the one thing from our original wedding that we were okay to keep. As Gabe said, his favourite colour would always be teal. Jackson pins it to my lapel, and I do his like Riley showed me, just as the first guests arrive.

Not like we have a large guest list, but when Margie steps out of the minivan dressed like the mother of the groom, I need to take a minute and breathe before greeting her.

"Margie..."

"Don't you dare make me cry before the wedding and photos, young man." Her voice hitches, and I hug her.

"Okay. I won't say anything until after, but if the man asks who gives me away, you better raise your hand." The gravel crunches next to us, and one of the young men currently staying with her extends a hand.

"Hi. I'm John. Congratulations."

"Thanks." I shake his hand and nod towards Margie. "Take care of her today. You take the front row. Your name is on a chair."

A few more cars arrive and follow the signs to the parking area. Jackson directs guests to the chairs under the tent while I greet the two men I don't recognize.

"Hi! Riley told us to just come ahead." He offers a hand in greeting. "I'm Charles, and I'll be performing your ceremony today."

"Thank you for coming on such short notice. We're super appreciative."

His smile is charming, and I immediately love how at ease he is.

"I've always wanted to see the Rocky Mountains, so it's perfect." He motions to the very imposing man next to him. "This is my husband, Dave."

"Nice to meet you. This is a great place," he says as he looks around. The man is a giant, and Charles rattles on about the ceremony while I watch the guy take a cookie from his pocket and eat it while he listens as well.

"I spoke to Gabe. He's so charming. He said you both had your own vows, and Riley said no religious readings, so I'm all set to get you hitched. If you don't have any questions for me, I'll go wait at the front."

"I'm good. Wander around if you'd like. The horses are friendly."

Things get a little crazy after that. Cars arrive and people are flowing in, taking seats, and while we only invited fifty people, it feels like there are five hundred here. Jackson keeps directing guests, and *finally*, Gabe's Lexus pulls into his usual parking place.

He doesn't get out right away, and the longer he takes, the more I sweat. If this was a dream, this would be the part where I wake up.

My heart beats triple time when he finally steps out and the breath whooshes from my lungs as I close the distance to greet him.

"Counsellor, you are a sight." My voice sounds like I'm chewing gravel, but I don't fucking care.

Gone are the suits from the first wedding. Both of us chose well-fit jeans and boots, with fancy sport coats and pressed shirts. He's fit so well into the country life, he didn't want to force me into something uncomfortable like last time. Gabe barely wears his suits to work anymore, either, and he says he doesn't miss it. Although sometimes I do, because it's hot to dirty him up when he's all put together with a tie and jacket.

"So are you," he breathes. I'm not waiting to kiss him, and I grab the back of his neck, pressing my lips to his.

"I told you we'd do it right and put your heart back together," I whisper across his lips.

"I hated waiting. For this...and to see you."

A throat clears, and Riley stands nearby in attire to match Jackson. "I don't care if you kiss before the ceremony, but try not to muss things up." He pats Gabe's arm. "Just watch for the signal from me. Enjoy these moments."

Gabe

When I pulled up and saw Hunter waiting on the front porch, hands clasped in front of himself like he didn't know what to do with them, I was frozen. Not with fear or an indecision, but with the reality of what was about to take place.

At our first wedding, the day of our first kiss, even, he was so stoic. There was no joy in his face, and his eyes didn't light up like they do now when he looks at me. Everything about that day was fake...except for the orgasms that night. We didn't fake those.

He was a poster model for what uncomfortable looks like. In a suit he hated and marrying a stranger, he was distant, and the little connection we had was purely physical.

Seeing him now on his ranch and watching the smile grow as I walk towards him is something I always wished for. I never knew how much until I met this man, and he changed my life.

"You can muss me up later," I murmur as Riley leaves us for a moment of alone time. Most of the guests have arrived and I'm happy to have this moment alone with Hunter. "I missed you last night."

Hunter dips his head. "I missed you, too." His thumb rubs across my knuckles before he brings it to his lips. "I'm so ready for all of this, Gabe. I never dreamed of being someone's husband, but no one else ever made sense to me."

"I know what you mean." Hunter was never supposed to make sense. He wasn't supposed to be anything, but I ended up liking him more than I originally planned. Hunter didn't just make sense. No one else could ever compare. "They say the best relationships sometimes start unexpectedly, and in this case, I think that's right. I didn't expect this, Hunter. I didn't think I'd fall so hard for you that I'd cry over divorce papers and ache so hard to marry you for real that I'd have anxiety over it."

Hunter kisses the back of my hand again, and he says nothing, but he doesn't need to. His eyes tell me everything, and I know he hurts sometimes still for making me sad, but he doesn't need to. It's easier for me to move forward from the past, but with time, he will, too.

Looking over Hunter's shoulder, I see Riley give me the wave that they're ready to start when we are.

"I'm ready to be your husband and kiss you in front of our friends, if you are."

Hunter glances back at the tent before turning back to me.

"Some kisses are worth waiting for, and that's one kiss worth the wait, Gabe." He squeezes my hand. "Let's not wait any longer to start our forever."

Twenty-Three
Hunter

The music is on point, the hot dogs and poutine were a hit, and my husband in my arms on the dance floor is the second best thing that happened tonight.

The first was hearing the words *'I now pronounce you husband and husband.'* A tsunami of joy rushed into me as I kissed Gabe so deeply and long, our guests started cat-calling and whistling. But I couldn't help it. This is the day we'll mark on the calendar and celebrate, even though the marriage certificate says something different.

Today is the day I'll remember as the day my life changed forever.

Gabe is the best thing to ever happen to me.

"Are you feeling more adventurous with dancing? How about a spin and a dip?"

Gabe chuckles, but his grin says everything. He will always try anything I suggest.

"We haven't done that before, but walk me through it." His eyes sparkle with a happiness I wish I could bottle.

"I'll raise my arm like this and don't let go of my hand." Slowing our steps, I spin him slowly, and he catches on with a peel of laughter.

"And then what?"

"Then I'll pull you back to me and bend you backwards...like this." Gabe doesn't stop laughing as I do exactly that while we stand still in the small crowd dancing around us.

"You won't let me fall?"

"Never, counsellor."

His smile shifts to something more tender as he leans in to kiss me. "Let's do it." His words whisper across my lips, and we share a moment. It was a rocky road for us, mostly my fault, but we made it.

"I love you, Gabe."

"I know, doll. I love you, too."

We pick up the music again—the two-step is what he's most comfortable with—and when I see the opening on the floor, I raise my arm for his spin. It's not flawless, but it works. When I pull him back to me, he immediately relaxes. He even kicks his leg up, but curls it around my waist as he smirks.

"Have you been secretly practicing?" I say as I pull him up, and he keeps his leg wrapped around my waist.

"I might have had a few dance lessons from a certain mutual friend." Gabe is quite pleased that he shocked me for a moment and pecks a kiss on my lips. "You're the only one who gets to touch my butt, though."

"Good to know. But who taught you?"

Gabe lowers his leg and glances towards the other dancers, specifically Diamond and Levi. It's very clear Diamond is trying to teach him some dance steps, and it's not going very well.

"Huh...probably should have guessed he likes to dance with those legs."

Gabe wraps his arms around my neck and pulls my attention back. "Do you mind if I dance with him for a while?"

The way Gabe asks me isn't for permission but more of a check-in since I haven't let him go all night except to go to the bathroom.

"Of course not. No butt touching, though," I joke, and he kisses me longer.

"Not a problem...husband."

With Gabe off to rescue Diamond from Levi's two left feet, I head to the bar where a familiar pair of denim-blue eyes meet mine. My gut flips not with butterflies, but with something next to regret.

"Sorry I'm late. The plane had a few issues and the traffic from the city is shit." Alec, the man I loved all those years ago, and who I was too afraid to stand up for, raises his beer to me. "Congratulations, Hunter. I wouldn't miss this for the world."

"I wasn't sure you'd come," I say with a shaky breath. "I wasn't exactly kind to you the last time we talked."

"No, you weren't, but I know how it is, Hunter. We have history, and that won't ever change. You were still fighting and figuring things out."

"Took me forty fucking years," I say with a small laugh and Alec just smiles.

"Better late than never." He takes a drink, and I'm at a loss for words. Yes, I invited him because I wanted him to come, but now that he's here, I'm unsure of myself. Sorry doesn't feel like enough.

"Did Zane make it with you?"

Alec's smile grows fond, and I know the look well. "Of course. I think he's outside trying to talk to a groundhog." We both laugh, and Alec tips his head towards the exit at the back of the barn. "Come on. Let's go outside for a bit."

When the barn door closes behind us, the quiet of the night is louder than the music inside, and I'm painfully aware of how much time he spent on this very ranch hiding himself because of me. All the times I was rude in public to cover my feelings for him aren't something I'm proud of. Those memories still linger here among the new ones I've made with Gabe.

"I can tell you're afraid of saying something wrong, so I'll start," Alec says as we walk to the pasture fence. He leans against it, his gaze looking out into the pasture that one time held cattle he helped tend to. "I don't regret choosing you, and I'll never regret my time here. We made a great team in the ring, but not so much as a couple. But our relationship helped me find what I wanted. Kind of like you and Gabe. Without you, I'd probably not be as happy as I am today."

Easing up to the fence next to Alec, I stare into the field as well. He's right, as always. I needed him to say something first.

"I'm sorry for being a miserable asshole and putting money before you. I always thought you were my biggest regret, but maybe that's not it at all."

"It's not." Alec's quiet and steady voice brings me back to all those years ago when he pleaded with me to choose something for myself just once. He didn't even press for it to be him. He just wanted something better for me. Alec believed in me long before I believed in myself. "We both grew up here, Hunter. You as a child, but both of us grew here in ways we couldn't possibly know back then. I regret nothing."

"You were my only actual relationship, you know. I never let anyone close after you." Puffing a breath, it just hits me finally. It almost steals my breath out here under the same moon that it began. "I was so afraid of someone else leaving me, I couldn't do it. I couldn't let someone close, but Gabe...it's like he knew that all along and just put up with my bullshit because he believed I'd figure it out."

Alec turns his head, shifting his gaze back to me. It's unsettling having this conversation now. It's been over ten years since we were close. When I made a half-assed attempt to win him back a few years ago, he had the same look now as he did then. I don't even have to look to know it's a gaze of shared sadness with an overlay of love. It's always love with him. Even at my lowest, he loved me.

"You're always a part of me, Hunter. That's something neither of us can let go, but that doesn't mean you have to keep away from me. I love Zane and you love Gabe. We found the right people for us. You'll always be my friend, and I'll always love you like one. Thank you for inviting us here to share this with you. It meant a lot getting that card in the mail."

"It seemed right...having you here."

From the corner of my eye, I see him shake his head with a grin. "You're forgiven, asshole. Let it go and enjoy life. You deserve it." He slaps me on the back, and I finally turn to him. His smile is genuine, and I know he's telling the truth.

"Thank you, Alec. For everything." I swipe at my eyes. "Jesus Christ, I'm not sure I like all this emotion shit. Makes my eyes water too much."

He laughs and elbows me as we walk back towards the barn. "Good to know the old ticker isn't all dried up then." With my hand on the door, he places his hand over mine and I turn to him. "You've always been a good person. Don't be afraid to show it more often. Now introduce me properly to your husband." He shakes his head. "Fuck, that sounds weird out loud."

I shove him off the door with my best scowl. But the scowl doesn't last.

"It does sound weird, but I love saying it. Come on. I want to formally introduce you to the man who stole my heart...my husband, Gabe."

Alec finally meets Gabe, and they hit it off immediately, as I knew they would. Gabe was the one who encouraged me to invite him, and it's just one more thing I can thank this man for.

Zane also welcomes Gabe, and those two would run amok out here if I let them. Thick as thieves, laughing and sharing stories long after most of the guests have left.

With the sun closer to waking up than the moon is to going to sleep, we finally end one of the most amazing days of my life. We're exhausted, but I've never felt the kind of contentment that sits in my chest right now.

Gabe, fresh from our shared shower, his cheeks still pink from the warmth of the water, slides into bed next to me.

"Today was perfect, Hunter. I'm biased, but it really was."

Smoothing the hair back from his forehead, I place a kiss there. "It was...husband."

"That word feels different now, don't you think?" Gabe's hands slide into my hair, and he nuzzles his nose next to mine.

"It does. I feel like it finally fits."

"You know what else fits?" His words carry the exhaustion of a long day, and he snuggles closer. "You. Right here in my arms. Tailor-made for me."

He forces himself lower, tucking his chin under mine. He drapes one arm around me and slides a leg between mine. My husband wedges himself into a position I'd normally find uncomfortable. Gabe really does fit like he was tailor-made for me.

His lips meet my skin, and he mumbles, "I'm too tired for the whole wedding sex thing. Wake me up with your dick somewhere on me and we'll do it in the morning. That's not a lack of romance either. It's a lack of my dick not being awake even pressed up against you."

My body shakes with quiet laughter as his breathing evens out. A soft snore sounds less than a minute later, and I grin into the dark bedroom.

Gabe's arm twitches and tightens around me, and I press a kiss to the top of his head. His arms around me are the safe place I've always needed, and even in sleep, he responds like he knows I need him there.

"Sweet dreams, counsellor. I love you."

Twenty-Four
Epilogue
Two years later

G^{abe}

"Hi fellas!" I hop out of the truck and wave at the cowboys here, attending the latest session of Jackson and Hunter's rodeo skills school. Most of them are fresh young men in their twenties with the baby face to match. They wave with a laugh and knowing glances, so I immediately change my path to meet their group.

"How did the school go today?"

Levi, Hunter's new roping partner, presses his lips together to remain quiet, but it doesn't last long.

"Hunter lost a bet," Levi blurts, and the guys all start laughing.

"Okayyy..."

Mike, one of the bull riders Hunter knew from his younger days, steps up next to me. He's a nice guy. Quiet for a rodeo cowboy, but he's polite and steady and helps keep the younger ones in line. He's been so much help as Hunter and I transition into running multiple businesses, his rodeo tour and, well, just taking the time we need to enjoy our relationship.

Since we got married, it's not all been rainbows, but when cloudy moments come, we've handled it well.

"Hi, Gabe." Mike nods and clears his throat. "You know how Hunter always challenges the new ropers to a contest that he never loses?"

I nod. "Yes. Best out of five or fastest time for a tie down?"

Mike hums. "That's the one. When he lost the first challenge...3-0 I might add, he made a bet that he also lost and right now he's out paying the debt."

Sounds right. Hunter is nothing less than competitive. If he lost the first contest, which he never does, he might have let his drive get the best of him.

"Do you have a lot of that anti-itch stuff? Like for mosquito bites?" One of the young lads says, and I nod.

"I think so. Do you need some?"

"No, but I bet Hunter will."

Now I'm just completely confused, but I turn when I hear the sounds of hooves and Hunter's voice.

"Lady Godiva ain't got nothing on me, you fuckers. I hope you're satis—" Hunter's gaze meets mine. "Oh, shit. Hey, babe."

The guys hoot and holler and clap and a few dollar coins get thrown his way because my husband is completely bare-ass naked on top of his horse. Well, naked except for his hat, and now I understand the question about anti-itch meds. It's still black fly season.

"You dared to ride naked if you lost a bet?"

"Not exactly." Mike chuckles next to me.

"Damn, Gabe. His balls must be chafing against that saddle. Gonna need more than anti-itch." Levi cackles, and I do my best not to laugh. I really do.

"What do you say, Hunter? Are your balls chafing up there? Need some Gold Bond?" one of the new guys yells out.

Hunter's hand goes to his naughty bits, and he attempts to cover himself since the crowd has stopped snickering and grown quiet as they ogle my naked husband. Which is hard not to, but I'm not loving him on display.

"Don't you guys have work to do or something?" I bark. Some of them excuse themselves, but most of them stay and laugh and grin as Hunter grows increasingly uncomfortable.

Maybe I'm a bit of an ass for making him sweat, but I don't think he'll mind later. It's actually kinda hot with him up there, reinventing the rustic cowboy image.

Since I know his first instinct is to always make sure we communicate when things get wonky, I shake my head and turn towards the house.

"Gabe, it's not —" A fresh wave of laughs and wolf whistles sounds. "Unless you want me to flash the goods, I can't get down, Gabe. Please don't be mad."

Turning around, I laugh as I walk to the fence. "I'm not mad, but why on earth would you bet to ride naked if you lost?"

"I didn't think I'd lose! Or that so many of these guys apparently wanted to see me naked!" He glares at the small crowd of men. We don't make it a point to ask them about their sexuality when they attend his school. What we do, though, is make it a point to tell them we're a married gay couple and if that's a problem, not to bother attending.

Clearly, we've acquired the largest group of non-straight cowboys in Alberta, since most of them can't seem to look away. We've moved beyond the shock factor and into open looks of appreciation.

"Honestly, I just wanted to know if he'd follow through." One man offers me a hand. "Hi, I'm Caleb. Seems like he's a man of his word."

I take his hand while I side glance at Hunter. "He's definitely a man of his word. Are you the man who beat him?"

"Yes, sir." Caleb smirks, and the cockiness is earned. Hunter never loses.

"Congratulations. I'm sure he'll bet more carefully in the future now." Caleb nods and waves to Hunter before turning back to the barn.

"You should probably get off the horse, Hunter. Where are your clothes, anyway?"

It's then one of the new guys bursts from the barn, arms full of clothes, as he runs down the driveway towards his vehicle. After he throws them in the back, he peels out of the yard, and I raise an eyebrow.

"Those were probably my clothes, and I'm kicking him out of the course." Hunter hangs his head with a laugh. "Lord, can this day get worse?"

"Doubt it, but I can definitely make it better."

"And that's my cue." Mike claps his hands and says goodbye while I jump the fence and walk over to Hunter.

"Truthfully, are your balls chafing?" We both laugh, and he adjusts himself on the saddle. "Yes, and my ass is sticking to it and the bugs are starting to get me, but I couldn't *not* follow through, Gabe. It was a bet, and they need to respect me, you know?"

"I know." I smooth a hand up his bare leg. He's so powerful and strong. Amazingly fit still, even in his forties. Dixie swings her head at me, and I say hello to her, too. "I'm not mad you're streaking on the back of a horse. It's actually quite the show."

Hunter snort-laughs. "I'm too old to let these young guns get the best of me. I can give you a show without the other eyes watching." He clears his throat and lowers his gaze.

"What do you need from me, doll?"

Hunter looks down at me and moves his hand away from his dick. Despite his situation, it's perking up. "Just stop touching me and looking all cute so I can dismount without...damaging something."

Immediately, I step back with my hands in the air. "Don't damage anything, and I'll help you recover." I turn to walk away, and Hunter calls out.

"Do you think you could bring me some pants?"

After hopping over the fence, I pause. "I think you can find something in the barn. This is your mess." Laughing, I jog back to the house with Hunter's laughter following me.

Hunter

Somehow, I get Dixie unsaddled and brushed in nothing but my cowboy boots. Thankfully, the little shit who stole my clothes knew better than to take my boots.

Why I made a bet to ride naked around the pasture is beyond me, but I wasn't about to not follow through. I'm a man of my word...even when they're stupid words that I regret. Although I'm quite fond of *'I'll Lady Godiva the shit out of this.'*

Gabe was home early and in that one instant where our eyes met, I panicked that he'd be mad, and I'd fucked up the best thing I ever had. What's he supposed to think when he finds his husband riding a horse buck fucking naked in front a group of men that doesn't include him?

My heart was in my throat as I tried to come up with a better explanation than the truth.

Then he smiled.

That fucking smile that makes me feel like I could fly to the moon.

"Sorry for all that, girl. You did not need me on your back like that." I pat Dixie and close the stall door. "Extra treats tomorrow. Maybe all week."

Are horses traumatized by human nudity? I sure hope not.

Walking through the barn with the air on my balls is different. Not sure I like it, but what the hell? If I owned the Lady Godiva act, I'd own this too.

With my hat on my head and boots on my feet with nothing in between, I strut from the barn to the house like a rooster on the way to the henhouse...and stop dead when Gabe opens the door with Diamond.

Both men freeze, Gabe with a twisted smile and Diamond with his jaw hanging open.

Grabbing the hat off my head, I cover my cock and balls and turn around.

"Oh, keep spinning sugar. Give me all the angles."

Gabe's laughter rings out, and I hang my head before turning around, only now noticing Diamond's orange Subaru in the lane. How could I miss that?

"Hey, Diamond. I didn't know you were here. Obviously."

"I was just dropping off a special something for you and Gabe. Clearly, it's not a good time to stay and chat, so I'll let you two get it."

He turns and whispers to Gabe. "Damn, Gabe. You get that every night?"

"Twice if I want it."

"I can hear you both!" I shout and walk towards the house with my swagger a little less than it was before.

Diamond waves with a smile and is on his way, and I'm finally in the house's safety. I hang my hat and pull off my boots, which is hard when you have no socks on. Gabe leans against the wall, watching me the entire time with a fond smile.

"Today is a special day. Diamond delivered so we could celebrate."

I freeze, running through the calendar in my brain. All birthdays accounted for. It's not our wedding anniversary or any of our friends that I'm aware of. Drawing a blank, I shake my head.

"Gabe, I'm sorry. I don't know what day it is."

He takes me by the hand and leads me to the living room. My favourite cheesecake sits on the table, and next to it is an envelope with my name. Now I'm really confused as he pulls me down on the sofa next to him.

"Three years ago, I moved in here and pretended to be your husband. A short eight weeks later, you sat where you are now with your feet on the table and a crossword book in your hand." Gabe reaches for the card. "I stretched out and rested my feet on your lap. You didn't push me away. Instead, your free hand absently rubbed my leg."

Gabe speaks softly as he tells the story of literally any night we spend at home, and I feel like an ass for not knowing what's so special about this day.

"Gabe...I'm sorry, but I'm not getting this."

He shakes his head, the fond smile never fading. "We celebrate our wedding, but we never celebrate little moments. It was at that moment, as you asked me another word for purple, that I knew I was in love with you. I'll remember it forever. It smashed into me so hard, more than any moment we've spent on the porch swing. I loved you. It had to be you."

Gabe passes me the card, and when I open it, it's an anniversary card, but he's scratched off all the words that say anniversary and replaced them with various words for falling in love, stealing his heart or whatnot.

And it chokes me up that he remembers the day so clearly and wants to celebrate it out of the blue. Hell, that he remembers it so clearly, and I didn't even know what was going through his head.

"And I ruined it by riding naked and showing friends and strangers my good parts."

Gabe laughs and takes my face in his hands. "You didn't ruin it at all. You reminded me why I love you and how lucky I am. I love everything about you, Hunter, and I always will. I didn't expect it, but that's kind of what all this is, right? Unexpected good things."

He kisses me. Deep and sweet, and I reach for him, pulling him onto my lap.

"Even when I walk from the barn naked and give one of our closest friends a full-frontal show."

"Especially then." Gabe kisses me all over my face. My eyelids, nose, and forehead. "Let's eat cake, and after that, I just want to be happy that I took the chance to tell you I loved you when you pushed me away." He kisses me and lingers against my lips. "I just want to remember that sometimes, when we take a chance, it pays off. And you were the best chance I ever took."

My throat bobs with a swallow, and I wish I knew what god to thank for this.

"Anything for you, Gabe. Always."

"I know, doll. Don't feel like you always have to prove that to me. I know it." He spreads his hand over my heart. "And *this* is the best part of you."

My husband presses his lips to mine and kisses me with the promise of forever.

"Can we eat that cake now?" I whisper against his lips.

"I figured since you were already naked, we could save the cake for later." He swivels his hips on my lap. "It's a cock-before-cake situation now."

My laugh is deep as I stand with him in my arms and turn to place him on the couch.

"I can definitely handle that, counsellor."

Acknowledgements

Thank you so much for reading Hunter and Gabe's story! I hope you loved them just as much as I did.

When I first wrote Hunter's character back in Alec's book, he sat with me. I just knew there was more to him and Alec didn't just have an asshole ex. Hunter had a story to tell and I'm so happy I waited for him to spit it all out.

Hunter has affectionally become my burnt marshmallow. (Thank you, April, for that!) Not a cinnamon roll, that's too soft. Hunter's scars run deep, and he and Gabe will always have issues pop up because of them. Under all the crispy and standoff exterior is a man so soft and gooey he regularly melts Gabe's heart. He's one of my favourite characters to date. I didn't see that coming, lol.

Huge thank you to Kyle Rodgers for the horse knowledge and helping me get the colic scene right. I appreciate the time you gave me to answer all my questions and read over the passage. And the horse photos!

Kota, I have to thank you for listening to me work out the plot issues in rambling voice messages that you somehow understood. I appreciate your feedback and the movie clips!

Thank you, dear reader, for once again turning the pages on one of my stories. Every time I publish a book and people read it, I get such a thrill. I always try to bring my best to you and I hope you enjoy these men.

Kissing Ridge isn't over.

If you're wondering if Diamond gets a story, the answer is yes. Bronc Riders Don't Fall in Love will come in 2026.

Thank you for reading and being awesome.

Much love,

RM

About the author

R M is an introverted Canadian author who likes to write about love while freezing in the winter. Her mission is to always make you swoon and snort laugh, sometimes even in public.

She talks to her cat, Moon, and sometimes people. She married her prince charming, who often inspires her characters, but still can't place dirty clothes in the hamper.

When she's not writing swoony men to fall in love with, she's in her garden providing mosquitoes with an alternative food source. She can also be found inventing new swear words on the golf course.

She also forgets to tell people to visit her website for exclusive stories.

rmneillauthor dot com

Also By

Want to read more by me? Scan the code
to find my back list.

Visit my website for signed paperbacks and merch!
rmneillauthor.com

www.ingramcontent.com/pod-product-compliance
Lightning Source LLC
Chambersburg PA
CBHW021043310726
48969CB00006B/1782